OKLA HANNALI

Books by R. A. Lafferty

Past Master (New York, 1968)
The Reefs of Earth (New York, 1968)
Space Chantey (New York, 1968)
Fourth Mansions (New York, 1969)
Nine Hundred Grandmothers (New York, 1970)
Arrive at Easterwine (New York, 1971)
The Devil Is Dead (New York, 1971)
The Fall of Rome (New York, 1971)
The Flame Is Green (New York, 1971; Minneapolis, 1985)
Okla Hannali (New York, 1972, 1973; Norman, 1991)
Strange Doings (New York, 1972)
Does Anyone Else Have Something Further to Add? (New York, 1974)
Not to Mention Camels (Indianapolis, 1976)
Where Have You Been, Sandaliotis? (New York, 1977)
The Three Armageddons of Enniscorthy Sweeny (New York, 1977)
Archipelago (Lafayette, La., 1979)
Aurelia (Norfolk, Va., 1982)
Golden Gate and Other Stories (Minneapolis, 1982)
Annals of Klepsis (New York, 1983)
Through Elegant Eyes (Minneapolis, 1982)
Ringing Changes (1984)
Serpent's Egg (London, 1987)
East of Laughter (London, 1988)
Sinbad, The Thirteenth Voyage (Cambridge, Mass., 1989)
The Elliptical Grave (Weston, Ont., 1989)

Okla Hannali

by R. A. LAFFERTY

With a Foreword by Geary Hobson

University of Oklahoma Press
Norman and London

Paper cover design by Sue Hollingsworth.

Library of Congress Cataloging-in-Publication Data

Lafferty, R. A.
    Okla Hannali / by R. A. Lafferty ; with a foreword by Geary Hobson.
      p.   cm.
    Reprint. Originally published: Garden City, N.Y. : Doubleday, 1972.
    ISBN 0-8061-2349-4
    1. Indians of North America—Removal—Fiction.   2. Five Civilized
Tribes—History—Fiction.   3. Choctaw Indians—Removal—Fiction.
4. Oklahoma—History—Fiction.   I. Title.
PS3562.A28O83   1991
813'.54—dc20   90-50692
                                                CIP

A MANIFEST
OF THE GOODS
IN THIS PACKET

v

3. Who eats Comanche potatoes? From Tukabatchee Town to Round Mountains. Kiowas smell like mares' milk. What do white men smell like?

4. Take a Snake Indian as old as the rocks. Cross with Coyote —and he is the Fox!

5. Gentlemen, that is shooting and that is talking. My brother is the wind.

6. A ring of bulls. A nation was being murdered that afternoon. Who knows the snake-hair plant?

FOREWORD

By Geary Hobson

Hannali Innominee's Century

R. A. Lafferty has been firmly established as a widely respected sci-
ence-fiction writer for well over twenty years. The winner of a Hugo
Award in 1973, he has been nominated for the same prize, and for the
Nebula Award as well, numerous times. Novels such as *Past Master,
The Reefs of Earth, Fourth Mansions,* and *The Devil is Dead* trilogy,
and the short story collections *Nine Hundred Grandmothers* and
Strange Desires, are testimony to his secure niche in the realm of
science fiction. Often overlooked, however, are Lafferty's historical
novels, works such as *The Fall of Rome* and *The Flame is Green,* and
especially *Okla Hannali.* Indeed, this last-named novel, published
originally in 1972, quickly became a major contribution to the surpris-
ingly small body of good fiction written about American Indians over
the past generation.

Unfortunately, *Okla Hannali* did not stay in print very long—
probably less than three years altogether. It is therefore pleasing to
booklovers and students of American Indian history that the University

of Oklahoma Press is bestowing on this novel a second life by reprinting it. For those who missed it when it made its debut, the treat of discovery is before them in this rather unusual, totally extraordinary book. And it is unusual, and it is extraordinary. The epic life-journey of the book's protagonist, Hannali Innominee, a larger-than-life Choctaw politician, businessman, trader, farmer, ferryman, town builder, fiddler, culture-keeper, and mingo (Choctaw for headman) is one which parallels almost precisely the turbulent history of the Choctaws in the nineteenth century.

Born sometime around 1800 in the Okla Hannali district of the Choctaw Nation, in the land that later came to be called Mississippi, Hannali Innominee (the accents for both names fall on the second syllable) lives almost the entire century, dying at last in 1900 at his home in an east-central Oklahoma community that had been, up to a generation before, an important town of the Choctaw Nation of Indian Territory. In the course of Hannali's life, a life always inextricably intertwined with the destiny of kinspeople in his tribal district (hence the book's title), the Choctaw Nation undergoes cultural changes that parallel the course of Manifest Destiny during America's "century of dishonor."

As one of the "Five Civilized Tribes," the Choctaws were in the nineteenth century, as historian Angie Debo has labeled them elsewhere, a republic, and as thoroughgoing a republic as could be found anywhere in the world at the time. Lafferty chronicles the tribe's history from the time of America's early process of nation-building and land-grabbing to the eve of Oklahoma's statehood, when it is assumed the Choctaws—and all other Indians in the region—merged into the dominant white society. Such an absolute, however, is far from the actual truth. In 1991, it is estimated there are approximately 250,000 Indians in Oklahoma—not an inconsiderable number for a "disappeared" people. As Lafferty delineates Hannali Innominee in the novel, there is something immutable about the Choctaw character that will always endure despite the racial intermixture and the superimposed laws and religions of the white American culture. On his deathbed, Hannali knows that his white-blooded granddaughter, Anna-Hata, with her "eyes like blue cornflowers and hair like corn," is indubitably Choctaw and that "the world had not run out of Indians yet."

Okla Hannali is, first and foremost, a novel about survival. Hannali Innominee and his fellow Choctaws endure the Removal era of the

1830s, the Civil War (and the attendant twelve separate little civil wars that beset some of the tribes during this time), the massive influx of the invading white settlers in the quarter-century following the war, the federally enforced termination legislation, and the culture-threatening land allotment system. At the end of the novel, Lafferty shows that, despite all these catastrophes, there are still Choctaws around.

Okla Hannali is an excellent fictional rendering of American Indian views (and in this case more particularly, the Choctaw view) of American history and Indian Territory during the last century. Anyone who has endured the milksop, watered-down, enwhitened view of Oklahoma history as taught in high schools all around Oklahoma is advised to read this book with extreme caution. Such readers are further enjoined to not be surprised to hear that there are indeed Indian versions of American history. *Okla Hannali* very handily provides such a version, and more of them are needed.

PREFACE

The trouble is that behind writing something like this there is only the story of long lonesome hard work: that isn't interesting. As to myself, I had no special qualification at all to write this novel. I'm not Indian. One quarter of the people in Oklahoma, a little over half a million people, had some Indian blood in them, but I haven't any. There were at least twenty thousand Choctaw families with grandfather traditions or letters of parallel events to those in *Okla Hannali*, but I had to come to them as an outsider. Some Choctaw should have written a Choctaw epic, as the great Osage writer John Joseph Mathews wrote *The Osages: Children of the Middle Waters* (University of Oklahoma Press, 1961), but none of them did.

I had already decided to write a series of works under the theme and classification of "Chapters of the American Novel." One of the earlier chapters would almost have had to be an Indian chapter, and I regard *Okla Hannali* as that chapter. I suppose that I chose the Choctaws because they were always there in the background, a little bit larger than life, and generally silent.

Anyhow, the facilities were available. The Gilcrease Museum (given to the city of Tulsa by Thomas Gilcrease, "the world's richest Indian") has an extensive collection of Indian artifacts, paintings, manuscripts, and books. The Civilization of the American Indian Series published by the University of Oklahoma Press then ran to about a hundred books, and I had read all but two or three late ones. There also were many good books put out by the Naylor Company in San Antonio, besides the popular Indian books which didn't need subsidizing and were put out by the regular houses.

My own earliest Indian connection goes back to the year 1899, fifteen years before I was born. At that time four youngish Irishmen from Iowa homesteaded on adjoining quarter sections somewhere north of present-day Snyder, Oklahoma. They built a shack in the middle of the section where the four quarters came together, and they lived there together. They were Hugh Lafferty, my father; Ed Burke, my mother's brother; Frank Burke, my mother's cousin; and a man named MaGuire. Ed Burke took a job at the Anadarko Indian agency (he was a stenographer as well as a farmer), and he knew very many of the wilder Indians (Quanah Parker and such) in their old age. He learned a lot of Indian lore, most of it apparently true. My father was also full of old Indian stories. My mother came down to Oklahoma several years later than he did, and with a high school diploma and a teacher certificate, she became a school teacher. With a third or so of her students Indian or mixed-blood, she also learned quite a bit about Indians.

My personal Indian connection began when I was four years old and we moved down to Oklahoma from Iowa (my family had moved back to Iowa twice from their earlier Oklahoma days). This was in Perry, Oklahoma, and early on our first morning there, I ran out into the street and there was a little boy about my size. "Hello" I said. He knocked me down, and I ran in the house crying. I told my mother that a mean little boy had knocked me down. "Don't play with mean little boys," she said, "just play with nice little boys." A minute later there was a knock at the door and I heard someone ask my mother if the little boy in there could come out and play. "Yes," she said, and she told me, "There's a nice little boy out there. Go out and play with him." I ran out again. Bang! He knocked me down again. He was the same blamed kid. He was a Pawnee Indian boy and was, as far as I know, the first Indian I ever met.

In every school class I have ever been in there have been several Indians. Mostly these have been Osages and Cherokees, but there were also a few Choctaws. I've known quite a few Indians quite well in my lifetime and have gotten some interesting talk and history from them. I know them well enough, most of the time, to know when they're kidding and when they're giving me the straight stuff. I've also learned that there's some whoppers about themselves that they really believe and that there's a lot that most of them don't know about their history.

Okla Hannali was first written in 1963. It was a torturous undertaking even though it wasn't much more than an overflowing of crammed notebooks: I wasn't a very good novel writer at that time. It has since been completely rewritten twice. In the various writings of it and studies for it, I have picked up quite a bit of the non-Indian history of my own region also.

—R. A. LAFFERTY

Tulsa, Oklahoma

PROLOGUE

*The history of the world in a pecan shell. The
sand plum was the forbidden fruit. As the White
Eyes count the hundreds.*

The first persons on our earth were two brothers—Chatah and
Chickasah. They emerged onto land from a cavern under the Gulf
of Mexico. From them are descended the Choctaw and Chickasaw
Indian nations and all other nations whatsoever.

It has been more than twenty generations but less than thirty since
the brothers first came up onto earth. There are those who pretend
to a greater antiquity for mankind on earth, but the fact is that we
are boys only and have all the awkwardness of boys. It was but the
day before yesterday that the two brothers established the nations. It
was yesterday only that the nations scattered. It was less than yesterday that several of these nations—much changed by their wanderings
—returned to their homeland.

The Choctaws and Chickasaws have always lived adjacent to each
other, often in tolerable friendship. Some blood they spilled, but it
was not as though they were enemies or strangers.

The forbidden fruit of the Choctaws was the sand plum. By eating
it, they lost the easy way and must climb the hard hill forever.

1

The Noe or Noah of the Choctaws was Oklabashih the great raft builder. The Flood was a Mississippi River flood of unequaled magnitude. It was at the time of the Flood, or as an immediate consequence of it, that the Choctaw Indians followed their brother Chickasaws across the river, from the west to the east side.

The Mound, the Babel, of the Choctaws after the Flood was Nanih Waiya (the Bending Mountain) in the Tallago Valley of Mississippi. There had been another Nanih Waiya in the old land before the Choctaws crossed the river to their new home. That one was the Mountain from the Beginning, this latter one was a memento of it built by hands.

The magic men of the Choctaws were the *Alikchi*. But the magic itself, the *Aleika*, could surround even a private man, and he then became a man of a special sort.

The patriarchs of the Choctaws were Homostubbee, Puchshenub-bee, Pushmataha, and Moshulatubbee. The Choctaws were still in the Age of the Patriachs when we begin our action.

The foregoing is the history of the world up to the point where we begin our tale, at the start of the nineteenth century as the White Eyes count the hundreds.

CHAPTER ONE

1.

*The birth and raising of Hannali Innominee. How
was it go to be a child then? Barua resigns from
the Pushmataha.*

Should we not now get a man to going? Chronicles are all very well,
but an epic—and we aspire to no less—has to have a man in the
middle of it.

The man is going. He is already born. He will be going it for a
long time.

In an unknown year (either 1800, 1801, or 1802 according to the
later recollection of his brother) was born Hannali Innominee of
the Okla Hannali District of the Choctaw Nation. Hannali would
be a big man and would almost exactly fill a century.

The Innominee family was of the Mishoweia town or clan, but
had now removed some distance from most of the Mishoweia. They
were of the Hundred Families, an odd minority along the Mishoweia.

Hannali's father was Barua Innominee. His mother was Chapponia. His brothers were Pass Christian Innominee and Biloxi Innominee. The names of the Choctaws had already begun their evolu-
tion into their mixed form. Hannali was the third generation of

Innominees. He had, of course, ancestors going back further than that, but the Choctaws had not used surnames further back than that. He was raised on a south-flowing river in what is now the state of Mississippi.

Hannali was a bulky boy, a Choctaw chuckler. And that is a thing that must be understood before we go on. Other peoples laugh or smile, some giggle. The Choctaws chuckle. An Indian agent, of a little later date, tells of a row of Choctaws sitting on a log for an hour, all as blank-faced as though they were dead. Then one of them began to quiver and shake, another, and still another. And all of them quivered and chuckled till they shook the leaves off the trees. They were the chuckling Choctaws.

They may have remembered a joke they heard the day before, or a week before; they may not all have been chuckling at the same thing. But it is a thing that distinguishes the Choctaws from other people, that they will sit silent for a long time, and will then begin to chuckle as though they would rupture themselves.

When very young, Hannali would sit on the black ground and chuckle till it was feared that he would injure himself. Whatever came over him, prenatal witticism or ancestral joke, he was seldom able to hold in his glee. In all his life he never learned to hold it in.

What did he look like? An early story tells it. Once when he was very small, Hannali was found in the company of an old she-bear. Papa Barua tried to get the boy away from her and was badly mauled. Then Mama Chapponia had to come in and smooth things over. She explained to the she-bear that this was not a bear cub however much it looked like one. It was Chapponia's own child and the bear made a mistake. You had but to snuffle the boy to tell that he was not a bear. They both tried it, and they both doubted the test. Hannali smelled like a bear cub and he looked like one. In a short time he would come to look like a great hulking he-bear.

The old she-bear remained around the farm for years, until she died, and became an intimate of the family. When the brothers would call to Hannali, "Your mother is looking for you!" he never knew whether they meant Mama Chapponia or the she-bear until they chuckled.

· · ·

"How was it go to be a child then?" Hannali's son Travis asked him years later.

4

"Everything was larger then," Hannali would tell his son, "the forest buffalo were bigger than the plains buffalo we have now, the bears were bigger than any you can find in the Territory today you call that a bearskin on that wall it is only a dogskin I tell you yet it's from the biggest bear ever killed in the Territory the wolves were larger and the foxes the squirrels were as big as our coyotes now the gophers were as big as badgers the doves and pigeons then were bigger than the turkeys now."

"Maybeso you exaggerate," his son Travis would say.

"Of course I do with a big red heart I exaggerate the new age has forgotten how I remember that the corn stood taller and the ears fuller nine of them would make a bushel and now it takes a hundred and twenty that doesn't consider that the bushels were bigger then the men were taller and of grander voice the women of a beauty to be found nowhere today except in my own family the girls sang so pretty with voices they walked so fine when they carried corn they could soft-talk you like little foxes those girls."

"You are joking it all, Father."

"Not like we joked then all the stories were funnier like the man who laughed till he split open one lung went flying out you think that stopped him his stomach and his little stomach came flying out then his liver out came all his entrails and the organs that an honest man doesn't even know the names of them should you not attend to him somebody asked his wife wait he stop chuckling said his wife I put them back before he stop chuckling then I have it all to do over again who will tell a story like that now you tell that and they look at you and say what is this a witless Indian things were funnier then my son."

Hannali did not speak in that manner because he was a clod, but because he was a Choctaw. Whether in English or Choctaw, all Chocs run sentences together with no intonation for either period or question. The educated Choctaws of that day—those who wrote in their own hands—punctuated either not at all or excessively. In official depositions one will find page-long screeds with no break at all. Or one will find random punctuation, with commas between almost every word, and perhaps a colon or semicolon between an article and its following noun. Someone had told them that they must punctuate, but nobody would ever be able to tell them how.

It is so even today with the removed Choctaws. Go to barrooms where Indians abound (First or Second Street in Tulsa, Reno or

California Street in Oklahoma City, Kickapoo Street in Shawnee, Sixth Street in Okmulgee, Callahan Street in Muskogee) and you will hear a man talk like that. Ask him. He will be a Choctaw.

"Mama Natchez says that you see with long time ago eyes and they magnify," said son Travis.

"True they magnify now we have forgotten how I know that I look back through the glasses of a boy who needed none a lens-grinder man has told me that this is an effect he cannot duplicate."

But that is the way it was in the early days. Everything was larger and was drawn with the old clear lines.

. . .

It was when Hannali was still a small boy that his father Barua Innominee changed the nationality of his family. Barua went to the tough chief Pushmataha and told him that he was resigning from his district. He said that Pushmataha had sucked the white men's eggs and still had the froth of them on his mouth. That was partly true. Pushmataha had become General Push to the white men. He held a general's rank for service in the War of 1812 and at other times. He had a general's uniform and he liked to wear it.

But he was a Medal Mingo for all that, a king, and a real king. Whether he was Mingo-Pushmataha or General Push, he was not a man to cross.

Barua Innominee was a very big strong man. There were no bigger men anywhere except for those few slow-minded, slow-moving giants who were sometimes born to the Choctaws. But Pushmataha could strike right through big men like that.

Pushmataha is described in a dozen accounts as of towering height and of great bulk. Indeed, he has described himself as such, and perhaps he believed that he was. But an early Indian agent has given it that Pushmataha was no taller than the average man and was on the lean side, that it was his burning intensity, his incredible speed and striking power with knife or short club or hand, his fabulous voice and his exciting mind that made him so outstanding and feared a person.

Nobody could kill a man faster than could Pushmataha. He made lightning seem slow, and thunder was a whisper beside his voice. He had hypnotic talents and great acting ability, and he scared men who didn't scare easily. To many he must have seemed of towering height. You don't call a man a giant unless there is something giant-like about him. And Barua had told him that he had sucked white men's eggs.

When crossed, Pushmataha would swell up and turn purple. Then he would either strike dead the man who had crossed him, or he would break into echoing laughter and it would be all over with. This time he did neither.

He finally let all of the air out of himself when he saw that Barua was unafraid. He told Barua that he accepted his defection, and to get out of his district at once and forever. This was the old Kunsha Okla Hannali Six Town District.

Barua told Pushmataha that he would *not* get out of his district physically, that he would get out only by declaring himself out, that he would continue to live on his same land, and that he would announce that land annexed to whatever district would have him.

Pushmataha told Barua that he would kill him and drag him out of the district by his dead heels. And Barua turned and walked away.

One does not turn and walk away from a Mingo without being dismissed.

Barua was in the saddle and a half mile gone when he heard the giant laughter of Pushmataha bouncing around the hills. Old Push was a fine fellow for all his fearsome aspect, and the Choctaws would remember him with affection after he was dead. Had he lived forever, the Choctaws would have done the same. And he later wiped that white man's egg off his face and became Indian of the Indians again.

Barua Innominee rode to Moshulatubbee, the Mingo of the old Okla Tannaps District, now named after him the Moshulatubbee.

Moshulatubbee was another very large man, and he had never sucked white men's eggs even to deceive them. He did not blow himself up and turn purple in the Pushmataha manner, but to one who had done wrong his appearance was equally disturbing. Moshulatubbee had a great grin that could not be fathomed. "It is like that of the nuthatch that has just swallowed a wild cat," one Choctaw said. Moshulatubbee wore that grin even when he killed a man with his own hand. As Mingo, Moshulatubbee was executioner for his district. He didn't love the job but he didn't shirk it. Mostly he was a pleasant man, and he was so now.

7

"You have ride slow the story have ride faster," the old Mingo said, "I hear you have call the old bull an egg-sucking possum now you have join our club."

"I have resigned from a district how have I joined a club?" asked Barua.

"It is a very small club," grinned Moshulatubbee. "It has maybe twenty dead members and you be only the fourth living one."

"What is make the club?"

"Those who have defy our good friend to his face Homostubbee did it and lost no sleep over it remember that about Homostubbee Puckshenubbee did it and it aged him ten years but it aged Pushmataha too I did it and my wifes have to burn my clothes after it I sweat so foully do you know what he was say about me after it."

"No I know nothing of that," said Barua.

"Pushmataha say that I leave my grin there grinning at him and walk out from behind it and take a ramble and a drink and a nap all the while he was hold his breath and swell up and turn purple and then I come back rested and slip into my grin again and so have him tricked I did not know to do this with him but since then I have done it with other men you want call me Mingo."

"I will join your district if you will have me if you will not then I will join Puckshenubbee if he will not have me either then I will be a man without a district."

"I will have you now you are my man I am your Mingo whoever touches you touches me you are now of the Moshulatubbee now you listen man Barua with every ear you have nobody ever resigns from my district I am not Pushmataha neither is Pushmataha Moshulatubbee I do not boast I do not blow up and carry on I tell you no four men no two men no one man ever cross me and live it is all a dead man club who have stood up to me you come see me some time tell me I have sucked eggs then we see some fun man."

The position of Barua Innominee was an awkward one. He had been hereditary town chief of Mishoweia Town though he had lived apart from that region. Even there he had been one of the Hundred Families—a minority faction. Now he announced himself to be a citizen of the Moshulatubbee, though still an Okla Hannali forever. He became almost a minority of one. Actually, five or six families, kinsmen and close friends, followed him in his new allegiance. But he set a pattern.

8

Later, his son Hannali would indeed become a minority of one, and he would maintain that he represented the correct and main line and that all others were following the eccentric.

2.

Where are your own horses' bones? Okla Falaya, Okla Tannaps, Okla Hannali. Incomprehensible ways. Even the stogie was sacred.

It was only yesterday that the nations scattered through the world, and less than yesterday that several of them returned to the homeland from over the sea, and greatly changed by their wanderings. Three of these nations were the Spanish, the French, the English. Interplay was set up between these returning nations and the Indians of the South.

The Choctaws were the central and most numerous tribe of the South, and their language (in its own form, and in that of the Mavila-Choctaw trade tongue of pidgin) dominated a wide region. The Choctaws were farmers, which is to say that perhaps one acre out of ten of their land was under the plow or the hoe. They had good hunting, good farms, and good livestock.

It is maintained that the Indians had no horses till the Spanish brought them. But this is a lie, one of the Chocs told me.

"The Choctaws always had horses," he said.

"Where are their bones then?" I asked him.

"Hog hominy hell how do I know where their bones are where are your own horses' bones the Chocs had horses as long as they had hoot owls."

The Chocs were the greatest Ishtaboli ball players in the world. They played with sometimes a hundred men on a side, and rival factions would bet whole towns on a game. When they scored a point, they gobbled like turkeys.

They had strong towns of timber and earth houses. They were such hardy warriors that they seldom had to go to war. Their presence imposed a basic peace on the old South during the Indian centuries.

9

So the Choctaws were the *Okla,* the People, until the white men returned to the land.

. . .

This is the chronology of that return:

In the year 1528 in the neighborhood of Mobile Bay, they made contact with Spanish men of the Narvaez Expedition. They threw stones but did not really fight.

In the year 1540 in the same neighborhood, the Choctaws under Tuscalusa met the Spanish under De Soto, and they did fight. In their chronicles, the Spanish claim to have won, and the Choctaws were not keeping chronicles.

In 1699, the French founded Biloxi in Mississippi. The Choctaws got on well with the French during the French century that followed.

In 1721, the first African slaves were landed in Mobile. Within a week, some of them escaped to the Choctaws and hid with them. For the next hundred years, Negroes from the white settlements would be slipping off to join the Chocs.

In 1726, the Jesuit Mathurin le Petit came among the Choctaws, the first priest of whom we know the name. The French missioners failed with the Choctaws, with one exception. In the Six Town District of Okla Hannali, One Hundred Families of the town of Mishoweia were converted. One of the Hundred Families was the Innominees.

The Three Nations of the Choctaws, coming from their ancient history into their confused medieval history, were these:

Okla Falaya, the Choctaws allied with the British.

Okla Tannaps, the Choctaws allied with the French.

Okla Hannali, the Choctaws confused unto themselves.

But their internecine wars were slight ones, only family affairs or town affairs.

In 1767 was born the particular Devil of the Indians. He would be responsible for the deaths of many thousands of them and for the dispersal of the remainder. The birth of the Devil was known to the Indians like an omen, and a shudder went through all the Indian South.

In 1786, the Choctaws made their first treaty with the new United States, the first of between thirty-five and fifty treaties depending on the way you count. None of the treaties was successful.

. . .

All Indians are philosophers but not very good ones. They ask all the questions but they do not find the answers.

"Where do I come from where do I go what is the purpose of it who thought of it?" Hannali asked his father Barua.

"God thought of it," said Barua, "and the ways of God are incomprehensible."

"What is incomprehensible is not a Choctaw word."

"Is French people word used by the priest," Papa Barua said. "I do not know what it means I believe the priest did not know what it means I believe the word itself means not know what it means."

"How can a bird move through the air and not be two places at one time?" Hannali asked his brother Pass Christian. "If it is one place one time and another place another time how does it move unless there are times between the times."

"I also wondered about these things when I was a boy," said Pass Christian. Hannali was nine and Pass Christian twelve years old.

In a laurel grove on a hill lived an old bear who was supposed to possess all wisdom. Hannali went to question the animal. The bear was sleeping, and Hannali hit it on the snout with a rock to wake it up.

"Old bear who know everything," Hannali sang out, "tell me what is the first order of business in the world."

The bear came out of the grove with a rumble, and Hannali was in the top of a tree without remembering how he climbed it. But he had his answer. "The first order of business in the world is to save your own skin," the bear told him, and not in words.

. . .

They smoke. Another voice takes up the linked stories of the Man and the Family and the Nation. Be you not restive! It is a hundred-year-long story they spin out, and it cannot be told in a moment. Take the pipe when it is passed to you, or light up a stogie. The pipe was sacred to all the Indians, but even the cigar was to Choctaws. Both tale and smoke are from the lips of great men, and some of them were Mingos.

CHAPTER TWO

1.

*When the Innominees were Choctaw rich. We are
not indolent we are lazy. Slave is for seven years.*

The thumb slips a bit, and we have riffled over a dozen years of a
life. Hannali Innominee was now a young man in his teens, and he
had come to a certain appearance. He would not change greatly in
looks for the rest of his life. He was a bulky Choc, and they are the
stockiest Indians of the Five Tribes.

Stocky! They are the fat Indians!

"There's a lot of them," a Chickasaw Indian said of them once.
"Not so many," someone protested, "only a few thousand of them
left." "I didn't mean in numbers," the Chickasaw said, "I mean the
way one of them's heaped together. Man, there's a lot of them!"

There was a lot of Hannali Innominee. Even when he was a boy
he was a lot of boy.

. . .

It is sometimes said that the Choctaws are indolent. "It is a lie,"
the Choctaws say. "We are not indolent we are lazy there is a

difference." There *is* a difference, but those who see things as all white or all red are not able to understand it.

. . .

The Innominee family had become Choctaw rich in those years. Barua Innominee did not seem an astute man, and he committed folly after folly. But after each of them, somehow, he ended up richer.

"Let us go ahead and build it," he would tell his three sons, "if we cannot use it for what we intend maybe we can use it for something else." They were great builders.

Barua built a grain mill on the south-flowing river on which he lived, but the Indians would not bring him their corn to grind. What were they, white men, that they needed somebody to grind their corn for them? They had their hand querns. Barua turned the mill into a dock and landing. He built flatboats and rafts and floated produce down to the Gulf. He built a station on the Gulf where pickups were made by coaster boats out of Pass Christian and Biloxi.

The Innominees were among the first of the Choctaws to put iron plows into the south sand soil of Okla Hannali. They were among the first to use draft oxen, and then mules. They were of the first to acquire Negroes.

There is a point about the Negroes to be cleared up. The Choctaws did not buy their Negroes. They acquired them. The white men said that they stole them. These were the slaves who escaped from the white settlements to the Choctaws.

All the Indians had had slavery, but not on the same basis. Slavery with them was almost never for life, and certainly was not hereditary. An indifferent or inferior slave would be run out of the tribe and back to his own Indian people, a superior one would eventually be adopted as a full citizen. Slavery of Indian by Indian in the old South usually observed the biblical limit of seven years, a limit that amazed early missionaries and was cited by cranks as proof that the Indians were the lost tribes of Israel.

2.

Hound is dog. Who pass law pigs can't run too?
Is not a proper fox hunt.

Pass Christian had brought his father Barua a bright red coat from New Orleans. It was such a coat as a Mingo might have worn. People, that coat was scarlet and splendid beyond believing!

For a few days Barua wore the coat only on special occasions— to weddings, to Istaboli games, to bear hunts, to pig geldings. He wore it with a white man top hat and with a red man turban. He wore it barefoot and booted, and when he felt particularly expansive he wore it to bed. But he did not wear it at trivial times, for he understood that it was a ceremonial thing.

Then an old memory of what he had seen or heard about came over him. He assembled his family and people to make an announcement.

"A red coat is a Master of the Hunt Coat," Papa Barua said. "I will wear my red coat I will make a brass trumpet nine feet long all assemble here in three days with horse and hound we will have a fox hunt."

"What is hound?" asked Biloxi Innominee.

"Hound is dog," said brother Hannali, but he was damned if he could understand what horses and dogs had to do with hunting their fox.

• • •

Papa Barua made a trumpet nine feet long. It took him two days. He had never made a trumpet before, but he had worked in brass a little, and he had a small trumpet of white man manufacture to copy. He finished it off, but it wouldn't sound. Undefeated, he modified it. He inserted the small white man trumpet as mouthpiece, and the great nine-foot length gave it resonance. He could play a lively tune on it, and it had a muted richness that the smaller trumpet had not had by itself.

Barua had sent for a certain man to instruct them in the fox hunt. This man, an Indian who had traveled much, had himself seen a fox hunt. That was in the Virginia country, and he had watched the hunt from a hilltop.

. . .

The women were up late the night before the hunt dyeing the coats of their men red, but not one of the coats was the equal of the New Orleans coat of Barua.

They assembled at dawn of the hunt day.

"Pass Christian get the fox," Barua said—they had but one fox in their town, "put a strap around her belly and a leader to that and drag her along to get her running Hannali and Biloxi get six dogs each belt them in like manner and drag them to get them started explain to them that it will be fun then the men on horses will start after them and who knows what the day may produce."

Pass Christian, the educated one of the Innominees, was at first embarrassed for his father and family. He knew that this was not the proper way to conduct a fox hunt. Then he laughed and went about it.

"What am I a white man," he said, "that I should be ashamed of my father and my family in their ignorance what am I somehow abashed for them who are bone of my bone and liver of my liver hell I want to have a fox hunt too I don't care if it is a proper one what am I get to be too educated to have fun."

Pass Christian went and got Fox, an old vixen who had born many whelps and was now old and cranky and deserted by her mate. He found her in the shade of the stump where she spent her mornings, and gave her a piece of pork to entice her. He put the strap around her belly and dragged her to get her running.

But Fox got hysterical at this treatment, and leapt up face high on Pass Christian and snapped him up on nose and cheek in an uncommon way. He ran hard to drag her along and take the slack out of her, but she bounded and yipped and turned over in the air snapping and gnawing at the line.

"They are going to have trouble with Fox," said a wise one among them.

Hannali and Biloxi had their dogs, but it is hard for a man to drag six dogs at any speed when they do not wish to go.

15

"Biloxi is too fat for it," said the man who had seen the fox hunt, "he will be out of wind before he is able to drag the dogs as fast as a horse is able to run."

"Biloxi is not so fat," Hannali told the man, "he is mostly feathers if you should see him plucked you would see that he is not fat at all." That was a joke, but the man was not a Choctaw and did not understand it.

Hannali and Biloxi dragged the dogs at such a rate of speed that the very ground smoked. It must be understood that these were not hunting dogs, nor had the Choctaws any such. They were little round yellow dogs that the Chocs kept and fatted to eat. Nobody understood the part of the dogs in the fox hunt, but the man who had seen a hunt swore that there had been hounds running.

Papa Barua gave a trumpet blast that almost lifted the ears of the horses off their heads. The red-coated huntsmen, there must have been twenty of them, were off after Fox and hounds.

People, that was the best fox hunt anybody ever saw. Pass Christian was remarkably fast of foot. He had to be to stay ahead of Fox who kept lunging up and taking pieces out of his rump till finally the whole seat of his doeskin pants was gone and he was exposed bloody to the world. Hannali and Biloxi went so speedily that their six dogs each stood out behind them flying on the ends of their tethers. At other times they bounced along the ground and high into the air, turning over and over and making a continuous complaint. The Choctaw horses set up a chortling neighing and horsey laughing and carrying on. They picked up the rhythm of Papa Barua's trumpet, "Whoopa, Whoopa," for Barua grunted into the trumpet every time he bounced on his horse. But he kept the nine-foot instrument clamped in his powerful jaws, and the brass caught the sun like a banner.

The Innominee pigs joined in, running between the dogs and the horses, and they were the runningest pigs in the whole country. The children got in the way too, for the hunt doubled back on itself time and again to keep in the rough brambled area and not to trample the standing corn.

"It is not right," called the man who had seen a fox hunt, "they did not use pigs they did not let the children get in the way they had only the fox and the hounds and the horses and the horsemen."

"Let them alone," ordered Papa Barua taking the trumpet from his mouth, "pigs like fun too children like fun too who pass law pigs can't run."

Hannali running hard blared like a bull moose and whirled his yipping dogs around his head on their tethers; somebody let the mean bull out of the corral and he began to toss horses and riders together; the boars tusked the horses after they were tired of chasing Fox and dogs; the girls began to throw throwing sticks at the hunters—all in fun, but those things can knock a man unconscious; the boys who had no horses ran tripping ropes across the course; Mama Chapponia loaded a shotgun with rock salt and let wham at the whole bunch of them not sparing her own man; the smaller girls threw rotten squashes into the faces of the hunters as they went by.

It was not a proper fox hunt. After a while it no longer pretended to be. But it was loud and violent and soul-filling. The three Innominee brothers, Pass Christian and Biloxi and Hannali, had not even begun to give out after hours of it. It would have lasted till dark if Fox had not taken matters between her teeth. In her crazy somersaulting on the end of her tether she finally worried that leather piece in two.

Then she cut back under the hoofs of the horses, throwing them all into a mill. Riders were toppled and horses fell on riders. Hardly a man of them but was trampled by the churning hoofs. Women came out and belabored their fallen men with swinging pots and pans, not from enmity, but just for the fun of it. A black girl named Martha Louisiana gathered Fox up in her arms to save her from further damage.

"Is the hunt over," roared happy Papa Barua, "how do we tell when the hunt is over?"

"I think it is over," said the man who had seen a fox hunt.

"If they have no grand gesture for the end of it then we ought to find out one for ourselves," said Hannali. "Who knows how to end it big how to put a crown on it?"

"They cut off the tail of the fox and wave in the air," said the man who had seen a fox hunt, "they call it the bushcht."

"I will cut it off and wave in the air," said Papa Barua. "I am the Master of the Hunt."

"No you will not," said the black girl Martha Louisiana, "the

17

fox has been abused enough. Sooner I let you cut off my own head than the tail of the fox."

"Is an even better ending," howled Hannali with kindly malice, "cut off Martha Louisiana head put it on the end of a spear it is the best ending of all."

"No. I joke. Better the fox than me. Have the dedamned little animal. Is not a proper fox hunt anyhow." Martha Louisiana had lived with the Choctaws most of her life, but often she did not understand their humor.

But Fox sent up such a whimper when Papa Barua began to cut off her tail that he cut off only the hair of it, bound it together with itself, and waved it in the air. And old Fox slunk off, shorn and shamed and disgusted, back to her tree stump.

. . .

Then it was late in the afternoon, and the Chocs had a very fair of it living over the events of the day: how Pass Christian the educated one of them had the seat of his pants eaten out and was exposed bloody to the world; how Papa Barua had lost his big nine-foot trumpet and had it bent and stompled on by hoof; how one man was thought to have been killed but later he got up and walked; how dogs and Fox had bounced along in the air; how this man had suffered a broken leg and another had his ribs cracked when a horse had fallen on him; how the pigs had kept on running after it was over with, and maybe the Chocs would never see them again—all such hilarity kept them occupied for a long time.

This was the only fox hunt those Chocs ever had. But they did have a lot of fun together in those years.

3.

The magnified years. The other end under your chin damn boy damn.

The Innominees became large farmers, and they had something of a trading station. They dealt in hides, pelts, pecans, corn, and cotton. Pass Christian became a boatman who went as far as New Orleans. Biloxi and Hannali remained with the father Barua in the expanding cultivation, in the saltworks, in the tannery. They lumbered, and floated it down. They imported both by wagon and water. Their landing became a store and depot, and they brought in a Frenchman or French Indian to run it for them.

This man was Silvestre DuShane, one a little beyond Hannali's age. He had connections in Louisiana, in Arkansas, and in the Arkansas West (later to be called Indian Territory). He was French, or he was Shawnee Indian, or he was both or neither. But he became a Choctaw and the Choctaws never repented of receiving him. He was the close friend of Hannali's young manhood.

They had high times—but we have to get on with it. These were the magnified years, and we are compelled to slide over them and enter the disturbed years that follow.

. . .

We riffle over a few more years of the lives. Hannali had now attained his majority. He was the best farmer in the Choctaw country. He was a mule man, a corn man. He was now in actual charge of all the Innominee production.

Into his notice at this time had come Martha Louisiana, a young girl of the Choctaw Negroes. It must be explained that Martha Louisiana was a strong, slim, rapid girl at this time. Those who knew her only in the middle years of the century, at Hannali House in the Territory, must be reminded that she was not always heavy and ponderous and measured of speech. You should have heard her sing while Silvestre DuShane played that little Louisiana mouth horn of his. And at this time they got a new music.

Pass Christian brought a fiddle back from New Orleans. He offered it to Biloxi, but that big young man would have none of it. Biloxi was slower of wit than the rest of the Innominee clan—a huge, slow-moving young fellow, almost but not quite one of those dim-witted giants who were sometimes born to the Choctaw families. Oh, Biloxi was all there, but he would never be one to play an instrument.

Pass Christian offered the fiddle to Papa Barua, but that older man said that his fingers had become too coarsened and stiff from the saltworks and the tannery.

"Give it to Hannali," said Papa Barua, "he will be the fiddler and do us honor why can't a muleman be a fiddler too Alapa Homa skins mules and plays the fiddle in Falaya we have not got no fiddler in our town at all the other end under your chin damn boy damn cut rushes spread them on the sand we will have a dance tonight go tell everybody my son plays the fiddle like nobody else in Okla Hannali I got the best sons in the country hear how he plays he never saw a fiddle before in his life kill the sick ox roast it we have a feed for everybody hustle out the fast pony spread the news man listen to my boy play."

And Hannali *could* play. He became a Choctaw fiddler. Not all Indians can play the fiddle. There are even some Choctaws who cannot, but the Choctaws were known as the fiddling Indians.

4.

Of fiddle tunes and larger events.

Did you know that whole years can go by like verses of a fiddle tune? A half-dozen years did go by as rapidly as that for Hannali, and they were good years. Martha Louisiana complained, it is true, that the tune was always the same one—that tune whose ending swirls up and breaks back to the beginning strains so that it goes on forever. Martha Louisiana had some idea about altering that unchanging tune, but it was altered by others.

But Hannali was as contented as he would ever be in his life. He was a muleman and a fiddle man and a corn man. He passed those early years in the hard prosperity of the sandy soil of Okla Hannali. There he was rated as a solid man of good family.

. . .

Then larger events plucked him out of all this. He was taken away on a long journey with his adopted brother the French Indian Silvestre DuShane, with Peter Pitchlynn of the Choctaws and Levi Colbert of the Chickasaw Indians, with men of other tribes, with several white men of official and unofficial status. When he returned, his old world would have been wiped out as though it had never been.

The men had a mission to examine and report on a new country.

To put it into context, this was just thirty-six years before the Civil War. It was the year 1828, and Hannali Innominee was somewhere between twenty-six and twenty-eight years old.

We must double back to the current of larger history to examine the reason for their journey.

CHAPTER THREE

1.

Behind God's Back. Near Doak's Stand on the Natchez Road. The Devil becomes President of the United States.

The Five Tribes were not wild. They had had their own agriculture for centuries, and they came quickly to improvements in methods of farming. At the time of their removal, they were better farmers than the white settlers of the same area. The tribes had maintained their peace over a very large area for a long time, and they were entitled to their peaceful increase there.

One thing must be understood. There was *not* a press of population or a shortage of land in the Gulf South states. There is not such today. The Indians had no great resentment against the white settlers coming onto the unoccupied land, even though it would abridge the hunting area.

But the white settlers did not want to clear the very good unoccupied land. They wanted only that portion of the land that the Indians had already cleared. They wanted the houses and farms of the Indians, their mules and cattle and pigs. A stubborn people who will sulk and die when put under whip slavery is of no use to anyone. The Indians must be killed, and more Negroes must be brought in to work the land.

Many species of game (and the Indians were a species of game to the white settlers) are hunted out by the use of captive members of their own species. They may be employed to capture their own kindred, as India elephants are. They may be employed as decoys or bellwethers. The analogy is not exact, but captive (white-blood) Indians were used to hunt out and penetrate their less pliable kindred.

The half-blood chiefs and advisers were used as wedges for splitting and shattering the tribes. Of the white-blood chiefs there would be Alexander McGillivray and William McIntosh of the Creeks, Major Ridge of the Cherokees, Greenwood LeFlore of the Choctaws, and too many others. We have no right to say of a dead man that, by his own lights, he was a bad man. Alexander McGillivray was quite a good man, and others of them meant well; but the white in them worked against the Indian interest. They wanted to see the Indians turned into white men. And the white men wanted no such thing.

How did it happen that the southern Indians were broken and murdered and driven off their land? Where did the breakdown come?

In October of 1803, the United States Congress ratified the Louisiana Purchase. The big-water French, the one people who had treated the Indians well, ceased to be their own people.

In the year 1816, the Choctaws were forced to cede all their land east of the Tombigbee River to the United States. As would always be the case in these treaties, it was pledged that they would be left in possession of the remainder of their land forever.

They had tossed one of their own limbs to the grizzled wolves to slow them down.

In 1817, Mississippi, the main homeland of the Choctaws, was admitted to the Union. There were conditions in the laws of the new state that spelled the destruction of the Choctaw Nation; there were clauses that spelled out murder plainly.

In 1819, Alabama was admitted as a state, and with something of the same tricks in the laws.

Also in 1819, Spain sold Florida to the United States. Thereafter, that special sanctuary of the Creeks and Seminoles and other Indians was thrown open to the despoilers from the states. Spanish and

French Louisiana and Spanish Florida had stood as witnesses. With these gone, the conscience of the Southland could be extinguished. No longer were there free outsiders to observe that rape that was building up. The Indian South became the Country Behind God's Back.

In 1820, "near Doak's Stand on the Natchez Road," the Choctaws ceded the large southwest section of their nation to the United States. This was to be in exchange for an equal area of land in the unknown West. It was a very bad trade, but it was forced on the Choctaws.

They had flung another of their limbs to their pursuers.

In 1825 in Washington, D.C., certain Choctaws signed a new treaty clarifying—so they were told—the earlier treaty of Doak's Stand. It clarified all their guarantees out of existence.

In 1828, the Devil of the Indians was elected president of the United States. By this, the Indians of the Five Tribes understood that many thousands of them must die and all of them be uprooted.

It was in the same year (1828) that a party of men from the tribes went to view the new lands in the West. Hannali Innominee was likely the least known man of this party, for most were town chiefs at least, or the deputies of district chiefs. But the party was to be representative of all sorts of Indians, and Hannali was the successful manager of one of the largest Choctaw farms. He would know about land.

This would be the first time that the Choctaws, Chickasaws, Cherokees, Creeks, or Seminoles had officially seen the new land for which they were forced to trade their nations. There would be a difficulty. The Osages, Quapaws, Caddoes, and other Indians who lived in the "new land" knew nothing of the United States giving their land to others; they knew nothing of the United States at all. And they were warlike Indians. The United States had traded land that it did not hold either physically or in real title.

We review the bare bones of the affair. We hurry through the details of the uprooting. It's a small matter to murder a nation, and these were but Five Nations out of hundreds. Three years, four, five, and most of it is ended.

We will go with the removed Indians to the new land and live with them there. We will be Territory Indians and know the Blue Stem Country and the Winding Stair Mountains and the False

24

Washita River and the Big House near the Three Forks of the
Canadian.

2.

*Dancing Rabbit Creek and the laws of unaccepted
testimony. Greenwood LeFlore and the Mingo.
One of the few remaining pleasures in his life.*

The end of it all would be the Treaty of Dancing Rabbit Creek
in 1830. By the time it was signed, many of the Indians would
already have emigrated to the new land.

In 1828, Georgia had extended her criminal laws over the
Cherokees within her borders (and Hannali Innominee was with
the Pitchlynn-Colbert Exploration in unnamed Oklahoma), followed by Mississippi enacting most peculiar laws over the Choctaws
and Chickasaws, and Alabama over the Creeks—and the Indians
were moving.

The laws of the three states declared all Indian treaties and
constitutions to be void, and the tribes to be extinguished. They
declared the Indians to be subject to the state courts under a
curious condition: no Indian's word would be considered against
a white man's word in those courts. The opportunities opened up
by this device were without limits.

The Indians found themselves evicted from their own farms by
forged deeds to white men whom they had never seen. They had no
recourse anywhere. The white man could swear in court, and the
Indian could attend but could not give testimony.

• • •

There is a black page in the plotting that preceded Dancing
Rabbit Creek.

In March of 1830, Greenwood LeFlore, the white-blood chief of
the Okla Falaya Choctaws, called a selected assembly of men from
all Choctaw districts. The requirement of this assembly, said the
enemies of LeFlore, was that all who attended should be traitors

25

to the Indians. LeFlore stated that in those trying times all the Choctaws should unite under a single chief.

LeFlore dealt with them shrewdly. He set up two puppets and then absorbed them. David Folsom, a weightless rival of old Moshulatubbee, was declared to be chief of his district. John Garland—another white-blood Indian and rival of Nitakechi (Pushmataha's nephew, Pushmataha was dead)—was stated to be chief of the Pushmataha District. Then both Folsom and Garland abdicated in favor of Greenwood LeFlore, and LeFlore was proclaimed chief of all the Choctaws.

The assembly drew up a treaty agreeing to give all Choctaw lands in Mississippi to the United States, and pledged all the Choctaws to remove to the western country. All of this was engineered by Major Haley, a personal envoy of President Jackson.

The treaty was carried to Washington, but the Senate refused to accept it. Defenders of the Indians insisted that any treaty must be made with the real representatives of the whole tribe. The Senate had the smell of the thing pretty accurately.

LeFlore was ordered by those who pulled his strings to make himself chief in fact. LeFlore and Folsom came down to Mushulatubbee's district with an army of one thousand men. They caught old Mushulatubby (he spelled his name all these ways himself, why should we not?) with an unarmed party at the "factory" of the Choctaw Nation—a collection of smithies and shops on the west bank of the Tombigbee River.

LeFlore said that Moshulatubbee must abdicate or die.

The old Mingo Moshulatubbee grinned weirdly at the white-man Indian intruder, and LeFlore must have felt uneasy even with a thousand men at his back.

What happened then isn't quite clear, except that Moshulatubbee did not abdicate and did not die. In some manner, the advantage passed over to him.

The only eyewitness account is a short one from a white frontiersman who (unlike most of them) loved old Moshulatubbee and hated Greenwood LeFlore. We follow it roughly.

The shabby old fat man Moshulatubbee had a presence that Greenwood LeFlore could never have, and he whipped him by his presence alone.

At length LeFlore trembled under the devious grin and silent chuckling of the old Mingo. His influence leaked away as Moshulatubbee faced him down. LeFlore turned away and gave the order to kill the Mingo, but his voice shook when he gave the command and his men laughed at him. They could not hear him, they hooted; speak louder, they said. They became Moshulatubbee's men as they stood there. In twos and threes, in tens and twenties, then in hundreds they shuffled across to the side of the Mingo. Moshulatubbee laughed out loud then and turned away with all the men, and LeFlore was alone.

The account may be colored a little by a partisan of the Mingo, but Moshulatubbee did win over all the Choctaws, and no shot was fired.

So that particular sellout was not successful, but the thing was certain as the Sun. Within the year, Moshulatubbee and Nitakechi would be compelled to put their own hands to an instrument conveying away the last of the old Choctaw land.

. . .

For a while the Indians found friends, but not strong enough friends, in the United States Senate. On February 11, 1831, the Senate requested that President Jackson should inform that body whether the Intercourse Act of 1802 (which guaranteed federal protection to the Indians) was being observed; and if not, why not.

On February 22, 1831, President Jackson delivered to the U. S. Senate a special message—one of the most dumbfounding messages ever. He announced that he was a champion of the state of Georgia (the outrage in question was one of Georgia against the Cherokee Indians) and of all other states in any controversy they might have with the Indians. He announced that he would *not* enforce the Intercourse Act or any other act or treaty that the federal government had ever made for the protection of any Indians, and that he would not permit them to be enforced.

And he won, for the Jacksonian revolution (the most misunderstood movement in American history) was in full swing. It was almost exactly the opposite of what is taught and believed of it. To describe it we must borrow the phrase of a better man about a more comprehensible revolution: It was the "Revolt of the Rich against the Poor." It was that and no other thing.

It embraced the illegal seizure of two hundred million acres of

Indian land in half a dozen southern states, and the turning of this land over to a few hundred already very rich men. It ensured that the seized land would be of the giant slave-plantation sort, and not of the freehold sort. It created the poor white and the poor black classes, which still endure.

The Jacksonian men were not the poor but honest frontiersmen. They were wealthy and powerful and corrupt, and they had found their leader.

. . .

Most of the Indian removal was in the years 1832, 1833, and 1834. About fifty thousand Indians moved or were removed from the old South to the new Indian country. And some twenty thousand others died on the journeys. The removal groups were always forced to go in the wintertimes. Harassments went from the petty to the murderous. White men accompanied by sheriffs with writs would seize the oxen and horses and mules of Indians for non-existent debts, and leave the Indians stranded with their wagons. But never mind, other white men with other writs would come and claim the wagons and other possessions. Indian stragglers were murdered. Stubborn Indians were declared black and enslaved.

Cholera had broken out on some of the Arkansas trails, but the Indians were compelled to use the cholera trails and not others. The sworn Devil of the Indians had aged suddenly; though he had attained the highest office in the land, he was an embittered man with little to cheer his life. But the news of the Indians' sufferings always brought a glow to him. It was one of the few pleasures remaining in his life.

Perhaps the Cherokees suffered most of all the tribes in the removal, but this is not an account of them. It may be that the Choctaws suffered least of the Five Tribes, for they left only 10 per cent of their people dead on the way.

And it may be that a Choctaw named Hannali Innominee suffered the least of all of them, for he began to have the luck of his father Barua on him.

CHAPTER FOUR

1.

*French Town and Five Luck. Hannali becomes
Louis.*

We had run ahead of ourselves a little, and now we must come
back to a straight account of our man. The year is still 1828, and
Hannali Innominee is in New Orleans on his way to view the
new land.

Hannali had cattle money and mule money, cotton and pecan
money, hide and timber money. He had credits and notes. He
converted a great part of it to French gold and Spanish silver—
still the main specie in the South and the Louisiana country—
which he deposited to his credit in New Orleans banks. Money was
one of the things that Hannali understood intuitively—like fiddling
and farming.

But he had to appear to better advantage, for now he would
be traveling with important men. He bought clothes shrewdly after
coming to New Orleans and was not taken. He got a white man
shirt and a cravat to go with it, a white buckskin coat, and cavalier-
style boots. He bought a canary-colored top hat, and a silver-headed
cane as heavy as an old war club. He made a good appearance

as he walked through the river city with his fiddle and carbine slung over his shoulders like twin bandoliers.

Hannali was a bigger man than he had believed, or else the rest of mankind had shrunken. The Frenchmen were neither so tall nor so bulky as the Choctaws, the town Negroes were smaller than the country Negroes whom Hannali had known, the Spanish were wiry but small, the Kaintucks and the men from Ohio and Tennessee were long and nervous but not really big. The Texans in town for trade were all of them small men, as they have remained to this day. The legend of tall Texans came later, and it was and is a legend.

Hannali walked through the town and was proud that he found no man so large as himself. Because of his size, and for another reason, he drew attention. He jingled dozens of gold coins in his big hand as he walked, and this interested people.

There was one thing about the appearance of Hannali of which he himself was unaware, and he would be mercifully unaware of it all his life: He was not handsome of face. He was not the ugliest man ever to come out of the Choctaw country. That honor belonged to John T who was a cousin of Hannali. But Hannali may have been the most strikingly ugly of all Choctaws. There was a majesty in his colossal ugliness. With his great body and huge grotesque face, he walked down into Frenchtown.

New Orleans has changed much since then, but the Frenchtown part—those ten blocks square—has not changed. Then, as now, there were quick-witted men in Frenchtown; they were found on Dauphin and Conti streets, they were alive and courteous, and they knew how to welcome a stranger.

Hannali, who stood to the men of that town as a bear stands to dogs, fell into easy conversation with a group of these gentlemen. They spoke to him in French, and he replied in Choctaw. They invited him by signs to come into an establishment and drink with them. It was also their disposition to introduce him to the game of dice.

Introduce a Choctaw to dice? What did they think the Chocs did for amusement? Had they never heard of *baskatanje*, the Choctaw game with the little cubed corn kernels? Anyone who has learned to roll the baskatanje kernels, crooked or straight, will have no trouble with precision dice.

Hannali played with the drinking gentlemen. There was the usual slow go when all parties try to lose a little for bait. Hannali let a number of his gold pieces trickle away from him, and he began to enjoy the game.

"*Le choc est mur,*" said one of the gentlemen to another, and Hannali chuckled. Did they not know that the Choctaws understand the speech of the French as easily as that of the mules or the Chickasaws? And this Choc was *not* ripe for the taking.

They played in earnest. Hannali took them all—steadily, and without speed or display. It is a pleasure to win money from such grand and free-handed men.

The gentlemen conferred with themselves. Then they gave Hannali a gracious green liquor to drink. They brought out the cards, and the chuckle of Hannali became an earth rumble. Choctaws and playing cards were made for each other, and the world was not really completed till they were brought together.

The Choctaw country was full of two-man logs to be straddled. The center space of these would be cut flat and smooth with adze and draw knife to make a playing surface. The Chocs had used shingle-thin wood cards, they had used cotton-cloth cards stiffened with pine resin. They'd trade a fat hog for a real pack of cards. And it was poker which the gentlemen mentioned, and it was poker that the Choctaws excelled at. Poker is a Noxubee Indian word, and it means five-luck or five-hazard; and the Noxubee Indians were Choctaw affiliates. The Eleventh Commandment for gamesters is: Never play poker with a Choctaw.

Hannali took them completely at poker. They were like little boys in his hands. The complete poker-face guising over the quaking body chuckle is disconcerting, and there is no beating clay-footed luck. Hannali took those gentlemen till they had not a bill nor a coin left.

But, curiously, the gentlemen stopped playing when they were cleaned, and they seemed displeased. They seemed not to know that under the bottom of the barrel there is always another bottom.

"The night is young," said Hannali, speaking French now that they had all come to a riper friendship, "is no use to call the night at an end the sun has only barely come up I play for mules I play for seed corn I play for pecans haven't you wives or hogs to put on the line I play for land who'll open with forty acres of bottom I go eight dollars American an acre of good land I play for Negroes I play for good yoke oxen I play for hides I play for somebody's wife my brother says it's time I got a wife I play for mortgage deed to town house I play for French boots I play for horses or cattle why should we stop play tonight the sun is not high hot yet."

But the gentlemen would not play with Hannali any longer. They were not the by hokey sports they had seemed. One of them, showing some exasperation, got a bung starter from behind the bar and coming up behind Hannali he gave him a terrific clout over the head with it.

But Hannali did not keel over from the blow as a Frenchman or an ox would have done. Instead, he chuckled with pleasure, got himself a bung starter, sat down astraddle a bench, and motioned the gentleman with the first bung starter to join him.

The gentleman was puzzled, and he appeared nervous over the whole business. Hannali explained it to him. This was a game the Choctaws played, he said. Two men would sit facing each other astraddle a log, and would begin to thwack each other over the head with such light clubs as these. They would begin with easy blows, as the gentleman had done, and gradually hit harder and harder till one of them called it quits.

But that gentleman had already called it quits. He said that he had promised his wife to be home early, and he left at once though the sun was not hot yet. He was pale and twitchy when he left.

The other gentlemen held a new conference among themselves. Then they told Hannali that they would give him a parting drink, the finest ever made. They fixed it up—a compendium of all great liquors and additives—and gave it to Hannali in a trophy cup that was as deep as a boot. Hannali drank it off, and he beamed all over his forceful face.

He looked at them. They looked at him. Hannali did not know the etiquette of parting, but his father had once told him that simple manners are always the best. He bowed to them and walked out, with his fiddle and carbine asling, with his clasp knife in his belt, and his gold and dice in his pockets.

The men followed him surreptitiously into the streets. He did not fall, and the knockout drops they had given him would have felled a blue-eyed ox.

"They are by damn gentlemen," said Hannali to himself, "every by hokey one of them is a gentleman how can they be so good to a stranger I bet even their little boys are gentlemen to be so kind to one who hardly have no friend at all in town to a clay-foot Indian not hardly housebroke they make me feel like a king they are so good to me."

. . .

The several Chocs were in New Orleans about three weeks, transacting various business and waiting for a boat that should take them up to St. Louis. Pass Christian Innominee, then a resident of the city, aided them all in various ways; and Hannali discovered that his brother had become an important man. Pass Christian could play the ruffle-throat silk stocking Frenchman, or he could still be the Choctaw. He was rich, more than merely Choctaw rich.

Hannali was baptized in New Orleans on that visit in 1828. His brothers, Pass Christian and Biloxi, had been baptized in early childhood, but the French priests did not come into the deep Choctaw country often. If you missed the priest, you missed him for many years. For Christian name he took Louis.

Hannali considered himself a member of the Church all his life, as his family had been for a hundred years before his birth. But it was mostly the Church of Silence to which they belonged. For nearly half a century—until 1874—he would have the opportunity of seeing a priest no more often than every five or ten years.

However, it is not true, though he often excused himself by it, that he was uninstructed in morals. When he acted infamously, he would sometimes tell himself that it was because he was a poor clay-foot Indian who knew no better. But it was a lie. He had received sound instruction from his father Barua.

2.

*Hatched out of a big egg. Peter Pitchlynn and
Levi Colbert. Pardoning your Reverences, it is not
worth a damn.*

Hannali Innominee, Silvestre DuShane (on the expedition because
he had been in the new country before), and several others of the
Choctaws now ascended the Mississippi by steamboat to St. Louis.
On the river voyage, the deck companions of Hannali Innominee
and his friends were many of them rafters and keelboatmen from
Missouri and Kentucky and Tennessee and Ohio and points farther
distant. There were French river rats who had come down from St.
Louis and beyond. There were French-breed Indians who had
formerly been employed at the heavy work of dragging and poling
boats upstream and who still followed the river trade after the coming of steam. Some of these worked their passage upriver on the
steamboat itself. Others worked for passage fare on the wood lots
between boats. The streamboats ran on wood—mostly on pine.

There is nothing like the smell of burning pine at night to bring
out the song and story in men. The big Choc fiddler and storyteller
was at home with the rough men of the boat, and some of his tunes
may still be making the rounds on the river.

The steamboat was named the *Caravan.* Its brothers on these runs
(for riverboats are male, whatever be sea ships) were the *Phillip
Pennywit*, the *Rodney*, the *Lamplighter*, the *Harbinger*, the *North
St. Louis*, and the *Choctaw*. We considered lying a little and giving
it out that Hannali and his party went upstream on the *Choctaw*.
But it is a true account we hew to, and the boat they went on was
the *Caravan*.

The places that are now towns along the river were then three
felled trees and a cabin. What are now cities might then have had a
dozen cabins. It is seldom realized of how short a period was the
ante-bellum South west of the Appalachians.

Baton Rouge was old, but its feature was still the fort on the
bluffs, not the landing below. And the fort no longer guarded anything.

Natchez was still called Fort Rosalie by the whites, but Natchez by the Indians. The Indian name would win out, the only battle the Indians ever won over the whites along that stretch of the river.

Vicksburg had been named Fort Nogales (Walnut Fort) by the Spanish, and Walnut Hill by the English. But as a proper town it was only three years old.

Memphis, "on the fourth or lower Chickasaw Bluff," was only two years established as a town.

Cairo was ten years old and predicted by her boosters to become the great city of the rivers, but St. Louis would beat her out. Cape Girardeau had French roots and was thirty-five years old. She also aspired to be the great city, but she would miss it.

St. Louis had already accepted the mantle. She was hatched out of a big egg and was already a metropolis in spirit. She was awkwardly situated, one hundred miles too high on the river for the Ohio branch, fifteen miles too low for the Missouri. There was no reason to build a city there, but she was built and thrived. What makes a leader of cities is no more known than what makes a leader of men.

It was in St. Louis that the exploratory party assembled—Choctaws from Mississippi and Alabama, Chickasaws from Mississippi and Alabama and Tennessee, Creeks from Georgia and Alabama and Florida. There were Cherokees present, but they were there unofficially and against tribal declaration and we do not know their names. There were no Seminoles known as such. They seem to have commissioned other Indians to observe for them. The Seminoles still swore that they would never move.

Peter Pitchlynn of the Choctaws and Levi Colbert of the Chickasaws were the leading Indians of the party. Young Peter Pitchlynn would serve the Choctaw people in many capacities until thirty-six years later (in 1864) when he would be elected chief of them in a time of their worst disaster, and after the title Chief was almost meaningless. The somewhat older man Major Levi Colbert (he held the title from the American Army in the War of 1812) will not be greatly involved in our account.

.   .   .

Hannali Innominee received an education by his trip to New Orleans and up the river to St. Louis. He now received another education by his association with the notables (Indian, white, and breed) who made up the Exploration party. Hannali's father Barua had associated with notables, as had the educated brother Pass Christian. But Hannali was country green at the thing.

There were forty-two men in the party. Most were important and very competent men, and they had come to contribute to a decision as to the future of the Five Indian Nations. The only one who has given any written account of most stages of it was a Baptist missionary named Isaac McCoy who spent a lifetime working among Indians.

They went south and west overland from St. Louis, with mule-drawn wagons, two jaunty buggies that broke down in the rough country, and most of the men on horseback. They came to the Three Forks of the Arkansas River (near present Muskogee, Oklahoma) in November of 1828.

They were then deep in the "new country." They had just crossed most of what would be the Cherokee District and were onto the edge of the future Creek District.

They saw a strikingly beautiful country, and it hurt them to say—as Peter Pitchlynn said it sadly—as Reverend Isaac McCoy mumbled it out of his long face—as Hannali Innominee growled it kicking a rock—"This isn't very good country."

They had come down through the Ozark Mountains using both the converging valleys of the Verdigris and the Neosho. They had seen the meadows with breast-high grass just turning brown, and had followed the sycamore and cottonwood creeks. They had come on sumac bush trees that barked like coyotes from the color in them. They saw the folded rocks above and below them, and the wonderful rivers.

"One can't eat district," said Peter Pitchlynn, meaning that one cannot eat scenery.

"It is fair to the eye," said Levi Colbert, "and, pardoning our Reverend, it is not worth a damn." The major actually cried in his disappointment. He was one who had urged the removal. He had said that the federal government could be believed that the new land would be of equal value to the fine farm land for which the Indians had traded acre for acre. He had pledged his honor and his manhood that the government could be believed, and now he said that he had lost both.

It was Hannali who had pointed out to them as they came down from the north that the lush grass grew out of very shallow and rocky soil. They dug and sampled, and it was the same in the very richest meadows. There was surface rock and subsurface rock, and ten inches down they always came to solid limestone. Geologists call it the Big Lime, and very few of the overlying acres would ever tolerate a plow. It could be pasture land and hay land, but never plowland or cornland.

The men of the party told each other how well the corn would grow in the river bottom lands, but they had to admit how narrow those bottom lands were, so shut in by bluffs and layered rocks. They visited the valley of the Illinois River. They went back up the Verdigris River and up the Arkansas. Hannali Innominee was joyed to find pecans; that was like coming home. But pecans are not enough.

They rode west for five days and came to prairies. It was wonderful grassland, but they knew with sorrow that it would be very indifferent cornland. They had no way of knowing that it would be the best wheatland in the world. The southern Indians hardly knew the name of wheat.

They went back down the Arkansas to the Three Forks. They went below the Forks to the place where the Canadian River joins in from the south and west.

Once more they studied the country and sighed, "This isn't very good land."

Though I be exiled from my own state for setting it down, I must agree that they were right. This beautiful eastern third of Oklahoma, from the Ozark Mountains and their striking valleys down to the Boston Mountains and the Sansbois and the really heart-filling Winding Stair Mountains, on down to the Kiamichi Mountains and the streams that run out of their flanks to the Red River, this country, pardoning your Reverences, is not worth a damn.

3.

I will marry the girl I forget her name. From Canadian River to False Washita. A bad report on the land.

Silvestre DuShane had learned the location of certain cousins of his in the Territory. With Hannali Innominee, he rode up the south Canadian River from its Arkansas River junction. They had ridden near a day when Hannali reined his pony, dismounted, and hobbled the animal.

"Why do you stop now?" asked Silvestre. "From my information, the place should be very near and possibly just around the bend."

"I know yes it is around the bend I smell the French and Shawnee smoke though for a moment I thought it was Quapaw smoke smell but from my information here is my place right here," Hannali said, and he cut a big stake. He whittled a flat surface on it. He carved the letters of his name on that surface and the year 1828. Then Silvestre had to show him how to form the month, for "Novembre" has many of the more difficult letters of the alphabet in it, and Hannali was not fully literate.

"Here I will build my house here I will live my life," said Hannali, "it is a no damn good country but this place is less no damn good than other land we have ridden over here is only fifty yards from the river and my landing will be at the bottom of the hill this is the river that goes all the way west they have a map that shows it is another one but the map is lie I will be back in the springtime and settle here all my life a man has to settle somewhere."

Hannali drove his stake. Then he mounted horse and rode with Silvestre. Around a bend of the Canadian River, and not two hundred yards from where Hannali had driven his stake, were the cabins and trading post of Silvestre DuShane's kindred.

Alinton DuShane was an old French-Shawnee. His daughter was Marie. There were a dozen other persons at the post, but they were dependents and employees, not of the family.

Silvestre and Hannali were not overly welcome. Alinton DuShane had once quarreled with his cousin, the father of Silvestre, and when Alinton quarreled with a man it was forever.

The post did not do well, and Alinton said sourly that he was ready to give it up in disgust and die and have done with it. There wasn't much that he traded any more, or much that he grew. Not twice a month would a flatboat or a canoe come to his landing.

Hannali asked Alinton DuShane one thing and had his answer. The maps were liars and Hannali was right. This Canadian River and not the Red River to the south was the river that went all the way west. By this river the Frenchmen had used to boat to within a day's portage of Santa Fe, and Alinton had been the last one of them to do it.

"I will do it again all the way to the Santa Fe when I come back several years after I come back," said Hannali, "when I come back in the springtime I will take charge of everything."

And they looked at him without comprehending him.

There was a lull. Hannali positioned his fiddle and began suddenly to play. He gave them a loud Choctaw scraping, much worse than he usually played. The hosts were shocked at the violence of the noise.

"Can you play *Femme et Chatte?*" Marie DuShane asked hopefully.

Hannali went into a real rouser of a tune. If that wasn't the tune, it was what that tune should be like.

"That isn't *Femme et Chatte,*" said Marie DuShane.

"What is not everybody know," explained Hannali still fiddling, "is that that girl had two cats and this is the tune of the brindled one." But Marie DuShane didn't appreciate it.

The father and daughter did not put themselves out too much for the two travelers. They regarded themselves as the last Frenchmen left in this particular world, and they had no interest in the first Choctaws. Time was when Alinton DuShane had been interested in everything. Now he was an old man, and that time was past.

Marie DuShane, the child of his old age, was sullen and closed. The daughter of a white mother and a part-white father, she was above these dirty travelers. So the conversation did not go well.

At dark (for they were not asked to stay), Hannali and Silvestre mounted horse again to leave the sorry place. But Hannali turned in the saddle and spoke as an afterthought:

"In the springtime I will be back to take over the post I will live here and wait a season before building my own Big House I will run the business and let you be able to die with a clear mind old man

I will marry the girl I forget her name be you get things ready for the springtime girl see you plant much corn old man the poor Indians who come will need it next year they will not have any money to pay you you must have corn for them in the spring I will be back."

They rode off, Hannali and Silvestre.

"I have never killed a man," said old Alinton DuShane. "I had hoped to be spared that in my life. But the oaf, if he return, will not have Poste DuShane."

"Better a bear or a boar than that lout," said Marie DuShane. "He will never have Marie DuShane."

Hannali and Silvestre rode through the night and came to the main party at sunup. And the men of the party went about their business of exploring. They were in the bear mountains and the buffalo hills that they had for their new inheritance.

They examined the land to the south for a month. They all realized now—(what the worldly of them had always known)—that the north-south distance was about a third of that represented to them, and that the undisputed domain of the Plains Indians was much closer than they had been told. *Three quarters of the land for which they had traded their southern acres did not exist.*

They began to lay out the districts in their talk—how it would be if they were really forced to move here.

The Cherokees would be north of the Arkansas River.

The Creek Indians would be between the Arkansas River and the south (or main) Canadian River.

The Choctaws would be between the Canadian River and downstream Arkansas River line and the Red River. The Chickasaws did not see any land they wanted at all. It was agreed, if it ever came to it, that they would somehow share land with the Choctaws.

The Choctaws talked of their three divisions, for there would always be three. One district would take the Canadian River as its north border and extend as far south as the watershed—the Winding Stair Mountains and the Jacksfork Mountains. South of the mountains, there would be two districts: one east of the Kiamichi River and one west.

They found a little better land in the South in the valleys of the streams that feed the Red River: the Washita (in those early days called the False Washita to distinguish it from the similarly pronounced Ouachita River in Louisiana), the Blue River, the Clear Boggy, the Muddy Boggy, the Kiamichi, the Little River, the Mountain Fork.

"It is better, but still not very good country," said Peter Pitchlynn. They returned to their homes and gave a bad report on the land.

CHAPTER FIVE

1.

*Old Indians in the new country. Masked men and
bull whips. Nineteen thousand five hundred and
fifty-four Choctaws.*

How did it happen that the Indian Territory was not already settled
by Indians?—that it could be considered as a new home for the Five
Indian Nations of the South? Were there not Indians living there
already?

There sure were. Three times the men of the Pitchlynn-Colbert
Expedition had been surrounded by very large bands of Indians.
These had treated them well, and their leaders had smoked and
talked with the leaders of the Expedition. But these resident Indians had laid it out quite plainly that if the intruders should come
in significant numbers they would all have to be killed.

And always the Expedition was followed, but so silently that even
sharp-sensing ones like Hannali were hardly aware of it. The Plains
Indians especially would come walking barefoot on the grass, talking
hand talk among themselves and uttering no sound. They con-
trolled their breathing, and when they practiced the easy-breathe

rather than the hard-breathe it was said that their scent nearly vanished. They were everywhere, there were a lot of them.

There were the splinter tribes, Anadarkos, Wacos, Kadohadachos, remnants of the great Caddoan Confederacy. There were some Pawnees, Wichitas, Comanches, Osages, Quapaws, and Kiowas in residence. Those great travelers, the Shawnees and Delawares, were to be found. There were Utes in the far West of the Territory. There were Poncas and Kickapoos and Tonkawas, and fragments of many tribes whose main bands dwelt hundreds of miles away.

But there were very few farming Indians in that country. This was hunting country, two thirds of it buffalo country, all of it deer country. As such it was adjudged as country not in intensive use. A country should support ten men farming where it will support one man hunting. So bring the southern Indians in and let the land support them. Let the hunting Indians hunt elsewhere, change their ways, or die.

But there were natural reasons why much of this land could never be farmed successfully.

. . .

Hannali Innominee returned to his old home and made preparations to move to the new Territory if it had to be done. His father Barua would not move. Barua had been a middle-aged man when he got his first sons, almost an old man when he got Hannali, and he was quite an old man now. The mother Chapponia was dead.

Brother Biloxi said that he would remain in Mississippi. He knew that he would be done out of his farm one way or another and must remain as a poor laborer or renter, but he would stay. Biloxi Innominee was a good-natured, simple, big-bellied man. The brother Pass Christian once said it correctly: that Papa Barua had left his brains to Pass Christian, his vigor to Hannali, and his pot to Biloxi.

Hannali found that things had been getting rougher in the Choctaw country and still worse in the areas of the other tribes. There were Chocs who said that all the Indians should rise even now. But there was a reason why it would be insanity for them to revolt.

There was not one Indian in ten who had a gun, not one in fifty who knew how to use one properly. Hannali learned that if he carried his own carbine openly in the Choctaw country he would soon lose his life. But every white settler had a gun and knew how to use it.

What store of guns the Indians did have was systematically dried up. One by one, Indian settlements were surrounded by large bodies of hooded men. These men hooted and howled like Choctaws, but they didn't have the same tone or timbre. They had white man boots and pants below their hoods, and they rode known white man horses.

These were not the first hooded men in the South. The Choctaws themselves had hooded-man and masked-man ceremonies and societies. And also, at an early date, the white-hooded Cagoulard society had crossed from old France to French Louisiana, and visitations by their men had been made on certain persons of bad behavior. Now the Peckerwoods of the South took it up in an extreme form to cow the Indians.

An Indian found with a gun was whipped to death. The Choctaws had more meat on them than other Indians and were able to endure longer under the lash. There were cases of a man taking a thousand lashes before he died, and the bull-whip wielders could deliver a blow with one of those things that was capable of shattering bones.

Were the Indians somehow effete to let this happen to them? Were they less men than the white men? No. Man for man they were more man than the whites. But they were unarmed except for bow and lance, and the white men had rifles and courts and sheriffs and armies. Though the United States in the person of its President Andrew Jackson had announced itself powerless to oppose the states in their assaults on the Indians, yet its army was quickly available to put down any countermoves by the Indians against the states.

Before the whole removal was completed, the Creek and Seminole Indians would have proved that their poorly armed men were the match for double or triple their numbers of regular white soldiers. But the odds would be raised still higher against them to the breaking point.

Nitakechi was the only Choctaw capable of leading a revolt. He could have found a dozen men of the caliber of his brother Opiahoma, of Peter Pitchlynn, or George Harkins, or Joseph Kincaid or Joel Nail as second echelon. Nail was Nitakechi's rival, but rivalries would cease on the call for an uprising. Nitakechi could have found a hundred men of the caliber of Hannali Innominee or John T or Albert Horse for third echelon.

Nitakechi was as brave as his uncle Pushmataha had been. He was better educated but less intelligent. He lacked the incredible speed of body and mind that old Push had possessed. And he had his poor people to consider.

Nitakechi threw the matter up to Moshulatubbee, and the old man threw it back to him. The old Mingo Moshulatubbee said that —old as he was (he was then more than eighty years old)—he would raise his people and give battle if Nitakechi would lead; but he would not himself give the word to rise. His hand and his mind had lost their craft, he said, and he did not know what to do. He said that it was a problem without an answer and had been so from the beginning. The day was past when a just peace could be maintained by strong men with staves.

It wasn't done. Revolt wasn't the answer. There was no answer.

When Hannali was convinced that there wouldn't be revolt, he put his alternate plan into action—that which his brother Pass Christian had planted in his mind the year before in New Orleans.

He would go to the new Territory and take along such founding men as he could get to go and establish themselves there. They would set up posts. They would plant all the acres of corn they could handle. They would amass droves of hogs and cattle, establish shops and smithies, plant cotton and set up spinning and weaving, and have turnips and potatoes in the ground. And Pass Christian Innominee and several of his associates would arrange for such financing as they were capable of.

When the Indians came to the new Territory there would be some food for them. The first settlers could carry the new arrivals over and get them started. It might work for a year. The second year, who could say? But when came the real flood of the refugees in the third and fourth years, then God help the poor Indians!

. . .

How many Choctaws are we talking about? The census of September 1830 (and it is believed to be accurate for all that it was made of bundles of sticks turned in by heads of families to town leaders and by them to the District chiefs) would give the numbers:

7505 LeFlore's District (Okla Falaya).

45

6106 Nitakechi's District (the Pushmataha, Okla Hannali).
5943 Moshulatubbee's District (Okla Tannaps).

Not quite twenty thousand Choctaws in the old South, and by then about a thousand had already emigrated.

2.

Of John T. Albert Horse, a gray-eyed Indian, and the little girl Natchez. Strange Choate and the star sparkle.

The only people that Hannali could call his own was a group of Choctaw blacks. There were about a dozen of these. But somehow the blacks numbered more than twenty when Hannali started them toward the Arkansas Territory. There was a good blacksmith among them, for instance, and Hannali hadn't had a blacksmith before. There were others of useful talent. Hannali had enticed several superior slaves to run away and go with his band to the new Indian country.

Hannali started them toward the Arkansas West in wagons, and he appointed the young Martha Louisiana to be matriarch in charge. He gave her casual instructions how to find the stake he had driven to mark his new homestead: to follow the river to the branching, to follow the new river to another branching, to leave the shore where three cottonwood trees form a certain cluster, and to look for the stake fifty yards back from the river bank. He gave Martha Louisiana one hundred dollars American money, enough to carry any party through any eventuality.

The blacks, some twenty of them, slaves by law, went through five hundred miles of slave country and direct to the stake with never a question of their not being able to find it. Their wagons and livestock were of value, as were they themselves, but they were not taken along the way. They had quiet assurance; they were challenged often but never overawed. It seemed impossible that they should get through untaken, but Hannali was a fool for luck and some of it rubbed off on his people.

Hannali then rode through the Choctaw country for a few days, conferring with the big men, becoming something of a big man himself as he accepted responsibility. He got a dozen capable men to promise that they would follow quickly with what parties they could raise; that they would set up farms in the new country and grow corn for the multitudes who would soon be coming over the trails.

Then Hannali himself started toward the new Territory accompanied only by two close friends: his cousin John T, and a strong, silent Choctaw man named Albert Horse. Hannali's cousin's name T was a name and not an initial. He himself pronounced it Tay. Later, in the new country, men would pronounce it Tee and John would have to accept it.

The three of them moved easily through Mississippi on horseback. They crossed the river and went into the Arkansas Territory up the Boeuf Valley. They were only a few days behind Hannali's blacks, and they had news of them from blacks of the land there and from Arkansas Indians.

The riders never met open hostility. They were three big armed men who always called out in friendly fashion when they approached cabins or clusters of cabins, and they avoided any large settlements. They could tell whether a cabin cluster was an Indian or a white man settlement, though perhaps they would have been unable to explain how they could always tell at a distance.

When no settlement was to be found near night, they killed fowl and piny deer, and ate and slept in the open.

.   .   .

One afternoon, Hannali was riding alone, and a mile or so ahead of the other two, when he came on a white man afoot who blocked his path. This man was possibly younger than Hannali, and he had a certain steeliness in his look.

"Get off that horse, you lout, and give me that fiddle!" the man snapped out in words that cracked like a mule whip.

Hannali was not about to get off his horse and give up anything he had, but there was something here that truly startled him. You'd look at a thousand men and you wouldn't see one like this. He was not a man to fool with, and he sure didn't seem to be fooling.

The man had a carbine, almost the twin of Hannali's, asling. Hannali was not at all sure which could unsling the faster. Many white men are very fast.

47

They locked looks, and locking looks with that man was like standing up to a lance thrust. But something drew a corner of Hannali's glance from the boiling gray fire of the man's eyes to lower down. Well, what do you know about that? There was something the matter with the man's stomach. It was as though he had swallowed a kicking pig.

By and by there was something the matter with Hannali's stomach also, much the same thing. Swallowed laughter can be held in only so long. The two of them erupted at the same time, and Hannali tumbled off his horse, chuckling and howling and talking all at the same time.

"You are no white man you are only white outside you be as much Indian as I am you are a clay-footed chuckler you could have hang me for a hog if I was onto you at first your by hokey gray eyes is what had me spooked you're no more a white man than I am what do you want my fiddle for."

"Show you how to play the clay-footed thing," the man chortled, and Hannali smothered him in a body press. Boys they were, the two of them. Who wants to be a man yet? They bear-hugged each other like brothers and became friends for life.

The big bluff was a game that Indian boys played when they met as strangers. They posted their dire threats and glared, and whoever broke and laughed first lost.

The gray-eyed Indian said his name was Chizem. He was not, as Hannali had believed, a Choctaw. His mother was Cherokee Indian and his father was Scottish. How could a Choctaw chuckler come out of a nest like that?

John T and Albert Horse rode up after a while, and they were not fooled as Hannali had been. They knew an Indian when they saw one. Hannali had been distraught that day or he would have known. It came on evening, and Chizem said that they should ride to the farm of friends of his.

"Yes I think that we should be with settled people this night," said Albert Horse, "it is that Hannali is act funny he talks funny and he rides off by himself there is something the matter with Hannali's head."

"Maybe there is nothing wrong with my friend Hannali," said Chizem. "Maybe Hannali is all right and the rest of the world is funny."

"That is not so," said John T, "I think he acts funny Albert think he act funny even his horse think he act funny there is something funny with his head."

They rode to the farm of the friends of Chizem. It was a cluster of cabins at night and the area was ablaze with pine torches. There was a hog scalding going on. This was the settlement of an old Cherokee Indian named Strange Choate and his wife Sarah and their family of four grown boys themselves with families; and of the little girl named Natchez.

There were a dozen slaughtered hogs strung up. A hog scalding should have a fiddler, and Hannali fiddled for them. It was funny music he made, though, not the sort he usually played. There was no doubt of it, Hannali was acting funny.

The Cherokee Strange Choate told them a little about himself and his business. He was of the western or early-removed Cherokees, as was Chizem. For a while he had lived over the line in the western Arkansas Territory, the new Indian country. Now he was back in the old Arkansas Territory, but barely over the line. (Hannali and his companions had not realized that they were so near their destination.) Strange Choate raised hogs. He provided salt pork for the garrison at Fort Gibson and for settlers generally. He had lived at the Grand Saline in the western country and still had a brother there. It was at the Grand Saline (Salina) that the little girl Natchez had been born.

"How has she her name," asked Albert Horse, "how is it be that a little Cherokee girl have the name of the faraway Natchez people she ought to have a different name."

"It is because she is small and scrawny like the Natchez that I call her that," said Strange Choate.

Chizem played Hannali's fiddle for the pig scalders. He had not been boasting when he told Hannali that he could show him how to play the clay-footed thing. On this night he played better than Hannali, for Hannali had indeed been playing funny.

It was early in the springtime. But spring had just come to Hannali Innominee and very late. There was something the matter with his head or with his liver, which the Choctaws believed to be the seat of the affections.

Hannali watched the little girl Natchez standing behind the torches. He noticed about her that, though she was quite a little girl,

49

she was not as young as she had seemed at first sight. She was marriageable. Hannali went to her father Strange Choate to give him this information and to ask him two things.

"How many do you have all together of pigs hogs shoats weanlings all of them together how many do you have," he asked Strange Choate.

"About three hundred," Strange Choate told him.

"I need a hundred of them to settle in the new country with," Hannali told him, "I will need that many to have pork for the new Indians coming over the trail and to have a drove of hogs growing for the Indians who will come the next year and the next I need one hundred."

"I will sell anything if we can agree on a price," said Strange.

"No you will have to give them to me," said Hannali, "who could buy a hundred hog animals out of hand like that I need my money for other things in setting up in the new country you will have to give me at least one hundred."

"Your friends said that you had been acting funny, young boy Hannali. Is there anything else you would like me to give you?"

"Yes the little girl your daughter Natchez have you looked at her lately do you know that she is old enough to get married although she is so little I want to marry her and take her to the new country with me."

"Go ask her," said Strange.

Hannali went to ask the little girl Natchez.

"I am going to the new country," he said, "I will need hogs I will need something else—"

"Maybeso," said Natchez.

"—to take with me what I want is a wife I was not think I would want a little scrawny one like you then I see you standing behind the torches—"

"Maybeso," said Natchez.

"—I want you to go with me be my wife maybe you will get fat and not always be so scrawny John T and Albert Horse say I act funny now I know why I act funny."

"Maybeso," said Natchez.

"If you would say yes I would go to your father to tell him if you was say yes we would settle it now."

"Maybeso," said Natchez.

Hannali went back to Strange Choate.

"What did she say?" asked Strange with an odd glint. He was not a chuckling Choctaw, this man. He was a twinkling Cherokee.

"She says maybeso what does it mean she keep say maybeso."

"She said yes," smiled Strange. He liked Hannali.

"Take the hogs and the girl in the morning and be gone. But come back often. We are now of one family."

They stood apart in the starlight. Choate—an odd, old, gray Cherokee of the given name of Strange—seemed to have some of that star sparkle on him. It was a bit like the aleika, the magic, that sometimes shone on a rare Choctaw. Strange was but a private man, and Hannali said of him later, "He is a Mingo."

. . .

In the morning, Hannali, John T, Albert Horse, and the little girl Natchez started to the new country with one hundred hogs, pigs, shoats, and weanlings. They were into the new country by midafternoon.

At Three Forks of the Arkansas, near Fort Gibson, Hannali married the little girl Natchez. Then he went with her and the hogs toward the stead he had picked for his home.

John T and Albert Horse angled off south to seek out homes for themselves. Hannali gave each of them a dozen of his hogs to get started in the pig business.

3.

Of three-forked lightning. What am I, an old boar coon? How Skullyville, Boggy Depot, and Doaksville became the capitals of nations.

And that is the story of the way Hannali Innominee took wife?

No! It is not! It is only one third of the story.

The rest of it is so amazing that we hesitate as to how it should be presented. Whoever heard of such a thing happening?

Listen to it! Let one ear droop for a moment and you'll miss it.

For two days later, coming to his black people set up at his homestead on the South Canadian River, Hannali married Martha Louisiana and made her people more completely his.

And, on the following day, he went around the bend of the river and married Marie DuShane.

That is it. It was like three forks of lightning striking down. Hannali was triply done for and he couldn't understand it at all. Just one week later he sat on a log and talked to himself about how it was:

"I am marry to three women and how did it happen to me I was not intend to marry at all Marie DuShane thinks that Martha Louisiana is my slave and Natchez is my cousin Natchez I don't know what she thinks only Martha Louisiana knows she says she will knock their heads together if they don't like it what am I a herd bull to have three calves coming all the same season God help me I don't know how I get into this I'm so dumb what am I a jack I get three colts in one year damn this is bad why was I not think what am I a cob turkey to have three hens they point me out boy you old jack you they say how you go to unfry fish how you go to unbake bread how you get out of this one Hannali what am I an old boar coon."

Spring had come very late to Hannali Innominee, but then it came in a torrent. What was there about the three girls that struck him like three-forked lightning? We have only a hint of the quiet acquiescence and sunny resiliency of Natchez, of the black-earth passion and blood friendliness of Martha Louisiana, of the sullen storminess and aura'd mysticism of the encounter with Marie DuShane—that white lady who turned into a breed Indian every time she blinked.

Hannali was married to Natchez by an Indian agent at Three Forks of the Arkansas.

He was married to Martha Louisiana by an itinerant preacher of one of the sects, a man who had with him an Indian orphan child whose language he could not understand and who was of a mother dead somewhere along the trail.

He was married to Marie DuShane by himself and herself in an old, and sometimes disputed, rite much employed by the back-country French, conditional to which was the requirement that the marriage be confirmed by the priest should one ever come.

The whole thing was wrong and Hannali knew it. He was not a savage man. Though he excused himself to himself as being a poor clay-foot Indian with no instruction, yet he knew what he had done and that it contained a fundamental canker in its spring bloom.

But in the eyes of the world he had done well. Like his father Barua, Hannali drew material prosperity from his follies. By Natchez he had the gift of one hundred hogs, an alliance with an established frontier people of some wealth, and entree into the nation of the western Cherokees.

By Martha Louisiana he had a people, and the beginnings of a settlement. He had the artisan blacks, the smiths and mechanics, and more of them would now accrete to him.

By Marie DuShane, Hannali had Poste DuShane. For Alinton DuShane did die quietly after turning things over to Hannali. With the post there went a good extent of bottom cornland and an excellent location. There was the downstream connection to the Arkansas River and thence to Fort Smith and Little Rock and Arkansas Post and all the way to New Orleans. There was easy access to Three Forks and Fort Gibson by both water and land. It would be, and Hannali was astute enough to see it, the crossing of the Texas Road (already in existence) and the California Road.

Here would be the meeting place of three Indian nations, for Hannali was also astute enough to see that the Creek-Cherokee border would be adjusted and that the Cherokees as well as the Creeks would be right across the river from him.

This was also the Three Forks of the Canadian River, not so clear as the Three Forks of the Arkansas, it is true, but within nine miles both the Deep Fork and the North Fork came into the main Canadian River.

Hannali had become a Cherokee Indian by his marriage to Natchez, and he would soon become a McIntosh Creek Indian by formal adoption. Through Major Levi Colbert he was close friends with the whole Colbert family, and Colberts would be chiefs of the Chickasaws for most of the following half century. He was close to Peter Pitchlynn, still a young man and the greatest of the Choctaws. He held the friendship of other men, such as Chizem, who were men with a future.

. . .

In the spring of the year 1830, Hannali Innominee had three sons:

Famous, by Natchez.

Travis, by Martha Louisiana.

Alinton, by Marie DuShane.

By this time he had his second corn crop in the ground. He was the biggest hog man in the Territory, and he had begun to build the Big House. Hannali also had another second crop working at the time when he left off doings in that field for the saving of his soul.

Hundreds of Choctaws arrived that year (1830), though their main migration would not be till two years later. Those who arrived now set up their territories and settlements by the names that would endure. And, as always, there were the three divisions of the Choctaws.

The Moshulatubbee District (that to which Hannali Innominee belonged) set up between the Arkansas-Canadian River and the Southern Mountains. The main settlements of the Moshulatubbee were Skullyville and Fort Coffee. Joseph Kincaid was the first district chief in the Territory, which old Moshulatubbee would never enter. He would be dead before removal was completed.

The Pushmataha District (that of which Nitakechi was chief) set up south of the mountains and west of the Kiamichi River. Its principal, hell, its only town, was Boggy Depot.

The Oklafalaya District retained its name, for Greenwood LeFlore couldn't impose his name on a district as Moshulatubbee and Pushmataha had done. It located south of the mountains and east of the Kiamichi River, and George Harkins was the first Falaya chief in the Territory. LeFlore remained in the old country, turned white man, and somehow had become possessed of sixteen sections of good farm land. Removal and despoliation were for others, not for himself.

The Oklafalaya was often called the Red River District. Its principal towns were Doaksville and Old Miller Court House. I am told that there never was any courthouse at Old Miller Court House. The settlement was named from the pretentious residence put up by an old half-breed named Miller. It looked like a courthouse, and the Choctaws called it Old Miller Court House.

The courthouse building was not old. Old Miller was old.

It is the small town of Millerton today. They will not let a good old name stand.

. . .

One day Hannali believed that he saw a Creek Indian named Checote riding away from Hannali's Big House, and at no great distance. This was odd, since Hannali had not seen Checote earlier nor spoken to him, and it was not like the man to pass close without stopping.

Then Hannali noticed—from the way that the man sat the horse—that he was not Checote. Hannali had never seen this man before, and now he saw only the back of him as he went away on horseback.

But Hannali knew who the man was. He had heard vivid descriptions of this unmistakable man by Choctaws who had encountered him.

The man was Whiteman Falaya. He was riding away on Checote's bay horse. Hannali's blood ran scared and his liver knotted up.

CHAPTER SIX

1.

*Whiteman Falaya. Hannali House. Twenty-five big
Indians and some generals. A Widdo were with
three Wifes.*

Hannali had been sitting on a massive bench, cleaning a gun on
his knees, and perhaps he had dozed. The bench was in front of
the only door to a certain strong room which he had constructed.
This was the place where he kept his gold and paper money, his
guns, his whiskey, several fine pieces of furniture when the house
had come to that point, and other valuables.

The door of the strong room was open, for Hannali had just
gotten two guns from it, one that he was cleaning, the other which
was loaded and leaning against the wall beside him, for he often
potshot game without ever getting off that bench.

Hannali knew that there was something wrong with his strong
room. He went in. He found a rough piece of paper stabbed into
the pine slab wall with a sharpened hickory spear piece. It was
lettered with a curious message, and Hannali knew what it said.

Hannali at that time could not read to a great degree, and the
man who had left the message could not write. But it is no great

trick to get the meaning of a written message. Shulush-Homa, a Choctaw chief of an earlier day, would run written messages against his cheek and announce to all present the meaning, though not the exact words, of the writing. And Hannali, holding the paper, held its meaning.

He took it to one of the blacks who could read. The words were: "Fat Man Hannali you have nowt but three bull calfs this year I will spoil you of one of your heffers when you have one I will spoil you of outher things I mean to cut you down your friend Whiteman Falaya."

Hannali Innominee was afraid of few things. In scuffling, whether friendly or serious, he had never been bested. He could kill a buffalo bull with a little one-handed club not half as long as his arm, and could drive a hand knife through eight inches of pine wood with a snap of his wrist. He had a good precision rifle at hand, and was the best shot of the Choctaws.

Was he afraid of Whiteman Falaya? He was afraid of no man else. But everybody was afraid of Whiteman, and Hannali came very near to being afraid of him. If this was not fear, then it was a new and exasperating emotion that left him breathing hard.

So Whiteman Falaya was in the Territory, and Hannali and others had believed him dead back in Mississippi.

Whiteman Falaya (three or four years younger than Hannali) had been born in Mississippi of a loose Choctaw woman. When asked the paternity of her boy, the woman had only said that the father had been a white man, and she named the boy Whiteman. But Whiteman was darker than most Choctaws, and it might not be fair to ascribe the evil in him to the whites.

Whiteman killed and looted and raped and burned because he had a passion for those things. And he left written documentation of his acts, both before and after they happened. The written notes are curious as coming from a man who could not write. They are in at least six different hands, and the writers of none of the notes ever came forward. The notes would be in one hand for a year or more, and then change to another hand. This leads to belief that the notes in each hand were all written at one time, and that the raids and murders of Whiteman were carefully planned and were not impulse things.

The fearful thing about Whiteman was his ability to enter and

57

leave places unseen and unheard. He had walked past Hannali Innominee who would have shot him on sight and gone into the strong room, stabbed the note onto the wall, and walked out again. Hannali believed that he had dozed for a moment, but how had Whiteman known that he would be dozing? Hannali could see miles from his bench, far across the river into the Creek and Cherokee nations. He could clearly see the house and pasture of the Creek Indian Checote whence Whiteman had stolen the horse.

The Reverend Isaac McCoy had said that Whiteman was sick, and should be regarded with compassion as one would a sick animal. Most of the Indians believed that the most compassionate thing they could do to Whiteman was to kill him as soon as possible, but they had never been able to do it. Whiteman Falaya was under permanent sentence of death by the Choctaw Nation, the Chickasaw Nation, the states of Mississippi, Alabama, and Georgia, and by the Ross Cherokees.

Hannali took his best rifle and mounted horse. He did not ride to the south after Falaya. Instead, he swam his horse through the river and rode to the home of the Creek Indian Checote. He said that he had seen, from a distance, a man riding on Checote's bay horse, and the man did not sit the horse like Checote. "Did you loan the horse Checote is everything all right?"

No. Checote had not loaned the horse and didn't know that it was gone. Maybeso it was another bay horse. But that of Checote could not be found. They raised a group and rode after the horse thief, trailed him (they believed) for fifty miles, and lost him. Hannali did not tell them that the man was Whiteman Falaya.

Nevertheless, from other depredations, it was soon known by all that Whiteman Falaya was in the Territory. There was a new cloud over the country.

. . .

George Washington once slept at Hannali House. This was Captain George Washington, the Caddo Indian chief. The only President of the United States who certainly slept there was Zachary Taylor, then General Zachary Taylor (it was in 1842). But there were personages greater than either of these who stopped over with Hannali at his Big House.

There were the great Indian leaders who visited him through

the years: Peter Pitchlynn who was a special sort of man, Israel Folsom, Pitman Colbert, Winchester Colbert (he looks like Abraham Lincoln in one picture of him in a top hat), Joseph Kincaid (when he was chief of the Moshulatubbee he had made Hannali his closest friend), Thomas LeFlore (a better man than Greenwood, he won back the chieftainship of Okla Falaya for the family and brought back respect to the name).

There was Nitakechi himself who said he had Moshulatubbee and Pushmataha for his two fathers. He was the last of the Mingos. There has been some dispute as to the meaning of the indefinite title Mingo. It meant to be a man like Nitakechi and his fathers. Not all chiefs were Mingos. The title had to grow on a man till one day the people would say, "He is a Mingo."

There were great Indians by the dozen come to Hannali House: Ya-Ya-Hadge, John Jumper, Captain Robert Jones, Roley McIntosh, Benjamin Perryman, Roman Nose Thunder, the great Cheyenne warrior. There was Gopher John—but he was a Negro, and not an Indian, you say—who started on a removal trek as a black slave and ended it as a Seminole Indian chief. That was one removal party that suffered unbelievable hardships, and had not Gopher John assumed leadership not one of the party would have reached the Territory alive. Gopher John later founded the city of Wewoka in Oklahoma.

Man, these were all big Indians, not the little Indians like you see every day. There were important Indians of the Plains tribes, Buffalo Hump, Pock Mark, Placido. There was John Ross who was chief of the Cherokees. There were good Indians and bad Indians who came to Hannali's: Benjamin Love, George Lowrey, Black Dirt, Bolek (Billy Bowlegs), Pliny Fisk. And Chizem, the gray-eyed Indian.

Prominent white men stopped at the Big House. Charles Goodnight was there several times. There was General Philip Henry Sheridan and Albert Pike with the black secret which he took to his grave. Devoted missioners such as the Reverends Isaac McCoy and Samuel Worchester were entertained by Hannali for weeks at a time, but only seven times in thirty years were Jesuits able to come. There were the Indian agents and the superintendents: Rutherford, Garrett, Drennen, Browning, many of them. Hardly a week went by that Hannali did not have guests at his house.

For, in the whole period before the Civil War, there was but one inn or hotel in the Indian Territory—that set up by Israel Folsom in Doaksville in the 1840s. Travelers had to stay at the houses or at the Army posts. In the Choctaw North the Big Houses were seldom more than ten miles apart, and most of the owners enjoyed having guests.

It took Hannali thirty years to build his Big House. It was not finished then, but he added no more to it after the Second Time of Troubles. Into the house went boatloads of limestone quarried north of the Three Forks of the Arkansas, sandstone, crab orchard stone, shale. There were even blocks of granite brought by wagon and roller from the Wichita Mountains. Hannali drove bargains in stone and timber in the course of his trading, and every addition to the house represented an era in his life.

It did not seem out of place when Hannali added New Orleans ironwork to a portion of the house, nor when he built the steepled lookout tower. It was not a distortion when he set in a ruby-red window. These things gave it force and power.

There was one visitor who said that the House looked like a giant turkey buzzard flopped down on the ground and ready to flap into flight again. This was not so. It looked more like a big barn owl, with its huge head, and wings spread out low.

For about thirty years, the peace in the Moshulatubbee Choctaw North was maintained by about a hundred strong settled men and their followers holding in such Big Houses. It was the feudal Middle Ages of the Choctaw Nation.

The House became a large part of the life of Hannali after he had become, as he once wrote, "a widdo were with three wifes."

2.

The end of the French wife. A Canadian River storm. Blood of my liver and clay of my clay.

It was early in her second pregnancy that Marie DuShane awoke in absolute fury to the true situation in Hannali House. She had been ignorant and blind. She hadn't even guessed that such a thing could be.

She had believed Martha Louisiana to be a slave woman whose son could have been fathered by anyone at all. She paid small attention to the little girl Natchez who lived with other Indians in one of the odd buildings being connected up to the main house. She believed Natchez's young son to be a little brother for whom she was caring, and took Natchez herself for only a child.

Marie DuShane was the white wife, and had no regard for Indians or Negroes. She was not consciously proud. It was simply that she didn't see them, any more than she saw the mules and the cattle.

But Hannali had been embarrassed several times when Marie DuShane reported Martha Louisiana for insubordination. Then one day, Martha Louisiana merely chuckled at a foolish command Marie gave her, and Marie stepped back aghast at it, but puzzled at her own confusion. Martha Louisiana had been insubordinate before. This was different.

It drifted down on Marie like white light, like snow falling on the hills. Marie nearly went blind when it struck her.

Martha Louisiana had chuckled with Hannali's own rumble. No other relationship could bring it so close. They had been intimate.

Marie DuShane set up a French screaming and activity and went after Martha Louisiana with a whip to show her how a slave should be. The French wife had gone wild, and she caught Martha Louisiana front on with a long stinging slash.

Martha Louisiana tasted blood running down her face at the first crackling stroke. Her dangerous chuckle turned into the exploding growl of a wounded she-bear and she moved in. Nothing could stop her when she moved forward. She overpowered Marie DuShane, took the whip away from her, and then slapped the white woman till she was near senseless.

"I am no slave woman. I am the wife before you," Martha Louisiana said heavily. She threw Marie DuShane to the earth and ground her unconscious with her heels.

And that was the end forever of the French wife of Hannali.

"He will have to put away the white woman. This cannot be," said Martha Louisiana sorrowfully to herself.

• • •

And that was the storm? Over as quickly as that? It was no such thing, it was only the little wind before the storm. The French wife was gone forever, but Marie DuShane was more than the white wife of a fat Indian. She had never been so white as she appeared on the outside.

Marie DuShane discovered herself—what she was. It was a sham she had played all her girl life. She was no French girl. She was a breed Indian—stormier than any full-blood and more savage than the fiercest white.

The Shawnee came up in her like a ghost, and a bloodier French than she knew that she had. She was a wild breed Indian, and she tasted her own blood as Martha Louisiana had done. The fury of Marie DuShane exploded into its second stage. She was a dangerous wild animal when she came off the ground, a wolverine, a she-devil.

Marie had a lithe strength that was unusual. She had once astonished big Hannali by hefting him onto her shoulder like a sack and whirling around and around with him. She hadn't the deep physical power of Martha Louisiana, but now she had a fire in her that Martha wouldn't be able to cope with.

Any person—believing a matter to be finished and disposed of and then finding it only begun—is at a disadvantage. Martha Louisiana was completely unnerved by the second assault of Marie DuShane after she had left her unconscious on the ground. In her astonishment she did not at first realize that this wild animal was the same woman, hardly that she was a woman at all. This was no longer the Frenchie who wore underclothes and would lift no hand in labor. This was a half-breed Canadian River storm.

Martha Louisiana was a very sturdy girl, one destined to become somewhat ponderous with age. In forward momentum she was relentless, but once she took a step backward she was lost. And she fell back before the ghastly assault.

Marie was sturdy herself and fast as summer lightning, and she bore Martha Louisiana down. The black girl could only think of keeping her throat from being torn out. She lost her confidence and went into panic, and wild Marie cut and beat her terribly and had her mouth red from Martha's blood. It was long and intense and gruesome.

When it was over with, Marie DuShane believed that she had killed Martha Louisiana who was blood-soaked and stark. And Martha Louisiana herself was sure that she was dead.

She lay in that witless confusion that comes just after death. She hadn't believed that the little white girl could beat her down and kill her, but the little white girl would never be that again. Martha Louisiana found herself stretched dead on the ground, and bleeding besides, and broken up and in great pain.

Marie DuShane had hardly started. It had happened once! It could have happened twice!

Things came into Marie's mad mind with perfect clarity. The second devil had come into her while she worked her murder on Martha Louisiana. Natchez was not so young a girl as all that! The maybeso girl had been Hannali's also. There were a hundred indications of it thronging into the mind—things that would have long since been clear to any but a blind woman.

Marie caught little Natchez—coming to see what the din was all about—and struck her down. She smashed the girl unconscious with one blow and believed that she had broken her skull. Marie was on the stricken girl with all four feet and almost beat her through the ground.

Hannali, running to pull Marie off Natchez, was quite sure that Natchez was dead. And it was close, for Natchez was unconscious for three hours and would not be able to walk for a week. Hannali hunched over her and sobbed out his clay-footed soul.

"The scrawny little girl that never hurt anything in her life she was so good you wouldn't believe it even the wild birds flew down when she called them now Marie DuShane have killed her all because I am a bad-hearted man who had done great wrongs she was the light of my life she was my first springtime now Marie DuShane have killed her the little scawny girl who would never get fat now I die too no do not touch her Marie DuShane you have killed her."

"No, I don't believe that I have, Hannali," said Marie DuShane, still trembling but beginning to be composed. "I hoped I had, but she's not dead."

"Do not touch my little girl she is broken like a bird the blood that runs out of her is my own now have God struck my family why have He not struck me who am guilty."

"It's all right to let me touch her, Hannali," said Marie DuShane. "The storm's gone out of me now. Why should I harm a little girl because myself was a blind woman?"

"You have killed her Marie DuShane for the sin that was mine."

"Oh, then I'll bring her back to life. Oh, she'll live, she'll live! Hannali, we'll fix up your little bird again."

"Permit that I see the child," said the bloodied Martha Louisiana, coming off the ground and forgetting that she was dead. "With you and with me it is one thing, Marie DuShane, and it may never be settled. But you should not have struck down the child. All your life you will regret it."

"May I have a long life to regret it in then," said Marie, "I see that I will have many things to regret."

Natchez did not die. And when she became well, she was the only well one of them. Marie DuShane and Martha Louisiana had both died a little.

It was three days later that Hannali and Marie DuShane and Martha Louisiana came to talk at the pallet of Natchez, for that girl was still too weak to get up.

"We will have plain talk now," said Marie DuShane. "All four of us are responsible for this.

"My husband Hannali is responsible for being a great springtime fool. It will do him no good to protest that he knew no better. He did know better! We are not animals. We are people, and we have not acted like people.

"I am responsible because I was a blind woman, and because I did not regard the others as people at all. I have done great wrong in not knowing what was happening.

"And Martha Louisiana has done great wrong because she *did* know what was happening, and she accepted it.

"And Natchez has done wrong because she is no such child as all that. One does not say maybeso when a big evil comes.

"Now then, Hannali, I will tell you exactly what you must do. And you will do it!"

"I will do whatever I must to make things right Marie DuShane tell me then I do not see anything at all no way to make it right."

"First you must put away Natchez and she no more be your wife."

"This I cannot do she is the light of my life she is my first springtime how could I ever put away a scrawny little girl like that," protested Hannali.

"You have to do it. There is no other way."

"It will kill me it will break my soul."

"Well then, it will kill you. And which of us deserves an unbroken soul? Say it, Hannali! Before God there is no other way."

64

"I will put away Natchez and she no longer be my wife," said Hannali heavily and with an empty face.

Natchez began to cry.

"Now finish it, my husband," pursued Marie DuShane. "The other thing must be ended also, however close it may have been. You must put away Martha Louisiana and she no more be your wife."

"This I cannot do she is from an earlier springtime she is my black people she is blood of my liver and clay of my clay."

"We are all of the same clay, I find," said Marie DuShane. "I will permit no delay in this. Cut the limb off, don't grind it off. This terrible thing must be over with. Say it, Hannali! You know what must be."

"I will put away Martha Louisiana and she no longer be my wife," said Hannali in dull agony. The weight had gone out of him.

Martha Louisiana sobbed quietly.

"It has been a terrible business, and now it is finished," said Marie DuShane. "I myself will be a better person. We will do all that we can to right this wrong. These two and their children be yet of our family, but not in the old way.

"And now, my husband, you have no wife but Marie DuShane, and we have long lives ahead of us. Gradually they may become more happy."

"I will put away Marie DuShane and she no longer be my wife," said Hannali as though talking in a dream.

And the whole world missed a beat at the echoing gasp of Marie DuShane.

. . .

But that is the way it would be. Hannali was unmoved in this.

"I cannot put away one wife I cannot put away two wifes I can only put away all three wifes a wrong such as mine cannot be righted by thirds in all my life I will no more touch woman will our lifes really grow more happy after a while what will it be for the children that you three are now carrying."

"Perhaps we should pray that we lose them or that they be born dead," said Marie DuShane disconsolately.

"Perhaps I will not permit that we pray to lose them not even that of yours, Marie DuShane," said Martha Louisiana solidly.

Hannali Innominee touched woman no more in all his life. And their lives did grow more happy after a very long time.

3.

The man with the talking horses. Name rolls is Indian stuff. The nations in him. Jim Pockmark and Timbered Mountain. Who else knew them all?

There was another element in the life of Hannali Innominee during the more than seventy years after his coming to the new Territory. This was his traveling life.

Hannali traveled every year of his long life in the Territory. Some years it would be no more than four or five weeks; but many times it would be four or five months, and twice he ran years together being gone eighteen months each time.

It was common for such settled farming Indians as the Choctaws to take a wandering year when they were young men. It was in memory of the centuries when they traveled always—a form of initiation that young men should go off in their time, singly, or in twos and threes, for an adventure year. Thereafter, the stories of his adventures were part of a man's stock in trade. A man must have adventures, or he must be able to fabricate adventures; and if he could not do either, then he was not a complete man. When a man told stories to his grandchildren he would begin, "It was in the Year of my Wandering."

Hannali had taken his own wandering year, while he was still in his teens, into Florida of Spain. Then he had taken another wandering year and another. And after he came to the new country, he wandered a part of every year, for this was one of the things he could not do without.

He came to know every big river of the West, and all the high plains, and the mountains, and the farther mountains. He knew every Indian nation of the West. But mostly he visited and lived with the Cheyennes—with them especially—with the Apaches,

66

the Caddoes, the Pawnees, the Kiowas, the Arapahos, the Comanches. And wherever he went he was accepted.

There was a duality about Indian hospitality: Those who needed it most were accorded it least. Indians were inclined to kill a lonely friendless traveler who seemed to be down on his luck. But a man of presence and front was accepted, and Hannali could always be such a man.

He came to be called, gradually over the years: Fiddling Bear by the Cheyennes, Big Frog by the Apaches, Laughing Bull by the Caddoes, Talking String Man (from his Choctaw habit of stringing words together without a break) by the Pawnees, Fat Beaver by the Arapahos, Mule Doctor by the Comanches, the Man with the Talking Horses by the Kiowas.

Hannali knew all the great Indians of the Plains for several generations. The names he could have dropped had he wished!

Leave us here and meet us again on the other side of the creek if you find such things tedious. But if you do, you will miss a hundred better men than any you will meet tomorrow. Cataloguing was as much a part of the deep oratory of the old Indians as of the old Creeks. Names are magic, for the name is the same as the soul. Name rolls is Indian stuff. They are woven into the fabric of this thing, and it will ravel if we tear them out.

Of the big Cheyenne men, Hannali knew Black Moccasin, High Wolf and High-Backed Wolf, Painted Thunder, Gray Hair, Dull Knife ("So tough he dull the knife" his name meant), Seven Bulls, Limber Lance (the name was given him by his wife who was an earthy humorist, but for all that he sired seven sons who were strong warriors), Left Hand Shooter, Wooden Leg, Walking Rabbit, Hail (Autsite), Wild Hog, White Elk, Sun Maker, Little Wolf (the Cheyenne, but Hannali also knew the Sioux Little Wolf), Roman Nose and Roman Nose Thunder, Walking Coyote, Crazy Mule, Crow Indian (who was a Cheyenne and not a Crow Indian), Raccoon (Mats-Kumh), Little Horse and Panther his brother-in-law, Porcupine Bear and his son Porcupine, Rolling Bull, Plenty Camps, Island, Black Moon (his name really meant Black Sun, but it must be translated as Black Moon from some old reluctance or taboo), Bad Face, Wearing Horns (Lahika), Lean Bear, Dry Throat, Six Feathers, Stone Calf, Tobacco, Gray Beard, Whistling Elk. Hannali knew every leading Cheyenne in their grand decades.

Hell, they were nothing but a bunch of horse Indians, you say. But from one view, there were no greater men ever than the horse Indians. They were the first All-American athletes, and they haven't been surpassed. They were the astute country-boy politicians whose wards ran from the Cross-Timbers to the Shining Mountains. They were the poets who could chant the empty plains full of buffalo, and who can do it now? They were the legendary lovers and clowns and storytellers.

The Indians were seldom baptized or formally named. A name grew on a man, and he might have several successive names in his lifetime.

Hannali knew the Sioux: Black Leg, High Backbone, Bloody Knife, Red Cloud, American Horse, Crow King, Crazy Horse, Spotted Tail, Cut Belly, Little Big Man. But he was never a Sioux man. With the Sioux, you like them or you like them not.

He knew the fine Arapahos: Left Hand (Nawat), Little Raven, Storm, Flat War Club, Crane, Bull.

And the Crows: Big Prisoner, Kit Fox, Standing Alligator, Plenty Coups. But the Crows were not his special people.

He knew the Anadarkos—Pockmark and Jim Pockmark and Jose Maria. And Nez Perces—Looking Glass, Tap-Sis-Li, White Bird, Joseph, Hush-Hush-Cute.

The Comanches—they were as fine as the Cheyennes—Bull Hump, Shavehead, Horseback, Paha-Yuca, Ten Bears, Traveling Wolf (Ishacoly), Shaking Hand, Morning Voice, Katemsie, Sun Eagle, Coyote Droppings (Ishatai), Mo-Wi, Black Horse, Toshaway, Quannah Parker.

Lean Apaches: Leading Bear, Thin Man, Taza, Zele, Victorio, Red Sleeve, Goyathlay (best known by his variant name Geronimo, but he hadn't that name yet when Hannali knew him, about 1860).

Serene Caddoes: Chowaw-hana, Quina-hiwa, Red Bear, White Antelope.

Pawnees with their eyes always watching you: Sky Chief, Pita-Leshar, Kokaka, Dusty Chief.

Kiowas—they were real men, and yet curious men: Satanta (White Bear), Satank (Sitting Bear), Little Mountain, Thunder Man, One Braid, Stiff Neck, Guibadai (Appearing Wolf), Light Hair, Big Tree, Eagle Tail, White Cowbird, Poor Buffalo, No-Shoes, Kicking Bird (Tene-Angopte—Striking Eagle was really his name), Timbered Mountain, Lone Wolf, Gotebo, Funny Man. The Kiowas were all funny men, but no one ever called them women. They could whip their numbers in anything.

It was with such Plains Indians that Hannali lived his other life—in the off-season weeks and months and years—for much more than half a century. He learned a dozen Plains tongues, he learned hand talk, he learned custom and medicine. He went to war with the Plains Indians and feasted with them. He taught them smithery, and what they taught him was more intangible and intricate.

There was Indian in Hannali that could never be satisfied with the settled life, with a single world, or half a dozen worlds. But some of the nations in him made satisfying contact with the nations of the Plains.

Buffalo meat piled high as a man in rows fifty feet long!

Comanche scalps fresh on poles before Cheyenne lodges!

Five hundred ponies taken in one night's raiding!

. . .

They smoke and they talk, and the Big Man is among them. Who else has taken the pipe from the lips of Timbered Mountain? Who else has passed it to Jim Pockmark?

Who else knew them all?

CHAPTER SEVEN

1.

*Luvinia, Marie d'Azel, Salina. Kill the big
Choctaw! The Whiskey Decade.*

In the spring of 1831, Hannali had three daughters born post-
humously, as it were—after the termination of his marriages. These
were:

Luvinia, of Martha Louisiana.

Hazel (Marie d'Azel), of Marie DuShane.

Sally (Salina), of Natchez.

Natchez had named Salina from the place of her own birth—
Salina (*Grand Saline*), the salt seeps of the Grand or Neosho River.

This was all the family that Hannali would have for that generation. In the later Territory days there was some mystery about this
family, and people wondered just what were the relationships. There
was confusion of surnames which were not yet fixed with the
Choctaws, or with any Indians. The Choctaw blacks still used the
patronymic form (the first name of the father becoming the last
name of the child), so Martha Louisiana called her children Luvinia
Hannali and Travis Hannali, rather than Luvinia and Travis Innominee. Marie DuShane had become a single word in the family,

and she was never called simply Marie; but outsiders still heard a family name in it. And the Louisiana of Martha Louisiana—though part of a double given name—also had the sound of a surname. So visitors wondered about the status of the strange triple family, and the Innominees themselves never bothered to clear it up.

But the explanation as given here, coming from one of the grand-sons, is the correct one. There had been three marriages of whom no one could say which was the true one. These three had all been terminated in a stormy family showdown, and thereafter the persons lived as one continent kindred.

· · ·

The main thought of Hannali Innominee that spring (1831), as the spring before and the spring before that, was to plant corn for the Trail Indians. There were difficulties.

One was the sod busting itself, the first plowing of the land that had never been broken. The grass roots were a thousand years old and so heavily entangled that they refused to be parted. The sod was so tough that it could be used for durable building blocks— earth and fiber one foot thick and unyielding. Most of the early Territory houses were sod houses

Hannali had the best mule in the world, a big black animal named Mingo. When he saw the second best mule in the world, Catoosa, a white mule belonging to a Creek Indian, he had to buy it. For the most stubborn sod, Hannali used both mules. But mostly he used one till it was weary, and then the other. And Hannali himself worked eighteen hours a day.

Another difficulty was the fencing. To build fences that are deer high, buffalo strong, and hog tight takes endless heavy labor; and barbed wire was a little more than forty years unborn. Hannali built miles of sod fences, rock fences, rail fences. Some of his fences can still be found in Pittsburg and Haskell counties of Oklahoma— standing up like walls of China in the bosky country. A dozen houses in the region have been built from the stones that Hannali carted in and built into his fences, and they've been using up his rail fences for firewood for a hundred years. Hannali was a mule for work.

The Trail Indians, coming mostly in the years 1832 and 1833, didn't call for Hannali's advertised free corn. The Indians stopped just inside the borders of their new country and would go no farther. They selected the poor lands of the eastern edge, too tired to travel three days more to better land. They were sick and weary, and one fifth of them had died on the removal. Hannali boated his corn down to Fort Coffee to give it to the starving Indians, but he wasn't permitted to do so.

Government distributors and licensed traders had been buying corn from Quapaw and Osage and McIntosh Creek Indians for fifty cents a bushel and selling it to the Trail Indians for three dollars. They would allow none of this free business. They moved to kill the big Choctaw.

Hannali escaped with his skin. He left his boat and his corn there and fled on foot where men on horses couldn't follow. Three good Indian trackers were put on his trail, but at a certain point they refused. As dogs will usually track a bear till they are onto him, but sometimes they will halt and tremble on the trail of a particularly savage beast, so did the trackers refuse to close on this animal.

It would be given out later that Hannali had killed three men on his breakaway near Fort Coffee, but this was false. The men said to have been killed were always men unknown or of made-up names.

It was no big event to Hannali, but he wouldn't allow himself to be killed while there were things needing doing. He sent out cautious word where he would make his next landing, at Round Mountain Landing twenty miles upriver from Fort Coffee. He gave away twenty barge loads of corn there in two years.

But something had happened to the Trail Indians. These were not the strong Choctaws of the old country, not the tall Creeks and the fine Cherokees. They were beaten animals when they came off the removal trail, and they had given up hope. The men of them were on the drink in a horrifying manner. Though starving, they would lie drunken all day; then, rising up, they would trade off their last pot or bushel or sell their last daughter as slave for another jug of spirits.

It is said that the Indians had no experience with alcoholic drinks before the coming of the white men, and that therefore they had no control. But, at this time, they had had experience with the white men and their alcohol for three hundred years; and before that they had had their own alcohol, corn beer, and cordial drinks from choke cherries and sand plums—though not strong spirits.

The Indians had been proper drinkers for centuries. They made joyous and selective use of the tricky old animal, and drunkards among them were few.

This degradation was a new thing—drinking to exorcise their unbearable misery. They had lost their country, their lives were uprooted, and death had struck nearly every family of them. It was then that the winged serpent turned into a venomous snake. They traded their last possessions and their manhood for the hasty whiskey sold them by profiteers along the way. It was the Whiskey Decade, the 1830s in the Territory, though it was over in far less than ten years. Missionaries were frantic over it, and some serious Indians considered the situation hopeless. Who can rebuild nations out of drunken animals?

A few of them saw it clearly, and one of them was Hannali.

"It is only the troubles they are snake-bit it is only a passing thing," he said, "give it three years and it will be gone they will wake up one morning and see that they are still alive they will see the sun and the grass they will build houses and farm the land give it three years and it will be gone."

2.

Green turban and red turban. Count in his castle.
Piano, loom, and eyeglasses.

Just how civilized were the Choctaws on their coming to the new country? Were they brownskin frontier white men, or were they still feral Indians?

There is a sketch of the Choctaws made by George Catlin in the 1830s, just after their coming to the Territory. It is of the Choctaw Eagle Dance, and it shows them painted and naked, hopping around in a circle, and they look wild. But that was a ceremony, a show put on for the visiting painter. How did they go daily? How did Hannali look when he went about his business?

Well, he wore cowskin boots and buckskin trousers both of his own fabrication. He wore a woven cotton shirt and a blanket over that on cold days, both from the talented loom of Martha Louisiana. Usually he wore a green turban, wound Creek-Indian fashion, on his head. This was not to make a splash of color. The Creeks wore red turbans, and the Choctaws wore green.

On very sunny days he wore a wide-brimmed manufactured felt hat. When important persons came to visit, he wore his canary-colored topper, and put on gloves. But was he a civilized farmer, or was he still wild Indian when he followed Mingo behind the plow and carried a long bow asling?

He didn't carry the bow because he was a wild Indian, but because he could fill the pot with it cheaper than with a rifle. He shot turkeys and rabbits with it as he went about his eternal plowing and fencing. He shot coyotes—all Indians ate dogs, and coyotes are dogs— and buck deer, geese, ducks, and coons. He had to be a good shot or the bow would be no advantage to him. It takes an hour to make an arrow in all its components, and if he missed often or lost arrows, it would not be cheaper than shooting a rifle.

Then he couldn't be called a wild Indian with a painted face? Let us not go too fast there. He painted his face about once a month, livid-red or chalk-white, usually after a dream telling him to.

But at least he wasn't a howling wild Indian? Sure, he was a howling Indian. He was a Choctaw, and the Chocs are Indians who have fun with noise. Who can refrain from answering the wolves and coyotes when they sound? Who but a dead man does not whoop a hundred times a day?

Hannali was a farmer, a blacksmith, a boatbuilder, a commercial shipper, a ferryman, a pork salter, a tanner, a miller, the founder of an estate that was a town. He was a count in his castle in the medieval setup of the Choctaw Nation. He was a banker, after he had a steel safe brought up the river from New Orleans. He was a carpenter and stonemason, a gunsmith and harness maker, a wainwright, cooper, fletcher, distiller, and brewer. He was a merchant with the first mail-order establishment in the Territory. He brought the first sheep and goats into the Moshulatubbee. He operated sawmills and quarries. He was a civilized man who sometimes painted his face and body and whooped and hollered with the loudest of them. He was a rude illiterate, but in five years' time he would no longer be that. He was the master of his own culture, and that is to be civilized.

Very early in his Territory years, Hannali began to send down-river for merchandise for his friends and neighbors. He assembled catalogues of the stores in New Orleans, and accepted produce for payment. His shipments were landed for him on the Arkansas River near present Tamaha, just below the Canadian River branching. He would go down and bring them up by keel boat, or send his boaters to do it. For his clients, he shipped down corn and pecans by the boatload.

He soon operated an unchartered bank, with Marie DuShane setting up a regular ledger of accounts and keeping them accurately. He paid and received interest, and had more gold on hand than any Indian in the Territory except the Chickasaw Pitman Colbert. And Colbert, according to true legend, had needed six mules and a specially built wagon to bring his gold from Mississippi to Doaks-ville in Oklafalaya.

With one of the first cargoes consigned up the river to him—after the change in his marital arrangements—Hannali brought three gifts, the things most desired by the three women. They were a piano for Marie DuShane, a manufactured loom for Martha Loui-siana, and a pair of eyeglasses for Natchez.

Natchez didn't need glasses. She could count the mites on a hawk a mile in the air and the microbes on the mites. She had once seen a rich Cherokee lady wearing eyeglasses, and she wanted them more than anything else.

All three of the women used the loom. Each, on occasion, wore the eyeglasses. Only Marie DuShane played the piano at first. She played like a Frenchie—the little tunes she had learned as a child at school. Then she tired of the instrument.

Martha Louisiana knew who the piano was when she first saw it— it was a person and not a thing to her. She played it like an ele-mental. Educated visitors later said that she played with genius, nor did they say this out of kindness; they were such as disapproved of a Negro woman being so mysteriously in the heart of a family.

3.

Come to the mountain. Seven hundred years old and blind. Oklafalaya was a magic word. Who summons by dream?

At the tail end of winter, after Hannali had been in the Territory for onto four years, he awoke one morning from a charismatic dream. It was the dream of the mountain Nanih Waiya, not that of the great mound that was built by hands in the Mississippi country, but of the older mountain of which the mound was the memorial. The last of the Choctaw magic men called to Hannali in the dream —"Come to the mountain."

Hannali told his women that he would be gone for two or three days. He took a sack of corn hominy and a little jerked buffalo, put some mule whiskey in his saddle bags, took his bow and rifle and fiddle, and mounted horse and rode south to find the mountain. He had painted his face—but only lightly—with streaks of green and orange.

Nanih Waiya was the leaning mountain. It would not be a particularly high mountain, nor grand for its sheerness and a suddenness of aspect. It was only a magic mountain.

As he rode south in the morning, Hannali was joined by other Choctaws, as he knew that he would be. Within a dozen miles he was joined by his cousin John T, by Albert Horse, by Inchukahata, by others—some twenty of them. All, of course, had had the same dream, and they rode without question on the journey.

In the afternoon they overtook a white boy riding a light pony. The white boy was frightened of them, but they spoke to him kindly and put him at his ease. He was about fourteen years old, and he said he was riding down to Oklafalaya. He mispronounced the name, but he said it with reverence. He was a pale boy with watery eyes; he was from Missouri; and his name was Robert Pike.

In American writings of before the year 1850, one will several times come on this enchantment of the name. Oklafalaya, Okla Falaya was a magic word. This was when the name Oklahoma was still thirty years uncoined, and Oklafalaya came near to giving its name to the whole Territory. In the popular mind it was an indescribably wild place, like an Africa in the middle of us.

It was the Indian land with wild mountains and forests. It was the land of the giant buffalo (though there were few buffalo east of the Kiamichi River in Oklafalaya itself); it was the land of the great bear (and it was); the land of panthers and real wild Indians.

They told the boy that he could ride with them, and that nothing could happen to him while he was in their company. They told him that they were going right to the border of Falaya.

"Are the Indians in Oklafalaya as kind as you?" the boy asked. He was afraid of wild Indians, but he had to go to the wild Indian country.

"No they are not," said Albert Horse, "they are our cousins and very like us but not such well seeming men they would not say ride along with us young boy they will likely say we will cut your ears off you young pup we haven't eaten boys' ears for a week."

"Will they harm me? Will they kill me?"

"They will not do either of those things they will only scare you till your liver melts but don't let them scare you."

"No, I won't let them scare me," said Robert Pike.

"They will have big knives they will whoop and holler and roll their eyes but remember they are laughing inside you laugh too."

"Yes, I will. I'll laugh at them."

"They will likely not cut your ears clear off," said John T, "they will cut them only half off and maybeso they will grow back again almost right just keep saying to yourself I won't let this hurt me even if it kills me a lot of times it doesn't hurt much to have your ears cut off if you keep saying that no no boy can't you see that we are laughing inside too we are also jokers the men in Oklafalaya would no more hurt you than we would they are our kindred and nearly as fine people as ourselves."

They killed a young buck for late dinner. They seared the meat and ate it near raw. Hannali, for it was his kill, gave the buckskin to the boy and instructed him how to dress it. Hannali played the fiddle for all of them as they rode rapidly through the afternoon. They covered sixty miles that day and arrived at their destination while there was plenty of sun left, for they had all started very early.

They had come down the Jacks-Fork of the Kiamichi. They skirted the Sansbois Mountains and now came to where the Winding Stair Mountains curled around from the east and the Kiamichi Mountains loomed distantly in the south. They began to climb into

77

a complex of the Winding Stairs—first on horse, then tied their animals and went up on foot. These were not high mountains, but were curiously curled mountains alive with color. None of the men had any doubt where they were going.

The rocks assumed odd forms as the afternoon sun picked them out. There was a rock above them that looked like a graven Indian man; they pointed and went up. One rock had looked like a buffalo, but the likeness melted away as the angle of shadow changed. One rock had looked like a woman bending over grinding corn, and then it had looked like nothing but a rock. But the image of the graven Indian did not change.

It was no graven rock Indian, it was Peter Pitchlynn, a great man among the Choctaws. He stood and waited for them, and a score of other Choctaws sat and lay about the mountain.

"Is this the place," asked Hannali, "we have ridden all day this white boy it is all right that he be with us he is a good boy and wants to see the Falaya country is this the place we are called to."

"I believe we are near the place," said Peter Pitchlynn. They were in a saddle between two low peaks. Then they heard a sharp whirring noise above them, and they knew which peak it was. They went up.

It was a rattlesnake, seven hundred years old and blind. Its sounding had been feeble, but they had been able to hear it. A very long time before this, the Choctaws had been a rattlesnake-clan people, before they had been a crayfish or deer or bear people. The rattlesnake was the oldest *uski* or clan of them all. This old rattler had been there many centuries, waiting to show them the place when they returned. Now, like the biblical patriarch, he looked on them and died.

Was this indeed the Mountain from the Beginning? The Choctaws, centuries before, had gone east across the Mississippi River, but they had come from a country of mountains. In the low pine country of Mississippi they had built (and it took them a hundred years) an artificial mound as memorial of the Bending Mountain— Nanih Waiya.

Were the Choctaws actually back in their original homeland? Or had a very shrewd and intricate man with a mystic involvement with his people contrived it all? Whether or not this was the Mountain from the Beginning, he had contrived it. He had sent out a manifold dream to a number of Choctaw men, and none had had that power for fifty years. He was the last of the Alikchi, the Choctaw magic men. He had called them to the mountain, and his name was Peter Pitchlynn.

They lit the fires in a pattern at dusk and kept them burning all night. These fires, from the top of one of the most westerly of the Winding Stair Mountains, could be seen by people in all three of the Choctaw districts: The Moshulatubbee, the Pushmataha, the Oklafalaya. All would know what the pattern of the fires meant, that the Friendly Mountain, the Bending-Down Mountain, lost for seven hundred years, had been found again.

But it wasn't in any sort of religious ritual that the men spent the night on the mountain. They passed it away with mule whiskey and fiddling and a great lot of shouting and hooting.

The Missouri boy named Robert Pike was in quiet ecstasy. He had become brother of wild Indians. He had seen the hills of Oklafalaya before the sun went down, and he would enter the district the next day.

. . .

The mountain, of course, was not a convenient place to set up a nation's capital. The site chosen was nine miles from there, but it could be spoken of as in the shadow of the mountain. It was near present Tuskahoma in Pushmataha County, Oklahoma. This would remain the real capital of all the Choctaws, even though the administration was moved at times to Armstrong Academy, to Doaksville, to Boggy Depot.

The mountain was as close as one could get to the indefinite junction of the three Choctaw districts. It was on the land between the Kiamichi River and its Jacks-Fork—where the main river begins to break up—and the Kiamichi was the dividing line between the Pushmataha and Oklafalaya. From the north slope of the mountain, all streams drained to the Canadian and Arkansas rivers; and all land that drained north belonged to the Moshulatubbee. The mountain was in all three districts and was not peculiar to any of them. If it were not the original mountain of the Choctaws, it was very much the sort of mountain they had retained folk memory of.

It was accepted. However you contrived it, Peter Pitchlynn, you contrived it well. It was the turning point. The Choctaws believed they were back in their original homeland, and they began to reconstitute themselves as nations.

CHAPTER EIGHT

1.

Fun in the old Moshulatubbee.

Three Indian boys are running a young buck in the jack-oak thickets on the south shore of the Canadian River. They'll catch him too.

But can mere boys catch a thing as swift and strong and enduring as a young deer buck? They can if they stay with it; they had stayed with it four hours. If three boys harry a deer and intercept him on every turnback, the deer must run three miles for every two of the boys, and he will have two boys ahead of him and one behind him every time he breaks back. Boys are smarter in pursuit than wolves. They are near as smart as coyotes.

The three boys are nine-year-old brothers: Famous, Travis, and Alinton—the sons of Hannali Innominee. They are of a size, and when you look at their faces you cannot tell them apart. Travis (of Martha Louisiana) is not darker than Famous (of Natchez) or Alinton (of Marie DuShane). All three have their father's face, but they have not his great broad head. Even though they have his face they are handsome, and he is not.

They will soon have their father's height, but not his bulk or great strength. They look so alike that Hannali can hardly tell which is which when they line up in front of him. But now he watches them from a mile away and he can easily tell them apart. They are three Indian boys, but when they run one is Indian, one is Negro, and one is white.

You may have noticed the thing about football players. There are crazy-legged white boys who can fake as well as any Indian, but they don't do it in the same manner. There are Negro blacks who are faster on the start, faster on the break, and faster on the straightaway. But nobody with eyes is ever confused as to which sort of boy is running. Watch a good Indian runner float down on an end who waits nervously wondering which way he will break. The Indian back will be by that end without breaking at all, and leaving him looking foolish. The runner changes pace without changing motion, and changes direction without seeming to. It is as though he ran a preordained course, and how did the tackler happen to be so far off that course? This quality of running can only be called floating deception. Louis Weller of the old Haskell Indians had it, Billy Vessels had it, many have had it.

The white runner dodges, the Negro breaks, the Indian floats by with no hand laid on him. Alinton could dodge, Travis could break, but only Famous had the queer floating deception. Alinton was the quickest; Travis was the fastest—not at all the same thing; but it was Famous who brought down the young buck. It looked as though the animal broke back sharply and ran right into the boy, but it was really an amazing capture that Famous made.

They threw the young buck down and killed him. They skinned him out, drew him while he was still hot, bled him and quartered him, built a hot fire, roasted him, and damn near ate him up in an hour.

Wherever could anyone have so much fun as in the old Moshulatubbee District on the Canadian River?

2.

Sequoyah and Moses. Ground to death between a
slate and a slate pencil. A cloud I had forgotten.

Marie DuShane decided that her nine children should learn to read
and write. Since the termination of their marriages, she had called
Hannali her father, and Natchez and Martha Louisiana her sisters,
and the six children were the children of them all. But now all
nine of them became her children for the hours of instruction.

One day one of Hannali's boatmen brought a strange package
consigned to Marie DuShane in a cargo from Tamaha Landing.
When the package was opened, the first thing to strike the eye was
ten red-trimmed school slates.

There were the slates and slate pencils. There were ten penny
catechisms. There were other books for the time after the catechism
was learned. There was letter paper, and wax and quill and such, but
these were put away carefully. They would spoil no paper till they
had first learned to write on slates.

Many Indians could already write. It was time that a great family
like the Innominees learned the art. Hannali already knew something
of the thing, though he would pretend not to and would learn
along with the other "children." At least he understood the theory
of it better than most. He explained the advantages that the Choctaws who had no alphabet had over the Cherokees who had one.

Before the removal of the tribes from the old country, a Cherokee
named Sequoyah did something that has been done only one other
time in all history. He invented an alphabet or something that was
very nearly an alphabet.

Sequoyah's invention was midway between an alphabet and a
syllabary; but due to the peculiar construction of the Cherokee
language they were the same thing in this special case. The eighty-
five symbols of Sequoyah (representing either a vowel or a con-
sonant and vowel combination) took care of every possible syllable
of Cherokee speech. It was an absolutely perfect vehicle for the
Cherokee language, and no other language anywhere has ever had a
system of writing that fitted it so well. It was the real and perfect
alphabet—for one language.

All other alphabets in the world (except that of Sequoyah) derive from one that was invented near lower Syria about twelve hundred years before Christ. A fundamental preacher once gave the theory that God himself invented that first alphabet, and that the Ten Commandments given to Moses on the tablets was the first alphabetical writing. Wherever he had his theory, it is near correct as to time and place. It happened about the century of Moses and in the Moses region.

But whether invented by God or not, that first alphabet had nearly everything wrong with it. It was a rough and uncertain thing, not to be compared with the perfect instrument that Sequoyah invented. The early alphabet had only one advantage: Any language on earth could be written in it by adapting it slightly. The Cherokee alphabet had one disadvantage: Only Cherokee could ever be written in it.

Hannali said that the Choctaws should leave off being jealous of the Cherokees (for they were jealous of them) for having a written language; the Cherokees were in a dead end and they would be surpassed in literacy by the other Indians. The Choctaws only had to learn to read one system and they would be able to read any language they could speak, Choctaw, Creek, English, French.

So now (about 1840) the Innominees learned to read and write. The six who were children in years were quick, and Marie DuShane seldom had to be impatient with them. She was afraid to show impatience with Martha Louisiana, but that woman displayed great aptitude for the reading and writing business. It was Natchez who was kept after school every evening, slaving over her slate and making the words again and again. It wasn't that she couldn't learn them, she learned faster than any of them. But every day she had forgotten what she learned the day before, and had to start at the beginning again.

"Is it maybeso I will have my death sitting on this stool and making the letters?" she would ask. "Is it that I will be ground to death between a slate and a slate pencil?"

If you are less than a hundred years old you won't know what a slate pencil is, but it doesn't matter. Commercial chalk had not yet come to the territory. The slate was like a small trimmed piece of blackboard and was made of slate indeed. The slate pencil was of softer slate, and would mark gray or nearly white on the harder slate, and could be wiped off with cloth or grass.

Hannali had no trouble with the reading or writing. Likely he had already partly educated himself in these arts, but in all his life he had never had trouble learning anything. But now he wished to make a bigger jump.

"You should have given me warning Marie DuShane," he said, "now it will be three months before I can get them here they should have come in the packet with the things for the children now I waste three months."

"What do you waste? What do you need, Hannali?"

"Eyeglasses a silver ink-horn paper with a crest printed on it quill pens from England they are the best all these things I need you should have let me know what you were doing how can I write to my friends till I have them."

"You need eyeglasses no more than does Natchez. So send for the rest."

Hannali asked a preacherman visitor to write down the books that an educated man should have on his shelf. But when he scanned the list, he had some doubts.

"Swift he sounds fine Montaigne he is French Marie DuShane can tell me the hard words Shakespeare sounds like a Grasshopper Creek Indian doing the spear dance Plutarch is the man Peter Pitchlynn reads Peter says that Plutarch invented great men and they have not yet appeared in life Irving he was a civil and well spoken man when he came to the Territory the Collected Sermons of Absalom MacGreggor the preacherman thought he would slip one in there but I caught him a History of Rome for the Young Student I will get most of them."

Hannali rode thirty-five miles each way to Three Forks of the Arkansas to buy such paper and pens as a man of importance might use. Those Marie DuShane had obtained were not of excellent quality. Then he sat down and wrote a letter to his brother Pass Christian in New Orleans. He labored all night over it. It was a good letter, and he spoiled only a few sheets of paper before he made his final draft.

He asked Pass Christian to send him such books as an educated man should have, and mentioned some of those that the preacherman had listed to show that he was not entirely ignorant of these things. He told the news of the Territory Choctaws—how it seemed that they might come out of their slumber and make new nations after all. He suggested that Pass Christian should bring his family and come up the river to visit, reminding him that families are sacred things and it is not right that their members should go a long time without seeing each other. He finished it up at dawn and gave it to a downriver boatman.

We will tell a secret—Marie DuShane herself could not read and write well. She spelled all languages by ear, but so did most of the frontier people of every color. It didn't matter with Choctaw—it was never to have a standard spelling. Choctaw tended to be spelled according to the English, and not the Continental, sound of letters. For this reason they came to write their own name as Choctaw, though linguists say that the original sound should be transliterated as Chatah.

The writings of Choctaws of that time in English have a humorous quality because of the spelling. But was it their fault that the English-language people had not had the diligence to update their own tongue?

· · ·

About this time (1840) Hannali found in a private room of the Big House a starkly lettered note from Whiteman Falaya.

"Fat man now you have three heffer calfs I mark one of them for mysef in tow years three years I will have her I kill anyone else who touch her you can nou way prevent me fat man Whiteman Falaya."

Hannali was shaken by this.

"How can I kill a ghost who comes and goes and nobody sees him how can I protect my daughters from Whiteman Falaya it is a cloud I had forgotten," he said.

3.

Sally for a Week, Hazel for Life, Luvinia Forever.

Already at nine years old the three Innominee daughters were noticed. In the following years their fame would come with a rush. Almost everybody in the Territory would know of the three pretty, bright-talking, little girls. It was increasingly because of them that so many visitors stopped at the Big House.

Unlike their brothers, the three girls did not greatly resemble each other. Marie DuShane said that Sally sparkled, Hazel glowed, and Luvinia burned, and she did not know which of her three daughters was the most attractive. Marie DuShane maintained that all three were equally everyone's daughters and that all in the family were of one flesh.

A crude-talking white trader said the same thing in his own words: that he'd like to have Sally for a week, Hazel for life, and spend forever in Hell with Luvinia.

But Sally would be anyone's first choice—so pretty and lively as to be sensational, as beautiful as her own mother.

As who? Natchez? Was she beautiful? That sound you hear is made by one thousand white men all rolling their eyes at once. Hannali had never suspected that scrawny little Natchez was beautiful, though his affection for her was boundless. Her father and family hadn't known it, and Martha Louisiana hadn't realized it at all. Marie DuShane, of course, had always known it. She would have been intensely jealous had not Natchez become her sister in the family arrangement. Indian scrawny is sometimes white man perfect.

Traveled visitors to the Big House, and they were men who knew what they were talking about, said that there was nothing like Natchez in all the Territory and that her equal would hardly be found in St. Louis or Washington, D.C. And Sally was coming to be very like her.

The others would have an attraction even deeper, though not so suddenly striking. There was really not anything like the three of them anywhere.

4.

*A dead man on a dead horse. Christ has come to
our house.*

In the year 1842, a skeleton man on a skeleton horse rode up to
Hannali House. He dismounted with difficulty, and he tied his horse
to the wind as they called it. It had no need to be tied or hobbled, it
wasn't going anywhere.

The sight that greeted the skeleton man would have affrighted
anyone who had not been looking death in the face for some time.
It was a monstrous huge man with a face more ugly than that of the
Devil. The monster was barefoot, and the skeleton did not wonder at
that. What shoes would go on those colossal feet? The giant wore
pants of buckskin—and surely it had taken the skin of many bucks to
provide them—and he was bare and near black from the waist up. He
was a long-haired Indian monster man, and on his head was an incredible green turban that was bigger than some whole people.

The skeleton man continued his examination, and saw that the
monster was reading Plutarch.

"You are Hannali Innominee," said the skeleton, "I am well met."

This was no poor traveler who would be fed in the off kitchen and
then bedded down till he was able to travel. Hannali knew at once
what sort of man this was, and he bawled for his family to come.

"Marie DuShane come quick it is come what we wished no longer
be we a deprived family Martha Louisiana find the children all this
is promised since before they were born Natchez you would not believe it Christ has come to our house."

The arrival was dying of tuberculosis, and what his horse was dying
of is not known. Neither of them would live to see another full
moon, and already it was well crescent. The man was a priest from
Vincentian Seminary (now Perryville), Missouri. He had been
traveling his large parish on horse for nine years and only came to
this extreme end of it in the week of his death.

He administered the sacraments to the whole family, to some of
the blacks and mixed Indians from the landing at the bottom of
the hill, to Creek Indians who swam their horses over the river—
called they did not know how, to Osages who always appear from
somewhere when a priest comes. Many of the Indians had had only a

tenuous connection with the Church for a hundred years and whole generations could pass without seeing a priest; but they were what they were.

"*In nomine Patris, et Filii, et Spiritus Sancti,*" the Latin was like rain on parched sod. Did you know that the Innominee family had their name as a mnemonic of the first words of the blessing?

The priest ate with them but would not stay the night. He had too many families to see in the time that was left to him. He went to mount his horse, and gazed bewildered when he discovered that the horse had died in the interval. Hannali gave him another horse, and the priest rode away just before dark.

He died four days later in the home of a Choctaw family named Durant thirty miles south. It would be ten years before another of them came.

5.

Aleika. Peter Pitchlynn was two different men. The men in Falaya have drunk mules' milk and are sterile.

Peter Pitchlynn came to the Big House in the year 1843 and stayed a week. It is time that we knew more about this man—who he was and what he was who reconstituted the Choctaw Nation. But we run into mystery in the beginning, in the middle, and at the end.

Pictures show him as a long-haired man, not very dark, with a great beak of a nose on him and yet not quite an Indian beak. He is handsome, the nose notwithstanding. There is something feminine in his features, though he founded and first led the Light Horse Indian Police in the Territory, and years later became (though against his inclinations) a competent military leader. He was certainly slim and probably tall. Even from a picture of him it rubs off on you, the aleika, the magic, what theologians call the indwelling of the spirit, and what others call personal magnetism. He was a special sort of man.

Pitchlynn is a white man name. All the historians who touch on the Choctaws, McReynolds, Grant Foreman, Angie Debo, and Cushman, I believe but I'm not sure, say that Peter Pitchlynn was the son of John Pitchlynn (white) and Sophia Folsom (Choctaw), and that he was born in 1806 in Mississippi. The worst of it is, for the outlandish theory that we are about to propose, that Peter Pitchlynn himself always referred to John Pitchlynn as his father. But we believe he was his father by adoption only.

Have we anything to base our theory on? Only one sentence by an English writer, and the feel that Peter Pitchlynn was not a white man, at least in the years when he was the Choctaw messiah. He was not a white man when he appears from nowhere at assemblies, nor when he summons men in dreams. But later, it seems that he may have been white after all.

Peter told the English writer Charles Dickens (they met on an Ohio River boat) that he had not learned English till he was a "young man grown." This couldn't be the case if he were son of white man John Pitchlynn. John Pitchlynn was not the sort of white man who becomes more Indian than the Indians. He wanted to turn the Indians into white men. He advocated educating the Indians and teaching them English. He himself taught English to the sons of dozens of other men. How could his own son not have known English till he was a young man grown?

There is a suggestion. This John Pitchlynn adopted or sponsored several Indian boys who seemed to him to be of unusual intelligence. Often in such cases, the Indian youth took the family name of the man who had aided him, usually having no family name of his own. It is certain that John Pitchlynn paid for the education of several Indian youths, and one of these could have been Peter. The first mention of Peter (other than an apocryphal story that as a young boy he refused to shake the hand of Andrew Jackson and gave a precocious criticism of his policies) checks with this.

In 1825 the first students arrived at new Choctaw Academy—twenty-one Indian boys arrived at Great Crossing (in Kentucky) led by Peter Pitchlynn. Peter was nineteen years old if his birth date of 1806 is correct, and he would have been a young man grown when he began to learn English at the Academy. These twenty-one boys were thought to be the most intelligent and promising in the Choctaw Nation and had been so selected.

How fast can even a young man of genius come along with so late a start? Very fast if he is a special man. In 1830 at Dancing Rabbit Creek, Peter served as chairman of all the Choctaw representatives and his "father" John Pitchlynn was present as government interpreter, but not as a Choctaw national.

Peter was twenty-four years old then. It was to him that the Choctaws turned to bring them together. He presided above the chiefs Moshulatubbee and Nitakechi and Greenwood LeFlore. Who else could have got Moshulatubbee and Greenwood LeFlore to sit down in the same assembly? Peter was already recognized as a special sort of chief of all the Choctaws, though he would not become chief in name till thirty-four years later.

Two white men of genius have given us descriptions of Peter. The painter George Catlin gave it in a picture, but also in words. It is from Catlin that we get the information that Peter's Indian name was Snapping Turtle or Ha-tchoo-tuck-nee. This may be near right, for Catlin gave Peter's white man name as Pinchlin which is close. The fetish for exactitude of names was never a weakness of the finest painter of Indians.

The second white artist to meet and be impressed by Peter was Charles Dickens. This was in 1842 on a steamboat between Cincinnati and Louisville. *American Notes* (Chapter 12):

"I asked him what he thought of Congress?" (Peter was returning from seventeen months of fruitless lobbying for justice for the Choctaws in Washington.) "He answered, with a smile, that it wanted dignity in an Indian's eyes . . . answered . . . that his race was losing many things besides their dress, and would soon be seen upon the earth no more . . . a remarkably handsome man . . . with long black hair, an aquiline nose, broad cheek bones, a sunburnt complexion, and a very bright, keen, dark, and piercing eye . . . as stately and complete a gentleman . . . as ever I beheld; and moved among the people in the boat, another kind of being."

Dickens was impressed by few things in the America of the day, but he was impressed by Peter Pitchlynn.

. . .

Peter was in admiration of the self-sufficient Manor House culture set up by Hannali and others in the Moshulatubbee, but he be-

90

lieved it should be only one of several elements of the reconstituted Choctaw Nation.

"The white man had this eight hundred years ago, Hannali," he said. "It was not enough, but they lost it in reaching for other things and became warped in a different direction. We need both the self-sufficiency and the wide-reaching commerce and manufactory. The merchants in Doaksville progress in trade, the Planters in Falaya will provide export surpluses with their bulk crop system. You are a merchant as well as a farmer, Hannali, and as a merchant you should work for the more open system."

"I chew the other side of the hog friend great man Peter," said Hannali, "too much trade is a bleed to death business what other storekeeper will tell his people do not buy this dress for your wife your wife already have a dress what other storekeeper tell his people go home and put that money in a safe place it will be a hard winter."

"You're unique in this, Hannali," said Peter, "but you may be mistaken when you discourage the people from buying. That is not the way of the white people nor of the Doaksville merchants. They say that trade will generate more trade and that dollars can be made to grow like corn."

"I am a banker and you are not Peter Pitchlynn you have no idea how rich I could be if I desired it's an irony thing that those who love the stuff so much have not mastered the simple arts of obtaining it I could be very rich and it would mean that other people would become very poor I say that no dollar can generate more than one hundred cents and I know more about giving and taking interest than do the men in Doaksville I say that they rub off a little bit of their soul every time they produce unusual surplus and have to buy back necessities."

"We will find truth between the two systems, Hannali. There is much to be said for the Manor system of the Moshulatubbee, and much for the open mercantilism of Doaksville and the giant cropping of the Falaya. I work always for Choctaw prosperity but I have trouble fitting the pieces in."

"There are more things than prosperity great man Peter let a man build up his own house it is the rind of his soul the men of Falaya have drunk mules' milk and are sterile theirs is not the way."

They disagreed on this, for Hannali could see no good at all in the runaway mercantilism of Doaksville or the slave-based cotton cropping in Falaya. Peter wanted to find a way to combine the two systems, and nobody has found it yet.

Peter Pitchlynn spent a week at Hannali's Big House in 1843. They entertained him royally, for he *was* their royalty.

. . .

The next year an equally intelligent man spent more time with Hannali. In the year 1844, Pass Christian Innominee brought his family up from New Orleans to visit.

CHAPTER NINE

1.

*Pass Christian Innominees. "Have I signed a paper
says I must swallow a kettle?"*

The children of Pass Christian Innominee were Peter, Marie Chapponia, Joseph, Catherine, John Barua, Therese, and Louis Christian. Some of them were older and some of them younger than the Hannali Innominees, for Pass Christian had not had all his children within one twelve-month period. They had become French, but they were still Indian also; and the cousins got together well.

Many other children came to the Big House in the weeks of the visit: John Sapulpa and Emily Sapulpa and Ophelia Checote—McIntosh Creek children from the north side of the river; Josephine Horse, Amanda T, Robert Harkins, Seoma Big—Choctaw children. There came Mary Choate and Lavaca Choate, nieces of Natchez, over from Sebastian County, Arkansas, for a visit. There were so many children and young people staying at the House that Hannali didn't have ponies for them all. Some of them rode around the country mounted on mules.

In one of Hannali's south fields there was a scarecrow that could talk and whistle. The children became partisans of the thing and carried to Papa Hannali its complaint that it needed a new coat now that winter was coming on.

"No I will not give him one," said Hannali, "my record show his field have suffered more crow damage than any other the crows call it Crow Haven it is all right a scarecrow learn to talk and whistle but first he must learn to scare the crows."

All the Innominee children of both families and Hannali himself were straight-faced in such daily carrying-on as this, for they were Chocs. But the two little Cherokee Choate girls would whoop and dance and giggle. They found all Choctaw jokes funny.

It was the snoot end of winter just coming in and you could have fun in the Territory. As in Hannali's own childhood, affairs came to the big focus. They were the bright, sharp days. The young people from New Orleans, having been on boats for many hundred miles, still could not get enough of boats. They learned to take Hannali's ferry across the river and back. They rode the keel boats and the barges for a dozen, twenty miles, and then walked back along the wooded banks. They were even allowed to fire up Hannali's big boat, the *Bashih*. They were not as you would imagine city children to be.

They were river rats. They could swim better than their Territory cousins. There was ice along the banks, and the water was very cold when the children swam in it. They lied through their chittering little teeth, they turned blue from the cold and nearly perished, but they swore that they weren't cold at all. Pass Christian had told them never to vaunt themselves, but to be as tough in all things as the Hannali children. Oh, they were all tough! It's fun to be tough.

The Pass Christians could ride well, though not so wildly as their cousins. They couldn't climb the big pecan trees as well as the Hannalis, but then none of the Hannali sons could climb them as well as John Sapulpa or George Hewahnackee. The Creek Indians were always the best pecan tree climbers.

Seoma Big could see through trees, and could say which trees had possums holed up in them and just where they could be found. Robert Harkins could knock squirrels out of trees with throwing sticks; he never missed.

The children drew the possums and squirrels and stuffed them with persimmons now turned purple with the frost, and roasted them till the juice squirted a mile. They noodled out Canadian River catfish as long as your arm. They chased bear cubs and Hannali's forest pigs. They nipped on stolen mule whiskey and told stories. Luvinia told the one about the panther who swallowed the girl.

"The panther didn't like it, after he had swallowed her, and the girl sure didn't like it," Luvinia said. "It was a big panther, but there wasn't very much room in there.

" 'I'm hungry, I have to have some corn,' the girl said after she had been in there all night. 'I can't eat the rats and things you eat. Swallow some corn.'

"The panther swallowed some corn but he didn't like corn very well.

" 'How am I going to eat this hard corn?' the girl asked him. I forgot to tell you it was hard, dry, last-year's corn. 'You got to swallow something to grind it with,' the girl said."

"Why didn't he dissolve her in his paunch and shut her up?" asked Nakni Pans-Hata. "That's what I'd have done."

"I don't know. I forget that part," Luvinia said. " 'I don't know anything about grinding corn,' the panther said, 'leave me alone.' 'All you got to do is swallow two stones,' the girl said. 'I'll grind it myself.' So the panther swallowed two stones and the girl ground the corn. 'Now swallow some water,' the girl said, 'I got to make the corn into cakes.' The panther swallowed some water, and the girl made the corn into cakes.

" 'Now swallow some sticks,' the girl said. He did. 'Now swallow some live coals,' she told him, 'I got to make a fire to cook the cakes on.' The panther swallowed some live coals, and the girl made a fire and cooked the corn cakes. But the panther began to feel he had made a bad bargain.

" 'Corn cakes are all right for breakfast,' the girl said after a half day had gone by, 'but what am I going to eat for dinner?' 'I don't know,' the panther said, 'let me alone.' 'I want some pishofa,' the girl said, 'swallow a pig.' The panther swallowed a pig.

" 'Now swallow a kettle,' the girl said. 'This I will not do,' the panther told her, 'have I signed a paper says I must swallow a kettle?' 'How I go to make pishofa without a kettle?' the girl wanted to know, 'I will give you no peace till you swallow it.'

"The panther swallowed a kettle, but by that time he wished he'd never swallowed the girl. She built a real hot fire under the kettle to make the pishofa. Then she began to ask for a lot of things.

She really needed some of them to put in the pishofa, but she just asked for the rest of them to drive the panther crazy.

"By that time the panther had enough. He reared back and brought up the girl and the corn and the two stones and the sticks and the fire and the pig and the kettle all in one big heave.

" 'Be careful, you crazy panther,' the girl said, 'you'll make me spill the pishofa.' "

"That is not a true story," said Marie Chapponia, for her own best story had been topped, "the panther couldn't swallow the girl all in one piece, and she couldn't talk after she was swallowed."

"Oh, but it is a true story!" cried Luvinia, and it was. "Top it, you children, try to top it!" Nobody could top Luvinia on a story. She'd learned to tell them from her mother Martha Louisiana.

2.

Can you bed down one hundred people at your house? Five Dollar Honest. Chikkih Chikkih. Weeping at Epiphany.

It was coming to the Christmas season, and the Indians had now begun to celebrate Christmas. They had always held potlatches at the four seasons, feasts with much visiting and gift giving. Now they made the winter one the biggest of the year. This was the year when everybody visited Hannali House.

Whole families came in—Choctaw families from all over the Moshulatubbee and even the Pushmataha, Creek Indian families from north of the river, several Chickasaw families recently arrived over the trails. White officers and soldiers came on holiday from Fort Smith and Fort Coffee, and from Fort Gibson at Three Forks of the Arkansas. Early cattle drovers (for the word "cowboy" was still unknown in the country) used the Texas Road and stopped at Hannali's for holiday visit. There were all sorts of visitors, many of them with no legal right in the Territory.

Can you bed down one hundred people at your house? Hannali could at his. For some there were proper beds, for others there were cotton ticks filled with corn husks, or straw on the dirt floor (for only a few of the rooms of the Big House as yet had timber floors) and buffalo robes for warmth.

Hannali brought a hundred wagonloads of wood up to the House to keep all the fires going. He killed a heavy pig every day and three steers a week. He brought three hundred pumpkins over from the Creek country. He even brought loads of wheat down from the Osage and Pawnee regions. The Choctaws had lately discovered the excellence of the unleavened wheaten bread of the middle Indians.

Hannali and his horse-crazy friends managed to drive two dozen wild buffalo into a corral that would hold anything. The animals were crashing around in there for weeks, foaming and heaving and hardly touching the hay tossed to them. They had a roomy space and a stream running through it, but they spent all their time crashing into the oak fences and rolling their bloodshot eyes up into their heads. Hannali had designed a spit that would turn a two-thousand-pound buffalo as easily as though it were a turkey. Many of the visiting Plains Indians would eat no meat but buffalo.

· · ·

One day, Marie DuShane harnessed up a spring wagon and took the thirteen Innominee children over the Ferry to North Fork Town. The town was five miles from Hannali's Landing, on the North Fork of the Canadian just below the branching off of the Deep Fork. It had become a large town with three stores. None of them had the bulk business of Hannali's own store, but they were longer on trifles and variety. They had things from the states— licorice, tea, snuff (Hannali had only tobacco twist and plug, and black-leaf cigars, and crimp cut), and coffee that was already ground. They had slippery elm for chewing and manufactured toys. Marie DuShane bought slippery elm and snuff for the children and many odd things for the house.

"Not Choctaw dollars, not Choctaw dollars," they told her, and Marie only smiled and laid out gold coin and watched them scurry up enough Mexican and U.S. silver to cover it. She even accepted two Choctaw dollars as part of her change, saying that Hannali knew how to redeem them.

"Choctaw dollars" were put out by a store in Doaksville, were impressively lettered in Choctaw and English (the Choctaw lettering on them said "One Dollar Honest" or "Five Dollar Honest"), and were generally considered as worthless. When Indians would get a few of them together and take them down to Doaksville, the men in the store there would say that they didn't know what they were and it must have been some other store in some other Doaksville that put them out.

Some of Hannali's friends had once been stuck with these, and he had redeemed them, being himself a banker. When he had a hundred dollars' worth of them he rode down to Doaksville. Not wishing to waste time, he rode his horse right into the store building and sat there, a big Choctaw on a big horse and with a devil grin on his face and a rifle across his saddle horn. The men redeemed the Choctaw dollars for him. He didn't even have to get off his horse. That had been the year before.

Marie DuShane and the thirteen children rode home from North Fork town at night in the spring wagon. They were most of them huddled in back with the merchandise and under the buffalo robes. It was snowing, and the ice tinkled when they drove the wagon onto the ferry and broke the ferry loose from its moorings. The children sang songs like "chikkih chikkih," and they gobbled like turkeys. It was a night to remember.

. . .

The wife of Pass Christian Innominee was Marie Delessert. She had been startled and silent when she first came to the House. But once she understood them, she accepted the strange arrangements of the Hannali Innominees. Previous to her visit, she had known of Marie DuShane only and had corresponded with her. On very first encounter, Marie Delessert was shocked by what appeared an unnatural situation, a Negro woman and an Indian woman sharing the place of her French sister-in-law.

Later, she became closer to Natchez and Martha Louisiana than to Marie DuShane. If it were possible, then Marie Delessert at the same time resembled both of them. She had the sudden wit of Natchez and the compassionate good humor of Martha Louisiana, the apparent weightlessness of Natchez and the certain bulk of Martha. She began a thought at the Martha depths and ended it in the Natchez trees. She was fair, for she was a white woman, and she didn't tempt the sun much.

She would never, like Natchez, have run out barefoot in the first snow to do the snowbird dance. She wouldn't, like Marie DuShane, have risen on a sleep-eluding midnight to mount and ride horse till after daylight. Like Martha Louisiana, she practiced the conservation of energy.

It was a big season and a big Christmas, for all that there could be no Mass and there was no priest within two hundred miles. The families exchanged gifts, they had been exchanging gifts for weeks, and feasted. And after a few more days, the visiting Innominees had to go.

The Pass Christian Innominees left Hannali's Landing on Epiphany of the year 1845, and returned down the rivers to their home. The children parted with weeping, for they were still Indian.

3.

The Year of the Big Thunders. Down the Texas Road. The clan thing Devil.

A year flicked by. It was a good year for Hannali and his family, the year when his three sons became men. They were coming onto sixteen years old.

The Indians later referred to this year as the Year of the Big Thunders. Meteorologically it was a very stormy year, one of floods on the Canadian and Arkansas rivers, or tornadoes ripping out of the Pushmataha and raking into the north, of lightning and thunder such as had not been seen nor heard since the days of the grandfathers, of hailstones as big as Ishtaboli balls. But it was a fertile year in all respects, and was the year in which the transported Indians finally got well.

There were gathering storms other than the physical ones. Schism of nation came to plague the Indians just as they came into their new prosperity. It rived every tribe in two. In the Choctaw country, the division was between the feudal, mostly full-blood, self-sufficiency Indians of the North; and the slave-owning, liberal, speculating, mostly breed and white-blood Indians of the Choctaw South. It was not that even one Indian in twenty in the South districts owned slaves; it was that a score of them owned from one hundred to five hundred slaves each, and they set the tone of that society.

At the same time, there came external war. In 1836, Texas had declared herself independent of Mexico. However it be falsified (and the falsification remains one of the classic things), there was only one issue there: slavery. Slavery was forbidden in all Mexico (including the province of Texas), and there were men who wished to turn Texas into a slave empire for themselves.

Mexico did not recognize the Texas independence. She was outraged by the bringing in of black slaves and by the murdering of thousands of Indians to make a place for them—for Mexico was of that same Indian blood. Between the years 1830 and 1845 there were nearly as many Indians who fled for their lives from Texas into the Indian Territory as had been brought from the old South to the Territory.

On December 29 of 1845, President Polk signed a resolution making the Republic of Texas a slave state of the Union. On January 13 of 1846, General Zachary Taylor was ordered to lead troops down to the Nueces River for an invasion of Mexico, and to create incident thereto. The admittance of Texas and the promise of war against Mexico were two parts of a package deal; no honest man doubts that now.

It would be exactly three months (all the while assuring Mexico of peaceful intent) before the United States would declare war on Mexico. It was the three months that had been calculated as the time necessary to mount the assault.

We are concerned with it here only because most of the army groups came south through the Indian Territory, and the most used road was the Texas Road that ran within sight of Hannali's Big House. There were raw-acting men in that army. Some of them were unruly, and some of the Indians were unruly in their turn. There were brushes.

On February 19, President Jones (the last president of the Republic of Texas) turned office over to James Henderson (the first governor of the state of Texas)—and already a United States Army was inside the new state and marching to create incident in the suddenly claimed and never seen Territory between the Rio Grande and the Nueces rivers.

In May when President Polk said that "American Blood has been spilt on American Soil," he lied grandly. It was the blood of the first Americans ever to see that soil, and they spilt it as they began their incredible invasion of that Mexican land.

. . .

One afternoon Sally was not to be found.

Her own mother Natchez was not worried about her. She said that nothing could ever happen to that girl, and indeed Sally often rode off at random. But her other mothers, Marie DuShane and Martha Louisiana, became unaccountably worried. They told Hannali that Sally had not been seen for some time, and that there were rough men in the neighborhood.

Hannali was standing rigid with apprehension and terror. He hardly heard them. He had already gotten the message in another manner. He cried out, and bolted from them to one of the fields. Already he knew what had happened to Sally and where he would find her. Several times in his life he would have such true dark visions.

He found Sally in a rock waste between two oddly shaped fields. She was badly mauled and torn, conscious though in shock. He carried her back to the house and gave her to the women. He knew that she wasn't to die from this.

He went to find what he knew would be in his inner room. It might give a clue, in its taunts, to the direction taken. He read the note, half with his eyes, half out of his intuition:

"Fat man I have had your heffer calf you will follow me at your perell I mean to cut you down I leave my notice and you sitting here sleepy in the same room and not even see me I hurt your heffer calf but not to die I will be back many times for her fat man you follow me you better trembel for your life Whiteman Falaya."

It was onto dark. Hannali calculated his way, and his intuition would carry him to the point of the showdown. Soldiers had been passing through the country all day. They would be bivouacked not much more than a dozen miles from there, south on the Texas Road. One thing Hannali knew—how Whiteman Falaya would be dressed.

Hannali mounted horse and rode off late in the night. He intended to come on the camped troopers a little before dawn.

CHAPTER TEN

1.

*Pardon my break in on you like this Commander
but I have come to kill one of your men. "Be
gone in five minutes or hang!" This bull will still
toss. Take you all at once or one at a time.*

In his senses Hannali was almost too Indian to be true. It is a question at what point very acute sensing and subliminal impressions will
pass over into intuition. Many of the intuitions of Hannali's life may
have been no more than this very sharp sensing.

He read the country like a newspaper as he rode over it in the
night. Indeed, to him it was yesterday's newspaper. He knew where
deer and cattle and horses had crossed his way. He knew which had
been the light Creek horses, which the Chickasaw steppers, which
the heavy Choctaw ponies, which the U. S. Cavalry mounts. He knew
just where John T had sat a Choctaw pony and warily watched the
cavalry soldiers pass the afternoon before.

Down near Gaines Creek, Hannali knew that he was near a con-
centration of men and horses. He caught the heat and scent of
horses, and the emanation and disturbance of men. Nearer, and he

heard the stir of predawn cooks and the clumping of a man walking a post through the brush. But the real sentinels for such a bivouac are the horses. They react to any intrusion and alert the guards. Only a horse Choctaw could have gone through the horses so easily without stirring them.

It would be a raggle force of men, but not a soft one. These weren't the reluctant recruits who would follow down the road a month later. They were the rough volunteer men who had jumped into the war with both feet.

"Be you at ease," said Hannali to the sentinel, coming behind him noiselessly on horse, "do not cry out do not turn around do not try to gun me I'd have you dead I want Whiteman Falaya."

"We've no man named that," the sentry croaked.

"He is with you under another name then we will wait here till the morning muster then I regretfully must kill a man of yours."

"Then we kill you, old bugger. We killed two Indians here last evening, and I didn't hear any regret. You have the drop on me, but I don't scare. Blink once, and I'll have you off that horse."

"I blink I still sit my horse whose are the footsteps who is it who comes."

"The sergeant. He is one man you won't take. He's rough."

"There are footsteps when he comes then he is gone again without footsteps he is the ghost what is his name."

"That is nothing to you."

"That is everything to me I will have his name from you easy or I will have you flat on your back and the snout of my rifle in your mouth when you say it what is his name."

"Whitman Long."

"It is the same his translate name is he a Choctaw Indian like me."

"I can't tell one of you buggy barstuds from another. He's Indian."

"I see the morning muster is called while we talk I will ride over to them and tell them my business do not shoot me in the back a young man whose voice shakes when he says he doesn't scare shouldn't try that one shot wouldn't do me."

"No. I don't believe it would, you old bull."

Hannali rode through the camp and up to the files of the muster. He dismounted and bulked up to the astonished major.

"Pardon me break in on you like this Commander," Hannali said, "but I have come to kill one of your men I will do it quick and then be on my way."

"That so, you bleeding Indian? Any particular man you have in mind?" The major didn't remain astonished for long.

"He is on your list as Whitman Long his Choctaw name is Whiteman Falaya I will kill him and then be on my way."

"I ought to throw the two of you in a pit together to see what happens. You're two of a kind," the major said.

"It would pleasure my heart to have him there or anywhere I cannot thank you enough Commander where is the pit."

"You mud-faced stallion. Do you think I'd let you at one of my men? Look yonder at that fresh dirt. Do you know what is there?"

"It is not fresh dirt it is last night's dirt two graves are there two Indians who are better than any men you have."

"Two sniveling Indians who came in with silly stories of their wives or daughters being assaulted by my horse soldiers. The fools believed that I should punish my men. There is their answer."

"I do my own punishing give the man to me now and I kill him."

"Look you here, bullhead; here is a noose. I know it is a good noose, for last night it did its work twice perfectly. And yonder is a tree branch that also knows its business. Do you understand me?"

"You waste my time mouth soldier I want that man now."

"Thunderation, you offal-faced ogre. Are you such a fool, or do you believe me one? I have two hundred men here. Do you think you can take them all?"

"All at once or one at a time I try it I want that man."

"You rot-headed fool! It is you who waste our time. There is room for just one more grave in that little hollow."

"True for the grave of the lean man I have in mind not for me it would crowd me I want that man now."

"You crock-headed Choc, I talk straight. *Be gone from this camp in five minutes or we will hang you.*"

"Who have a watch," Hannali asked softly.

The major took out a fine gold watch and laid it on the tree stump that served for a muster table.

"There it is, you old bluffer," the major roared. "The noose is getting itchy. When that hand gets to there—"

"I know time," said Hannali.

Hannali stood with his hands in his pockets and gazed at the watch. They played the minutes out. A dozen men, on a nod from the major, loaded and leveled rifles at Hannali should he do something rash. Three men stretched out the line and the noose and made it ready. A lieutenant studied the hanging tree and gave it a shuffling kick as though to tell it to get ready. The time was running.

The major chewed his moustaches as seriously as though he sat at poker, but he was playing poker with a Choctaw. Hannali stole the game by his presence. They didn't know when it had happened, but for several minutes now they had all drawn back from his menace, and only Hannali could see the watch.

The time seemed triply long. The men lost their edge as they waited and doubted the thing, and they fell into frustration. The only sound was horses clanking their hobbles as they grazed.

"Five minutes go," Hannali announced.

The Adam's apple of the major bobbled, but he voiced no order. It was balanced on the edge there. A ripple ran through the men, but they did not quite come to action. Hannali continued, with his hands in his pockets, to gaze at the watch; and the fascinated men still gaped at Hannali.

"Five minutes a little bit more," said Hannali heavily, and the men stood dry-mouthed and nervous.

"Five minutes quite a bit more," said Hannali after a while.

He spit on the watch. He looked as though he would spit on the nervous major, but he did not. Instead, he seemed to wake with a start.

He shook his head in bafflement. He smashed a big fist into his palm so loudly that it echoed.

"Today I have lost God give me another day," he said. He turned and walked wearily to his horse, his face slack with defeat.

"That man have tricked me," Hannali announced sullenly with the bridle in his hand and one foot in a stirrup, "I know something have changed and I do not understand it that man is no longer in your camp he is no longer in the dress of a horse soldier he may be in a Creek turban or a Pawnee slouch hat he has slip away while I played a boy's game with boys I am a fool not to know what it meant when his scent was gone he is nine miles gone now and he is the man that nobody is able to track I will have him one day today I have miss him."

Hannali went to mount, then paused once more.

"This bull will still toss," he announced to the soldiery multitude, "this bear will still smash the dogs what I say stands I take you all at once or one at a time which man make move."

He gazed at them out of his powerful face for a long time. No man made a move. Then Hannali mounted slowly and walked his horse out of the camp, eaten up with frustration.

2.

Welsh Indians. Robert Jones and the five hundred slaves. The man named Six-Town is the other pole of it.

There is a whole recondite literature grown up about the "Welsh Indians." It will bulk nearly as large as the literature connecting the Indians with the lost tribes of Israel or with the people of Atlantis.

The story is that Welshmen (under Prince Madoc) came to America long before Columbus, went inland, and intermarried with Indians. They left a progeny of blue-eyed and hazel-eyed people much lighter than other Indians, and with Welsh words in their languages.

It was not the experts who compiled the corresponding word lists, but the amateurs. Usually the comparison is with the Mandan Indian, for the legend connecting the Mandans with the Welsh grew stronger after the Mandans were wiped out by smallpox and their faces and speech could not be closely studied. There are many words which seem the same in both languages—*ni*, we, *chwi*, you (but the Welsh not pronounced at all like the Indian), *buw*, to live, *cysgu*, to sleep, *ceffyl*, a horse (but the Welsh is from the low Latin *caballus*, and the Indian from the kindred Spanish *caballo*), *afor*, a river, *trof*, a town, *coch*, red, *nos*, the night, *modryb*, aunt, *cwch*, a boat, *mawr*, big, *tebot*, a kettle (the compiler didn't realize that the Welsh word is from the English teapot, a much later borrowing than the purported Welsh intrusion of America), *cryf*, strong, *carreg*, a stone.

But the game can be played with any language, and it has been played by others with Hebrew and Phoenician and Basque and Ainu —relating them to Indian tongues.

We do not believe in the pre-Columbian Welsh intrusion, but we do believe in one very early in the colonial period. And there *are* Indians who, in a sense, may be called Welsh Indians—the Choctaws. Just as the Cherokees were mixed English and Ulsterman Indians, and the Creeks were Scottish Indians, so were the Choctaws Welsh Indians. We have no idea why so many of the colonials who came among the Choctaws were Welshmen, but they were.

There is a long list of Choctaws who carried Welsh blood: Robert Cole, Robert M. Jones, George W. Harkins, Sidney Bowen, David Folsom, John Morgan, George S. Gaines, William David, W. N. Jones, the Pitchlynns, the Kincaids, the Pebworths, John Garland, George Hudson, Frank Owen, S. D. Griffiths, F. G. Wynn, W. A. Williams. These were Welsh Indians.

A Welshman is more canny than a Scot; he will not let himself have the name of being canny. He is more stubborn than an Englishman, though letting it be thought that he is amenable. He is neither an explorer nor a seafarer nor a pioneer, but whenever the pioneers come to the ends of the earth they always find a Welshman already there and running a store.

Among the Choctaws, the merchants at Doaksville and Boggy Depot and Skullyville were usually these Welsh Indians, blue-eyed and hazel-eyed and lighter than their fellows. It was they who set up the toll bridges and the toll pikes and who took tribute at the fords and passes. They were the inventors of the leased-land device in the Territory, of the affair of entering non-existent Indians on the rolls for allotment payments, of the trail-driver grazing fees, and much else. They were the big planters and the rich man Indians. They were the slaveowners.

The greatest of these Welsh Indians among the Choctaws was Robert M. Jones. He was the richest man in the Territory, and one of the really rich men in the whole country. He came most typically to represent one of the two aspects of the Choctaws, so we must have an account of him.

He was a half-blood Choctaw, born in Mississippi in 1808 of a wealthy family. With what he was born with, and what he acquired variously along the way, Robert M. Jones became about as smart a man as was ever to be found anywhere.

On coming to the new Territory as a young man, Robert Jones selected Doaksville as his base. He served a swift apprenticeship with a French-Canadian trader named Berthelet, going on trading missions to the Plains Indians, the Wichitas, Wacos, Caddoes, Comanches, Anadarkos, and Cheyennes, comprehending all the intricacies of the trade, and learning the languages of all of them in one year.

Berthelet then took Jones into his store as full partner, and their company soon surpassed Doaks and Timms Mercantile Company as the leading establishment in Doaksville. Berthelet soon passed from the picture, and Jones owned it all. His monopoly on trade with the Plains Indians and his political influence over them remained one of the strong sticks in Jones's hand.

Jones acquired credit and went into the slave and cotton business. His first plantation, three hundred acres near Fort Towson on the Red River, was only a start. By the time of the Civil War he had six large plantations: Rose Hill, Boggy, Root Hog, Shawnee-Town, Walnut Bayou, and Lake West. Lake West is mentioned as having five thousand acres, and it may not have been the largest; it was at the Rose Hill plantation that he built his fine house.

Robert Jones owned five hundred slaves, and they were contraband blacks new from Africa. The Negroes were landed in the Sabine Estuary, driven through the wild piny country to a Red River point in Louisiana, then brought up the Red River by boat to the landings in Oklafalaya. Importation of new slaves was then forbidden and slaves brought a very high price in all the South, but Robert Jones went into the big slave business cheap.

But one secret of Jones's success was that he came to own many of the Choctaw Indians more completely than he owned his own Negroes. By his wealth and his mind and his methods, he became the most powerful Choctaw of them all.

He had everything, a mill and sugar plantation in Louisiana, stores in Skullyville and Boggy Depot as well as in Doaksville, his own steamboats on the Red River, a great house at Rose Hill with furnishings imported from France and with formal gardens laid out in the high English manner. He built alliance by marrying into the first family of the Chickasaws, and thereafter their chiefs were always Jones's in-laws, so involved with him in business deals that they had to be his partisans.

When the moment of decision should come in a few years, it

would be the weight of this one man Jones who would tip the balance to a wrong choice and the eventual destruction of the Five Tribes Indians.

Robert M. Jones, politically liberal, devoted to the fevered and exploding economy, slave-driving, white blood, operating by political deviousness and entangling loans, selfish and shriveled, represented one pole of the Choctaws. He was the biggest of those men of Falaya of whom Hannali had said that they had drunk mules' milk and were sterile.

And the man with the given name of Six-Town, Hannali Innominee himself, politically conservative, economically feudal, free-holding, full-blood, compassionate and chauvinistic, perhaps represented the other pole.

3.
The day when Hannali was no longer ugly.
Famous Innominee and his brothers. The Big
Decade. Alabaster Hills and Great Salt Plains.

It was Abraham Lincoln who said that every man over age thirty is responsible for his face. He will have formed it by then. If he has an ugly face it is because he is an ugly man through. But there came a day when Hannali Innominee was no longer ugly of face. The details of that great bulk had now formed themselves into a thing so curious, so intricate, so interesting in its topography and so deep in contour that it was in no way ugly. He looked like the figurine of some chuckling God, but no longer of an ugly one. Later visitors at his Big House have said that he was a man of deep charm and power, and of most pleasant and exciting appearance. Earlier visitors had said that he was a bedamned spooky devil till you got to know him. The new Hannali had come onto a certain intensity of life and vast inner resources.

. . .

The three sons of Hannali had been sent off to school. The Choctaw academies had now been set up, one in each district. Hannali sent his three sons to three separate schools, not from a desire to separate them, not to keep one from standing in the shadow of another (for they were of near equal ability), but that they should know the various parts of their own nation.

Alinton Innominee went to Spencer Academy in Oklafalaya.

Famous Innominee went to Fort Coffee Academy in Moshulatubbee.

Travis Innominee went to Armstrong Academy in Pushmataha.

This (from about the years 1847 to 1860) was the Great Decade of the Innominee family—a baker's dozen decade. They multiplied their friendships, extended their connections, and increased their own numbers. Hannali could do no wrong in material things. His prosperity grew.

In fact, it was a period of prosperity, the only such period they ever knew, for all the Territory Indians. In population the Five Tribes had made up the losses of the twenty thousand persons left dead on the removal trails. They had learned to farm and ranch in the new country, and the weather and prices held well for them. Education was moving forward. It really seemed as though the Indians had discovered a way of accepting the best of what the white people had to offer, and rejecting the worst.

Famous Innominee became something of a Territory dude in his time at Fort Coffee Academy. He had a certain advantage over his two brothers—a living grandfather, Strange Choate. The family of Famous' mother Natchez was now accessible to him. From Fort Coffee Academy to the Choate holdings in Sebastian County, Arkansas, was only a two-hour drive, and Strange Choate had given his grandson Famous a flamboyant buggy and two fine trotters to drive it in often. Some of the rough Choctaw bumps were knocked off Famous by his smooth and pleasant Cherokee cousins. Also Famous brought about a new cementing of the friendship between Hannali and his father-in-law Strange.

Strange Choate was a Cherokee of the full-blood faction. His beliefs were those of Hannali, but more fully worked out. Both, in the years of crisis, would be Freedom Indians. Each would always know that, however bad things got, there was one other Indian standing firm forever.

It was on the advice and counsel of Strange Choate that Hannali entered politics. Politics had not yet taken its modern form, and campaigning was not so competitive. Hannali simply announced that he would devote his time and talents to a particular service if so be it he was selected for it. But it pleased him when he was chosen.

It was the crown of the success and respect that he had won that Hannali Innominee became (for the first time in the early 1850s) one of the twelve members of the Choctaw Senate. Later he served a term as congressman (there was one congressman for every one thousand Choctaws), and still later a second term as senator.

The views of Hannali in the Choctaw Senate were usually minority views, but he gave expression to the basic philosophy of the free-stead Indians. Today he would be called a conservative and damned for it.

The Big Decade of the family was such a large and pleasantly juicy thing that we must bite into it from all sides to get the varied flavor. We may seem to skip around in treating of the Innominees in those years, their connections, their travels, their increase. But, people, people, how the Innominees themselves did skip around!

They became almost tourists with Hannali's own love for travel. They visited the Alabaster Hills and the Great Salt Plains and the Wichita Mountains. They consorted with Osage friends at Hominy Falls, with Caddoes on the False Washita, and with Creeks at Lokar Poker Town on the Arkansas. They were town Indians and country Indians at the same time, they went in four buggies and a big red wagon, they reached out their hands to touch everything. They were an expansive family in the Territory that had begun to seepen and vary.

The first of the sons to travel far was Alinton. Like Famous, Alinton also had a second grandfather. Old French Shawnee Alinton DuShane, long dead, still lived in his grandson Alinton Innominee. And Alinton reverted to a dream of his dead grandfather. He announced that he would take boat and trade goods and go all the way up the Canadian River to the Santa Fe portage.

CHAPTER ELEVEN

1.

About green Indians. The Canadian River goes to Santa Fe. The California Road.

Have you heard about the green Indian named Pickens? He got a stock of goods from a trading post, and he went to trade with the prairie and Plains Indians.

Pickens is a Cherokee when the Creeks tell the story, a Creek when the Choctaws tell it, and a Choctaw when the Chickasaws tell it. None of them will admit that an Indian that green could be one of their own.

Pickens had nine pack animals laden with goods. He knew all about what gifts must be given to open a parley; he knew how to ask for beaver pelt in Arapaho and for foxskin in Wichita; he knew which Indians will accept cigar coupons for Territory money, and which will buy bear grease for Chippewa honey. He knew how to deal with the ignorant brush and Plains Indians. Some of those fellows are so ignorant that they will take a trader's mules and food away from him, not realizing that he will die without them.

One day Pickens came to a Kiowa Indian and gave him a block of soap for parley gift. The Kiowa began to eat the soap. "No, no,"

Pickens yiped at the man, "it is not for eating." "Tell me not my business, boy," said the Kiowa, "you should see what we eat at home."

The Kiowa gave Pickens three beaver pelts for three more blocks of soap. Other Kiowas came and each of them gave him three more beaver pelts for more soap, for a grindstone, for a yellow rock that he said was Cherokee salt, for a sack of pecan shells which he said would hatch into quail if you put them in creek water, for a broken chamber pot with little cherubs on it, for a left-handed glove for a left-handed Indian. He traded all sorts of odd articles to the Indians, the dasher out of an old butter churn, a child's broken doll, a little lead soldier, and for each of the things he got three beaver pelts.

"I bet I have three thousand beaver pelts," Pickens cried when he had traded off the last of his unusual articles, and he turned around to look at his pile. But he didn't have three thousand pelts, he had only three. Each Indian had come behind him and stolen the pelts and then walked around a rock and traded the same three pelts back to him.

"It is a green buffalo!" one of the Kiowas yelled, and Pickens ran up to the top of the hill to see it. While he was gone, someone stole the only three pelts there were. "Where is it? Where is it?" Pickens called from the top of the hill.

"It wasn't a green buffalo at all," the Kiowa said, "I think it was a green Indian."

Pickens came to some Caddo Indians one day. The first one came and took a bundle of merchandise—"for a parley gift," he said. He took a second bundle "for gift for my wife." And still another bundle "for gift for my second wife." "Stop! That's enough! How many wifes do you have?" Pickens cried. "Is it your business how many wifes I have?" asked the Caddo, "with all these bundles I need one of your mules to carry them." And he took one of Pickens' mules away.

Other Caddoes came and took bundles from Pickens for parley gifts, loaded them on his remaining mules, and led them away. And Pickens was left alone and destitute in the wilderness.

But not for long! Cheyennes came to him and asked for parley gifts. "The Caddoes have stolen all my merchandise and left me destitute," said Pickens, "I have nothing left for a parley gift." "How can a man with a little sack of corn to eat say that he has nothing for gift?" asked one Cheyenne, and he took the little sack of corn. "How can a man who has a jug of water to drink say that he has nothing for gift?" asked another Cheyenne, and he took the jug of water. "How can a man with a shirt on his back say that he has nothing for gift?" asked another Cheyenne, and he took the shirt off Pickens' back. And still other Cheyennes took the hat off Pickens' head, the trousers off his shanks, and the clout from his loins. Then one took his shoes away from him.

"Let me keep my shoes," Pickens begged. "How can a man walk in this terrible country without shoes?" "I tell you what," said the Cheyenne, "a man that hasn't any corn to eat or water to drink or clothes to wear and the sun burning like it is today, that man isn't going very far anyhow. He don't need shoes." So the Cheyenne took Pickens' shoes and left him to die in the wilderness.

You think that was the end? You don't know those Plains Indians. A Pawnee came and said, "How can a man with meat on his bones say that he has nothing for gift," and he began to cut the meat off Pickens' bones to feed to his dog. "What will I have to cover my bare bones with," Pickens' dead body asked, "if you cut all the meat from my bones?"

"If I'd gone as far with it as you have," the Pawnee told Pickens' dead body, "I don't believe I'd worry about my bones." And, as it happened, he needn't have worried. A Comanche came and began to break loose Pickens' bones and toss them in a hamper on his horse. "What will be left of me if you take my bones?" said Pickens' bones. "Am I a philosopher?" asked the Comanche, "how do I know what will be left of you? We will break these open and my wifes will make soup from them. Thank you." And the Comanche carried off all Pickens' bones.

No, no. That wasn't all of it. An Anadarko came by and caught Pickens' soul in a sack made out of a deer's stomach, and carried the soul away.

And that was the end of the green Indian named Pickens—until the next story. The thing about it was that all these stories were true: Those ignorant Plains Indians were pretty smart, and they'd pick a trader clean if he let them. Alinton Innominee had heard these stories from his father before he started out, so he only grinned when the Plains Indians said to him—as they said to every new trader in their country—"Here comes Pickens, the green Indian."

It took Alinton only three days to discover, as his father Hannali had tried to tell him, that the trading trip up the Canadian River was impractical. But he continued on. He would go to Santa Fe for adventure, if not for profit.

Well, why was it impractical? Wagon traders and mule-pack traders had been doing well with the western Indians. And in the old French days, the boat trade had beat any other sort. Now there was more profit than ever on the big rivers. Why shouldn't there be a middling profit from a middling river?

On the third day, Alinton and his companions tied the boats to a cottonwood shore, climbed the banks, and saw the reason. That was where the country changed, where one goes *up* from the eastern mountains to the western flatlands. West, north, and south it was green and level as far as one could see.

The thousands of miles of eastern and middle rivers had all run through forested and tangled country where one would have to hack his way for wagon or even pack animal. But here was a good level road, one thousand miles wide, going west. It was ten times as easy to get out and walk as to pole a boat up that river. The Canadian River was not practical.

Well, they gave away all their boats but one small one. They got a little, but not much, for their merchandise. They continued west by river for adventure.

Alinton had a map that his father Hannali had drawn him. He also had a map of the United States Government, and it was plain that one of the maps was in error. The reason that the government map was wrong was that the mappers themselves had not visited that country, and that they had been misled by a confusion of names.

There is the Red River that flows into the Mississippi in the Louisiana country, and which farther upstream is the border between Texas and the Indian Territory, and it comes from the vague west. And in Spanish New Mexico there is a fine little river starting out and flowing east, and it is named the Red River. And the map makers had assumed that they were the same. They weren't.

The Red River itself comes apart into the Cache Creek Branch and the Prairie Dog Town Creek Branch, and the Elk Creek and the North Fork and the Salt Fork and the Deep Red Run, and it really doesn't go very far west. But the Canadian continued west three hundred miles farther than the government map showed it. There was another thing that misled them: The Upper Canadian River does look like the Red River farther down—flowing through treeless rolling or flat country; it does not look anything like the Canadian River farther down—flowing through its woodland.

Nevertheless, it pleased Alinton Innominee to take a trade boat over three hundred miles of dry land according to the government map.

The boys and young men of Alinton's party several times believed themselves to be in mortal danger. There is one aspect of all Indians, civilized or wild or gone feral, that is seldom emphasized: All the Indians are born kidders. The tough Plains hunters loved to spook and frighten such a bunch of boys and would never pass up an opportunity for it. What sometimes seems unsufferable arrogance, incredible boorishness, intolerable menace of the Indians is most often nothing but this rough kidding. They were initiations, hazings, things to be done. Sometimes visitors died from such kidding, but not often.

In New Mexico, the boys pushed their last boat almost to the top of the Sangre de Cristo Mountains. Those flatboats would float on a mirage or a heavy dew. They made packs of their last cargo, and undertook the portage to Santa Fe. Hannali had said that the Canadian River could be navigated to within one day's portage of Santa Fe, for he himself had done it. It could be, but it was a hard twenty-hour-long day portage.

To Santa Fe, the end of the line. No. No. They hardly stopped in Santa Fe. It was early in the year 1848. The word had not got back east yet, but it had reached Santa Fe.

The boys bought wagons and more mules. They took the California Road to find gold.

This was Alinton Innominee's wandering year—extending more than a year. We do not go into it in detail, for it is *his* property and not ours. A wandering year was to be part of a man's stock in trade. It was the mother lode from which he could mine stories and lies for the rest of his life, and it was not supposed to stand up to the close examination by an outsider.

2.

*Tow-headed Choctaw. A Durham bull and a wife
named Helen. Barnful of children.*

Jemmy Buster was a young cattle drover who came up the Texas
Road. He was a tow-headed Texan who was part Choctaw. He first
rode to Hannali House in 1848. He was a white boy on the outside, and Hannali moved to meet him and give him a short welcome.
There had been disreputable white men in the neighborhood and
some of them had stolen livestock—"drifted" them along with their
own herds.

Jemmy Buster had heard of the cantankerous big Choc and of the
deep hospitality that he gave—if he accepted one. Jemmy was sick,
his herd in bad shape, and he needed that hospitality. He didn't
know how to begin. He stammered and stuttered, but he stuttered
in Choctaw and Hannali practically adopted him on the spot. Jemmy
Buster would be the first of the several additions to the Innominees
in their time of expansion.

He had started up through the Territory with three hundred
steers, one scatter-witted white youth for helper, and only two extra
horses. Fifty of Jemmy's cattle had been seized by Indians. Every
family through whose land he passed took one steer for passage payment. "One steer is too much," he protested to the first of them.
"Ah well, give me half a steer then," said the Indian. "I am interested to see how you will drive the other half of the steer along
the trail." Jemmy would have been plundered deeper if he hadn't
been able to talk Choc, but he'd have gotten through free if he'd
looked like one. Now he had lost confidence in himself, and was
afraid to continue farther north where the Indians were not even
Choctaw.

He stayed at Hannali House for a week. His herd recovered on the
good grass along the Canadian River, and he himself was cured of his
sickness. In that week he acquired another sickness, but a more
pleasant one.

Jemmy's problem about traveling through the northern Territory
was solved by Famous Innominee, the Territory dude. For several
months Famous had been somewhat jealous of his brother Alinton
who had gone on a journey. Now it was agreed that Famous should
accompany Jemmy north. The two had become close friends. Famous

was a Cherokee as well as a Choctaw, and he said that they need give no steers to the Cherokees. They went up the road that had been the Osage Trace, that had been the East Shawnee Trail, that was now the Texas Road.

They drove deep into the Kansas country, selling steers to feeders as they went. They followed down the Little Osage River into the Missouri country, and sold the last of their steers there. They had finished their business. Well, why didn't they come back home then? They lingered there for three weeks, in spite of the urging of Jemmy Buster that they should be gone back south.

When they came back, Famous Innominee did not come empty-handed. He brought back an amazing Durham bull that must have been worth a thousand dollars American. He also brought a wife named Helen Miller, and her value was incalculable.

"It isn't quite a hundred pigs shoats hogs weanlings but you have done well," Hannali told his son with humor, but this was one of the few times that Famous didn't understand him.

The ring had been broken. The Innominees had entered on the period of their increase. It would be the time of the great harvest.

Here we must compress. These were the great years, and we must press them down to a small space, squeeze them till the juice runs out of them by the bucketful. The periods of plenty are never given fair space in history, and we will not go against the proportion of history here. We row upstream too often against her accepted current as it is.

Events had come in clusters. Jemmy Buster held pledge wedding with Hazel Innominee, and Jemmy and Famous went into the cattle business in a large way. In 1850, Travis Innominee took Rachel Perry of the Creek Indians for his pledge wife. In the same year, Luvinia Innominee was joined to Forbis Agent, an itinerant preacher and bookman. The first impediment of the man was removed by the stern instruction of Marie DuShane; the second remained, but it was not regarded as a serious drawback. Forbis could work, as much as was needed, for other members of the family; and he could still be a bookman. It isn't necessary that all should create prosperity; there was enough of it to go around.

Sally Innominee had become indrawn during those years. White-man Falaya had visited her again, but she said that he came as a ghost or devil and not as a man.

Alinton Innominee finally returned from his very long wandering year in Santa Fe and California and other places. He had a wife, Marie Calles. And he had returned rich.

Even his father Hannali would never be able to determine whether Alinton was really rich or only Choctaw rich. He did have a sudden spread of money and he did make a great splash with it. But he was too good a boy to keep that up long. There were sometimes the sound such as a pocket makes just before the bottom is reached; but Alinton never came to that bottom, and it may be that the warning sound was only imaginary.

Alinton bought into a store in North Fork Town. He talked Hannali into closing his own store. It had been set up to aid the destitute Indians who were no longer destitute, it had lately been operated at a loss and had to be supported by the farming, and Hannali's heart had never really been in it.

Alinton also took over the landing and maintained what freight boating was still worth-while. He put money into the farming enterprises of his brother Travis and the stock raising of his brother Famous. He helped his brother-in-law Forbis Agent build his house, and it is suspected that he aided in Forbis' support always. They were close; Alinton was something of a bookman himself.

From an old account book we have the names of the grandchildren of Hannali Innominee born in this time of prosperity.

To Jemmy Buster and Hazel Innominee: James, Marie-Therese, Henry-Pushmataha, Bartholome, and Philip-Nitakechi.

To Famous Innominee and Helen Miller: John-Durham, Famous-George, Francis-Mingo, and Strange-Joseph.

To Travis Innominee and Rachel Perry: Louis-Hannali, Peter-Barua, Jude, and Matthew-Moshulatubbee.

To Forbis Agent and Luvinia Innominee: Mary-Luvinia, Martha-Child, Gregory-Pitchlynn, and Anne-Chapponia.

To Alinton Innominee and Marie Calles: Charles-Mexico, Pablo-Nieto, and Helena.

Whom have we forgotten? Hannali had twenty-one grandchildren when the time of troubles began, and one is missing from the list. Hannali would never have failed in the listing, but we have missed one in the copying from the old account book. Which of the children have we forgotten?

The only cloud over the Innominee family was the shoved-back,

119

always suppressed nightmare of the ghost-crazy Whiteman Falaya and his visitations.

But what if one thousand men of such serpents' seed should appear? Who could measure the desolation that they would bring to the Territory? How if the sick lions should be turned loose on the people?

It happened. They came—the ghost-crazy killers, the sick lions, the devil-men of the weird seed. And even now who can measure the desolation that they wrought?

CHAPTER TWELVE

1.

*Moth-eaten Moses. The sick lion. The man who
lost his magic.*

Contemporary and entangled with the Civil War in the United
States there occurred the murder of the Five Tribes of the Terri-
tory. We will give some of that stark thing here. But this is *not* of the
Civil War—not of the one you are minded of.

In the ruination of the Territory, three men played large parts:
General Albert Pike, a white man.

General Stand Watie, three-quarters Indian by blood, but all white
by inclination.

Chief Peter Pitchlynn of the Choctaws.

Here are three men of elemental sorts. Each suffered tragic changes
and became less than he was; each died broken in his way and
leaving the unanswered question "Why did you do it?"

We see an empty pompous man taken over by a secret evil. We
watch a surly man turn weird and ravening. We see an excellent
man ("Peter, will you also go away?") become no more than an
ordinary man. We take them up, the least of them, Pike, first.

There are certain men who are sacrosanct in history; you touch on the truth of them at your peril. These are such men as Socrates and Plato, Pericles and Alexander, Caesar and Augustus, Marcus Aurelius and Trajan, Martel and Charlemagne, Edward the Confessor and William of Falaise, St. Louis and Richard and Tancred, Erasmus and Bacon, Galileo and Newton, Voltaire and Rousseau, Harvey and Darwin, Nelson and Wellington. In America, Penn and Franklin, Jefferson and Jackson and Lee.

There are men better than these who are not sacrosanct, who may be challenged freely. But these men may not be.

Albert Pike has been elevated to this sacrosanct company, though of course to a minor rank. To challenge his rank is to be overwhelmed by a torrent of abuse, and we challenge him completely.

Looks are important to these elevated. Albert Pike looked like Michelangelo's Moses in contrived frontier costume. Who could distrust that big man with the great beard and flowing hair and godly glance?

If you dislike the man and the type, then he was pompous, empty, provincial and temporal, dishonest, and murderous. But if you like the man and the type, then he was impressive, untrammeled, a man of the right place and moment, flexible or sophisticated, and firm. These are the two sides of the same handful of coins.

He stole (diverted) Indian funds and used them to bribe doubtful Indian leaders. He ordered massacres of women and children (exemplary punitive operations). He lied like a trooper (he was a trooper). He effected assassinations (removal of semi-military obstructions). He forged names to treaties (astute frontier politics). He was part of a weird plot by men of both the North and South to extinguish the Indians whoever should win the war (devotion to the ideal of national growth). He personally arranged twelve separate civil wars among the Indians (the removal of the unfit). After all, those were war years; and he *did* look like Moses, and perhaps he sounded like him.

. . .

Stand Watie of the Cherokees. He was really a white man who happened to be an Indian chief. There remains divided opinion about him. Was he the sick lion? A diabolical sadist? A pathological killer? Or was he only a very good fighting man, taciturn and determined, and stubbornly following out a brutal war policy?

Was he the greatest military genius ever produced by the American Indians? Very likely he was. He repeatedly led charges against seasoned Indian and white forces five times the numbers of his own men, and often carried the field. He was a man where Pike was only a mannequin. Had he not taken his peculiar stand, the Territory Indians would not have been ruined at that time or in that manner. He was a turning point.

. . .

Peter Pitchlynn of the Choctaws. We are back with our friend Peter, the man who once had magic—and lost it. He was the last of the Choctaw magic men who could visit his people in dreams and who could summon by dreams. How can the magic flake off a man who once had it?

Peter Pitchlynn had a long interview with Abraham Lincoln shortly after the inauguration. It was on March 12 or 13 of the year 1861 that they met. Here were two men, both flaked with the aleika, the magic, though neither of them wore a full mantle of it.

At this meeting, Peter Pitchlynn told Lincoln truly that he believed in the Union. He said that he would endeavor to hold the Choctaws and other Territory Indians to the Union, and that he believed he could do it.

But while Pitchlynn was in Washington, his policy was undercut at home. He soon came to accept and join that undercutting. Why did he do it?

Peter Pitchlynn owned one hundred slaves. And thereby he changed.

Naturally he was kind to his slaves, and naturally he employed stewards who were not notoriously cruel. But this was a business to Peter Pitchlynn, and there is no such thing as benevolent slavery.

It had been necessary that Peter put himself on a sound money basis. He maintained himself in Washington at his own expense, once for more than two years, several times for more than a year at a time. He was an unpaid lobbyist for justice for the Indians, and he had to meet the highest capital society on its own level. A white man, if he had real ability, might go shabby and still enter that society; he would be no worse than an eccentric. But an Indian must be elegant, or so Peter believed.

Peter had a sharp and direct intelligence and real ability in any field he chose to enter. He had acquired the common fund of knowledge and civilization almost intuitively. When he put himself to acquire the wealth that he believed the necessary basis for his mission, he acquired it quickly and directly. There was only one way to do this in the Territory—to join the big men of Falaya in the giant slave-grown cotton speculation.

But Peter Pitchlynn owned one hundred slaves. He had given hostages to fortune. He had acquired a vested interest in a thing that went against the grain of his soul.

2.

The Freedom Indians. Forbis Agent and the broadsheets. The snake we cannot kill.

Some of the Indians, as outsiders able to view it objectively, had seen the Civil War as inevitable before most white men had. And the opinion of most Indians was: Stay completely out of it!

Chief John Ross of the Cherokees put it clearly: "Do nothing, keep quiet, comply with treaties." This sounded uninspired, but actually it was an impossibly heroic position to maintain.

The Indians loved a war nearly as much as did white men. It was intolerable to stand on the sidelines when there was a good fight brewing. One jibe of Albert Pike's—that the Indians were afraid to face white men in real battle—always brought howling results.

But in the immediate family here there were several men strong enough to hold out against involvement and to face all the defamation and pressure that a neutral position would draw. Hannali Innominee always proclaimed himself a Freedom Indian, and by this he meant freedom from the creeping involvement. Strange Choate, Hannali's Cherokee father-in-law, had been a blood-spilling warrior in his youth; now he rose to greater heroism in holding against the thing. Famous Innominee—the son of Hannali, the grandson of Strange—was an impassioned fighter for complete neutrality. Forbis Agent—the husband of Luvinia Innominee, the son-in-law of Hannali—tried mightily to convey this Freedom Indian thesis (to which he himself had contributed much) to the Territory Indians. Four men! Enough for a nucleus.

Forbis Agent was a slight man. He did not know who he was, and we cannot know. He looked white, but look again and he was an Indian. He was a Territory orphan raised by a white missionary. He was the bookman who had a good but informal frontier education. For his work now, he had broadsheets printed up on the press at Baptist Mission. Then the southern sympathizers had him cut off there. For a while he inserted reasoned articles in both the *Choctaw Intelligencer* and the *Choctaw Telegraph* (these were the only two Choctaw newspapers there were); then Robert Jones, who owned a piece of everything, put a stop to the Forbis Agent articles. Jones would allow no neutralist sentiment where he could reach, and he had long arms.

Forbis Agent wrote out his broadsides by hand then. Hannali rigged up a waxed-stone, grease-carbon apparatus (a primitive mimeograph) that made copies. A few of these, but not enough, were legible. So the whole nation of the Innominees went to work writing out copies by hand. And Forbis Agent rode around the country passing out these handwritten broadsides.

By this activity, Forbis Agent (a slight man in himself) became a nuisance to the big Indians of the Choctaw South and to the Texas men who had made alliance with them. They sent men to kill him while he was on his rounds.

Albert Horse learned of the plot to kill Forbis. Albert did not— as he would have done six months earlier—go to Hannali with the information. Albert did not want murder on one side any more than on the other. He went to Hannali's son Famous Innominee who had become a man as tall as his father when no one was looking. Famous Innominee and Albert Horse gathered up six other men and ambushed the ambushers—those who had been sent from the South to kill Forbis.

The ambushers had followed Forbis into a draw. They were in no hurry; they did not intend to take him for several miles yet. They were drifting along saddle sleepy in the sunshine—and Famous Innominee had the drop on them and had his men all around them. Famous told them to fall off those horses, and they fell off.

Famous was as tall as his father, six foot five, and this day he wore jack boots that added many inches to this height. Famous was afoot and his men mounted, but he stood on a little rise, and he looked down into the eyes of the hired killers. He was lean as a lance except for big hunched shoulders and massive hands; he had a crooked grin and a whip-lashing voice, he scared those men.

But they didn't kill the intruders, although those men had come to kill Forbis Agent. Albert Horse and one other man held guns on them; five men beat them almost flat into the ground with staves; and Famous Innominee spooked them with his grin and flayed them with his voice.

Those men lay near dead for that evening and the night. The next morning, Albert Horse managed to have them discovered and helped by men passing by; so they returned to the South. One of them reported to his masters that Famous Innominee could lash a man with his voice alone so as to break him open and make him bleed.

A vengeance had now been vowed on all the Innominees, but it wouldn't be effected carelessly. Famous Innominee had become almost as feared a man as his father Hannali.

. . .

Several men of good minds were met one day at Hannali's House to discuss affairs. We know them all.

"I am reminded," said Peter Pitchlynn, "that the persecution of our people was really by the government of the North. It was the northern national thing that drove us out. Now we have promises —I cannot credit them fully, but I do give them some credit—that we will receive fair and equitable treatment from the Confederacy."

"Our persecution was not by the government of the North," said Hannali, "it was by the everywhere government but it was by the states of the South and the men of the South it was in the South that it happened it was South lands that we were robbed of but it was the government entire you cannot say that it was of the North."

"Its continuation is the government of the North," said Peter. "This is the snake we cannot kill. We know we will not have justice from the North, though presently they have a just man. The North passes. Why is it wrong that we choose the future thing?"

None of them doubted that the South would win the coming conflict.

"We must choose neither of the perditions," said Strange Choate.

"We must remain uninvolved, and it is the hardest choice we will ever make. Our only chance of survival rests on this standing apart."

"Why have it come to the people again," asked Hannali, "why are the people to have never peace that we be desolated once more have God forgot us that we try to be good people we have had our destruction and our death it should not come to us the second time even Christ was crucified but once."

"It may not be so severe as that, my father," said Famous.

"Yes, it will be as severe as that, my grandson," said Strange Choate. "We will be extinguished, ground to death between two stones. I am old enough to be able to see over that hill and I see our disappearance. But if we must go, let them remember us as we were. Let us stand up clean in this matter away from the mud of the North and the gumbo of the South. How is it that you waver, Little Peter?"

"They close in on us and we are compelled to take sides," said Peter Pitchlynn. "We are not masters of our fate. It may be presumptuous to suppose that we have a fate. We become, all at once, people of no moment."

"I am a man of moment," said Famous, "my father is and my grandfather is. You are wrong, Peter."

"No, I am right. There is a man who says that the Indians are only a satire on the white men, as the white men are only a satire on the gods. It may be that we are no more than a caricature of a caricature."

"I know who is that man," said Hannali, "he have a big beard and he lie into it he is the man who speaks of gods and know not God he is a caricature of a man it is not we who are he is the second Devil of the Indians do not listen to the big crooked man friend Peter he is a mouth man he is not a real man may we not ever come so low."

But Peter Pitchlynn had been listening to many sorts of men. He had often talked to Robert Jones and other rich white-man Indians of Oklafalaya; he had talked to the Texas men and the Arkansas men who now began to have great influence in the Territory. He talked many times with the government Indian agents: Douglas Cooper of the Choctaws, William Garrett of the Creeks, Samuel Rutherford of the Seminoles, George Butler of the Cherokees. These white men had always been friends of the Indians, and they had all thrown in with the Confederacy.

He had talked to all sorts of men, and he was confused. The magic was flaking off him like bark from a sycamore tree.

3.

Which woman have wet mud feet? I remember every blade of grass that I have ever seen. The boy with the watery eyes.

The dates were various: the secession of South Carolina on December 24, 1860; Jefferson Davis becoming President of the Confederacy on February 9, 1861; Lincoln inaugurated twenty-three days later; the first noteworthy shots fired April 12; and on April 15, Lincoln declared that insurrection existed and called for troops. So it had begun.

In our Indian Territory, Union forces were withdrawn from Forts Washita, Arbuckle, Cobb, Gibson, and all other posts in July of 1861. This made the Unionist Indians feel that they were abandoned. It lent strength to the contention of the trusted Indian agents that the Confederacy had now succeeded as the legitimate government of the Territory. When the Union Army was withdrawn, these agents had been the only government men of any sort remaining in the Territory. Their defection had great influence. The Indian Territory did not leave the Union; the Union left the Territory.

The Union soldiers in the Territory had been good fellows, young, rough, easy-going. They had always gotten on well with the Indians. Yet, as soon as they were gone, and in several accidental cases a little before, there was a wave of hatred against them; they became cowards, jayhawkers, niggerheads, thieves. Well, somebody was turning out the words, and we know who. The wave of hatred was a very contrived thing, but it could kill.

In that same July 1861, a man or an apparition was seen near Hannali House. Then he was not seen again for several years.

This specter had the appearance of a Union soldier—a straggler from the withdrawal. Newly fervid Confederate Indians led by white men had followed this man or apparition to kill him. These men had wounded him but not brought him down. They tracked him through a muddy ravine near the Canadian River. Then the tracks ended in a confusion.

This was good mud and wet sand, and the markings were clear; it was the interpretation of those markings that was foggy. For the tracks of the man ended. There were short steps as though he had stopped and teetered—about to fall. And then no more mark of him.

But there were also the footprints of a woman there. These came almost to the point where the tracks of the man ended. Then they turned around and went back whence they had come.

"That man he could not have fly," said one of the Indians, "he was too bad shoulder-shot to fly."

The white man in charge looked at the Indian angrily. He never knew when these wooden-faced fools were joking. But the tracks of the woman led to Hannali House, and the tough Confederate captain from Texas—with two other white men and nine Indians—came to the House right at dawn. They demanded to search the place.

Hannali Innominee refused them entrance. His son Famous came and supported the father with a steel voice edged with derision.

"So. A man has been tracked to within a half mile of here, and now you can track him no further? You are no Indian trackers. You are white men with ocher smeared on your faces. You could not track a goat if he wore bells."

Those nine Indians didn't want any part of Famous Innominee, not on his own ground. They knew that the dude was a swift strong man who could bad-eye them till they froze like ground squirrels before a bull snake. They feared him as their fathers feared his father. The captain from Texas had also heard of the Innominees.

"I don't understand about those tracks," said the captain. "I agree with the tall bucko that these men aren't the best trackers in the world. I know blue-eyed Texas scouts who'd track a man through the air if he went that way. But I'm pretty sure that the man we're after is in your house, and I mean to search the place."

"You have no idea how strongly I mean that you will not search my house," said Hannali. "Nobody will search my house while I live."

"We may fix that too," said the Captain.

"Another white man officer once put a term on my life but he did not call it when it was due," said Hannali.

"I'm familiar with the tale, and I'm impressed by it. Well then, Senator Innominee, what is your suggestion?"

"I will not see any soldier man of either side in my house while there is war," said Hannali, "this is my sworn word you cannot search my house with the men you have here we spook you my son and I your Indians look at my house and count on their fingers they do not know whether my other sons and daughters' husbands are in the house or not it does not matter two of us are enough we whip you we chill you now take my word I will not see any soldier man of any sort in my house while there is war I swear this."

"I'm inclined to believe you," said the captain. "Even your enemies—and you have more of them every day—say that your word is good. And it's a wild idea that the man could have gotten to this house. It's a wild idea that he could have gotten anywhere, but he's gone."

The men wrangled awhile, and then the Southerners went away without searching the house.

"Which woman have wet mud feet," Hannali asked of the family.

"It does not matter which woman, Father," said Famous, "it's done."

But Hannali saw the answer from his own doorstep. He had only asked the question to mask his feelings. He knew the marks of every shoe in his household. Hannali knew the answer, but we have not been able to learn it. It remained a family secret.

Even little Natchez—she was strong as a colt in spite of her small size—could have done it. Marie DuShane had once hefted big Hannali onto her shoulder for a joke, and Hannali would weigh more than twice as much as this wraith. Martha Louisiana could have lifted a horse. Sally could have done it easily. Hazel, Luvinia, Helen Miller, Rachel Perry, Marie Calles, any of them could have done it.

One of them had gone out before sunup that morning—knowing that someone was in trouble—had found the wounded man and had seen that he was being hunted down to his death; had taken him up on her shoulders and carried him—so as to leave none of his tracks—the half mile to Hannali House. And the Indian trackers, of course, had understood it all. They knew why the footprints of the woman were deeper when going back to the house. Whichever woman it was, she had carried the man into the house, and he was there now. This was the man they would look at and not see for several years.

Hannali went to his strong room and found what he had expected, but by his word he did not see the man at all. He called loudly for warm water and oil and unguent and linen and whiskey—such things as are needed for the wounded. And after he had patched the man up he spoke softly to himself.

"Never could I believe that such a darkness would come over my eyes it is almost as if there were someone in the room with me and I can see no one I am give my word that I will see no soldier of any kind in my house while there is war it is sad that my poor eyes should fail me I have been proud of my seeing."

"If your sight has failed, how about your memory?" a tired voice asked somewhere in the room. "I have an advantage over you. A man is remembered as a man, but a boy is not always recognized in the later man."

"My memory is unimpaired it is only my eyesight that have failed," said Hannali, "I remember twenty-eight years ago this springtime a man spoke to me and twenty others in a dream come to the mountain he said I arose in the morning and rode to the mountain on the way we picked up a white boy we frighted him with the notion that the men of Oklafalaya would cut off his ears now it comes to me the notion that those same men would cut off his head and it not be a joke."

"The name of the boy?" asked the voice of the wounded man.

"A voice comes to me out of the air," said Hannali, "it asks do I remember the name of a boy I have just say to myself that my memory is unimpaired I remember every name or word that I have ever heard I remember every blade of grass that I have ever seen every scent that I have ever smelled every object to which I have put my hand every notion I have ever had in the dark of night my memory is unimpaired only my eyes grow curiously dim."

"What was the boy's name?" again asked the voice of the man that Hannali couldn't see.

"His name was Robert Pike he was a boy who rode down from Missouri he was fourteen years old a pale boy with watery eyes he wanted to see the wild Indians in Okla Falaya he didn't know that the Indians in Okla Falaya were not wild then it comes that now they are."

"I have found that out," said the voice.

"I dream the face of that boy before me now," said Hannali, "I fancy how he would look when he had become a man I build up in my mind what would be that face it is almost as if I see that face before me now."

The wounded Union soldier was Robert Pike from Missouri. The Innominees kept him hidden in their house for several years. They maintained the fiction that they could not see him. They were Freedom Indians and they could give no harbor to any soldier while there was war.

CHAPTER THIRTEEN

1.

The United Nations was established at North Fork Town in 1861. There are men here today who would lead us like sheep. Robert Jones owns the Choctaws.

The United Nations was established at North Fork Town in the Indian Territory in June of the year 1861. Its members were the Creek, Seminole, Caddo, Chickasaw, Choctaw, and Cherokee Indians.

Like another organization of identical name that was established four score and four years later, the first and original United Nations was conceived partly in deceit and partly in sincerity. It was announced that it was to be a continuing assembly where the nations could discuss their common problems and advise as to common actions. Some good men remained in the organization for its duration. But from the very first the apparatus was rigged, contrived, subverted, and made the tool for a peculiar and alien policy.

We will not pursue further the parallel of the two organizations, but we do not lay off for fear of giving offense, only to get on with our main account.

"It is fun to give offense," Hannali Innominee said boldly at the first assembly of the original United Nations, "it is fun to throw the truth rock and hear which hit dogs howl what are we sheep that we should allow ourselves to be led by false shepherds there are men here today who would lead us like sheep."

The big Choctaw with the given name of Six-Town or Six-People (Hannali) was delegate to this new Six People affair called the United Nations. The assembly grounds near North Fork Town were only five miles from his own Big House, and he lodged many of the delegates with him.

The United Nations was not the great show that it might have been earlier. The last of the old assemblies had already been held; this was the first of the new sort. There was Indian oratory, but not the old deep Indian oratory. There was the Chinese-sounding tone speech of the Cherokees; proclamations in the Caddo that sounded like the barking of happy dogs; and measured eulogies by men of the other four tribes who all spoke languages of the Muskogee family—languages that are jointed and ordered and sounded something like our own. Then the Indian stuff had to go.

The languages of the nations would have no place in the United Nations after the introductions. There were certain white men there —not white-man Indians, not Indian agents, certainly not delegates —who were running the show. They ordered gruffly that the Indian nonsense should stop and everybody should talk English.

But nobody can orate in English, certainly Indians cannot. English could only be the prose to their poetry. It has no real song or sweep to it. One cannot play it like an instrument.

The hell one cannot! Just two weeks later they would hear Albert Pike do it. They would hear a deep white man orator who used English as a compelling instrument. They would be swayed by his great voice as no voices had swayed them since those of Pushmataha and Moshulatubbee. They were hungry for high oratory.

But there was none of that high business at that first United Nations assembly. There were only things written into the minutes that were not spoken on the beaten ground of the assembly; there were rulings that this man might not speak, and this other man might; there were things not even discussed, and written down as voted on and settled.

The preacherman who gave the invocation had spoken out of the Psalms:

"My heart hath uttered a good word, I speak my words to the King; my Tongue is the pen of the scrivener that writeth swiftly." But many of the words there were not good, and sometimes the pen wrote too swiftly words that had not been spoken at all.

Most of the honest Indians got mad and went home. A few remained to try to add their leaven to the mass. The meeting broke up without any decisions, and with only a loose promise of future meetings.

But immediately it was published that the Six Tribes of the United Nations and all their members present had declared for the Confederacy. Even the hundreds of honest Indians who favored the Confederacy were outraged by the high-handed operation.

With the Choctaws, the matter had already been thrown into the fire in March of that year. For the Choctaw-Chickasaw meeting at Boggy Depot, Choctaw Chief George Hudson had prepared a neutrality message. Copies of it had been passed around, and most of the leaders had read it and agreed with it, but it was never delivered.

Robert M. Jones arrived and put a stop to all that. Jones held no office, was not a delegate, did not need any office. He owned five hundred Negro slaves, but he owned many more Choctaws than that. He was a great money lender, and most of the delegate Choctaws had acquired a taste for luxury. Jones reminded them on the floor of the assembly that they all owed him for the very finery they wore, for the houses that they lived in, for the education of their children sent to eastern schools. He told them that he owned the very shirts on their backs and the breeches on their flanks, and in most cases he did. He owned a majority of the delegates by his judicious money-lending, and he owned them damned completely.

He had had the big Texas men there to back him up. These were the men who paid the Choctaws and Chickasaws ten cents per steer driven through their territory, who sold them the illegal whiskey, who rented their lands for grazing, who would be coming into the land in force. The Indians had better get right in their thinking, the big Texas men said.

Robert Jones was a furious, stumbling, stuttering man, but he owned the Choctaw delegates except for the freehold men of the North. The Colbert families cracked the same whip over the poor Chickasaw delegates. The two tribes made treaty with the Confederates. Hannali and others rode home in seething fury, but there were so few of them who were not owned by Jones.

2.

You can buy a lot of Indians with that. Who forged Opothleyahola's name? Brutus is something out of Dumas.

Albert Pike, when he began his operations as Confederate Commissioner of the Indians, had a slush fund of one hundred thousand dollars with which to reason with those Indians. It was the Indians' own money which had been withheld from them by the Indian agents who had defected to the Confederacy, and was comparatively small payment due on old land adjustments. This was only the opening ante given to Pike. A half year later (January 28, 1862) Pike wrote to Elias Rector, superintendent of Indian Affairs at Fort Smith: "I have $265,927.50 in specie." You can buy a lot of Indians with that if you are as closefisted a man with money as was Albert Pike.

There were no U.S. government men in the Territory at all. All the agents had gone Confederate, and Texas and the Arkansas territory were Confederate. A fourteen-year-old boy on a horse could have ridden through the territory with a proclamation and a sheaf of forms and signed every tribe to the Confederacy within a month, if a straight game had been intended. That was all Albert Pike had to do, but he was not capable of playing a straight game. His aim, the aim of all the men of his sort, was the total destruction of the Indians.

Pike began his mission in late June of the year 1861. He visited many Indian tribes and made a number of treaties. When it is stated that Pike made a treaty with a certain tribe of Indians, it is always that he made a treaty with only one faction of that tribe or with a single subchief (then to be accepted by the Confederates as the full chief), or that he somehow got names on paper to bind one faction, and sent the other faction away angry.

On July 10, 1861, Pike signed a treaty with the Creek Indians that they would adhere to the Confederacy and would raise troops in her support. The Creeks who signed this were Samuel Checote, Motey Canard, and a variety of men of the McIntosh families. It was *not* signed by the Creek chief himself, Opothle Yahola, nor by the second chief, Oktarharsars Harjo. These men and their names are found on the treaty in addition to the others.

Pike forged the names of the two men to the treaty. Even for astute frontier politics it was a little raw. Perhaps the two men would have signed if they had been present, but in that case there would not have been created a civil war among the Creek Indians. These two were not such men as would accept the forging, and Pike knew that they would not.

Opothleyahola (the name is written joined about as often as separated) was like a man struck by thunder when he returned and saw his own name signed to the treaty. He said that he had had a bad dream when he was in the Antelope Hills. Perhaps he had flown back those two hundred miles when in the grasp of the bad dream, signed his name, and returned to the hills. In cases like this, he said, it is really the Devil, and not the man himself, who signs. Opothle Yahola was correct in this latter guess. Opothle said that he would not be bound by his name signed by the Devil to a paper.

On July 12, Pike got his full treaty with the Choctaws and Chickasaws. The agreement wrung from them in March by their own Robert Jones and by the big Texas Men had compelled them to accept the Confederacy as the government in fact, the continuance of the Union authority. This July treaty forced the two tribes to raise troops for the Confederacy, and to make war on Unionist Indians and white men, and also on neutral Indians.

A few hundred of the Choctaws and Chickasaws rode off by night to join the Union Army in Kansas. Others of the Choctaw North believed that they could remain neutral and that nobody would break up their strong houses. But most of the men of the tribes, now that the agreement was made, went into war with enthusiasm. They were strong fighters and would never be beaten by equal numbers of white troops.

On August 1, Pike got his treaty with the Seminole Indians. This was signed by John Jumper, George Cloud, Tacusa Fixico, and others. But it was *not* signed by Billy Bowlegs, Alligator, or John Chupco. These three men had been ready and willing to sign, they were old enemies of the Union (they had fought it in the old days through the swamps of Georgia and Florida when the tamer Seminoles had submitted); but somehow these three were shuffled off and insulted. Jumper, Cloud, Fixico, men of no standing, were invited to sign in place of them and were accepted as chiefs in place of them. If this was some mishandling or clumsiness on Pike's part, then it was a clumsiness that would be repeated twelve times with other tribes. If it was a deliberate pattern, then it became a most consistent one.

But Pike served two masters, one of them still secret. His first aim was to raise up exterminating civil wars in every Indian tribe. Only secondarily did he care about binding a majority to the Confederates.

Pike made his rounds, riding in a carriage, always dressed in his bewildering pseudo-Sioux Indian trappings, which mystified the Territory Indians, and with Brutus, his top-hatted, frock-coated Negro servant at his side.

Brutus would remain in the carriage when Pike descended. Whatever sort of servant Brutus was, he was not a footman or groom. Pike would provide the hard work and high oratory for swaying the Indians, and Brutus would sit in state the day through. When they consulted, it was Pike who came to Brutus, not Brutus to Pike. Pike was the florid front. He was the Moses who brought the wilderness to the people. But there had to be a committee behind that front, for Pike never showed enough intelligence to carry such a double thing through by himself. Brutus was the custodian of the money boxes, and he may have carried their other asset in a box of his own. There is a Dumas-like suspicion that Brutus and not Pike was the master. It did seem to all observers that Albert Pike took his instructions from the enigmatic Negro Brutus.

The treaty with the Kichai Indians (August 12, though it is given mistakenly in history books as July 12) was signed with one Ki-is-qua, the *second* chief of the tribe. Angry and insulted tribesmen rode off to find the first chief who had been decoyed away from the meeting. Another civil war was created.

On the same day, Pike got one Ochillas to sign a treaty for the Tawakoni Indians and to become puppet chief. So there was civil strife among the Tawakonis.

On the same day, at Wichita Agency, Pike obtained a number of other Indian treaties. Four of them are of interest.

He signed a treaty with Jose Maria for the Anadarko Indians. But Jose Maria was only the leader of a minority faction, the Mexican Consensus, of the tribe. There was now civil war made among the Anadarkos, for Jose Maria by his unconsulted act seemed to be setting himself up as leader above Pock Mark and Jim Pockmark.

Quinahiwi signed as chief for the Caddo Indians. But the Caddoes had a dozen chiefs and no high chief. The other chiefs made war on Quinahiwi and his followers.

The name "Cashao" was written in as signing for the Aionais or Hainai Indians, but we don't know who wrote it. It was intended to represent the man "Kutchaw" who was chief in fact and who was literate enough to write his own name—always as Kutchaw, not as Cashao. Someone with a tin ear for Indian pronunciation had signed that one. It was Kutchaw who led the Union side in the Hainai Civil War that followed.

Isadowa signed for the "Ta-wa-i-Hash people of Indians, now called by the White men Wichitaws." But Isadowa had the right to sign only for the Leeper Creek settlement of the Wichitas, and his signing for all caused some hard feelings. The Wichita Civil War was a fizzle, however; one of Pike's failures. The different Wichita clans had affection for each other and could not be induced to make war, though a second later attempt added fuel to it. In all, Pike secured treaties with eleven tribes or factions on August 12 at Wichitaw (the final W of the name was still used officially) Agency.

The big man Albert Pike had hardly begun. His next big bag— though he had good hunting all along the way—was at Park Hill in October of 1861. He had a new advantage working for him: On August 10, the Confederates had won a solid victory over the Unionists at Wilson's Creek near Springfield, Missouri. This assured the Confederates a free hand in the Territory, and confirmed the prevalent belief that the South would win the war.

On October 2 at Park Hill, Pike got a treaty with the Big Osages. It was the sort of double victory that Pike enjoyed, for the Little Osages were rejected and alienated. So the Little Osages became fanatical Unionists. This Osage Civil War was important to Pike for there were more Osages in Union Kansas than in the Territory, and this ensured terrible raids and extinctions across the border for years.

Also in October at Park Hill, Pike got a treaty with the Sandusky Seneca Indians with two odd names signed to it. These were Little Tom Spicer and Small Cloud Spicer. Someone with that tin ear for Indian pronunciation had been forging again, for the first of these should have been Little Town Spicer. These were not names (though Spicer has now become a Seneca surname in the same manner that King became a surname); they were titles and meant approximately "Chief of the Little Town Band" and "Chief of the Small Cloud Band." But they served the purpose of names on treaties whether they were names or not and whether the men were present or not.

On the same day or the next, Pike got a treaty with the Mixed-Band Senecas and Shawnees, signed by Lewis Davis and Joseph Mohawk—two men ambitious to be given the command of troops. Two thirds of the Sandusky Senecas and the Mixed-Band Senecas and Shawnees escaped from the trap of the Confederates and their new quasi chiefs and got to Kansas. Some were permitted to remain neutrals there, others were pressured into becoming Unionist.

Most of the Absentee-Shawnees (that was the going name of one tribal division) had already got to Kansas before the Mixed-Band Senecas and Shawnees. A John Linney had signed them to the Confederacy back at Wichitaw Agency (one of the eleven treaties procured by Pike on that memorable August 12), but the Absentee-Shawnees did not recognize the treaty. Linney was a hanger-on around Wichitaw Agency and no more a chief of the Absentee-Shawnee Indians than you are.

On October 7, Pike pulled his master stroke. He got the two mortal enemies, Chief John Ross and Stand Watie, to sign a treaty binding the Cherokee Nation to the Confederacy. It was a triumph for Watie who was a Confederate to his bones. It was a triumph for Pike. And it was complete defeat for Ross; not only was he forced to give up his neutral position, but he was forced to take in his blood-enemy Watie as a sort of co-chief. This created the slickest civil war of them all. It is possible that Ross could have been forced to adhere to the Confederacy without Watie. Now he was compelled to break away from it, to be on any side that Watie was not on, and he could be branded as a traitor when he broke away.

The work of Albert Pike was essentially completed. He had signed Confederate treaties with more than twenty Indian nations, and he would represent to the Confederacy that he had bound twenty great tribes to the cause. But he had not bound any tribe completely, and he hadn't intended to. Every one of those treaties was touched with fraud, since Pike worked for divided ends. There was one man (not an ardent supporter of his) who said that Pike poisoned every spring he passed. But it must be admitted that he did it skillfully.

3.

Fashions in Hatred. The Territory Indians die fifty-two times. Thirteen Civil Wars.

It had been a hot summer. And riding on the simmering heat there were waves of hatred for the neutralist, full-blood Indians; the Territory was poisoned by it. There are fashions in hatred, but this sudden and explosive hatred of the white-man Indians for their full-blood cousins remains inexplicable. It had been instigated and fanned, and the catchwords of it were of known white man coinage. But it was not like the Indians to be taken in by such transparent fraud. The full bloods had always been called the Pins, the Sticks, the Snakes; but now these traditional names took on livid overtones. The white-man Indians came to regard the full bloods as less than human. Stand Watie would report several times that he had killed so many men (white men or white-man Indians) and so many Pins. Watie did not kill women and children of the human species, but he killed those of the Pins wherever he found them. He killed all the Pins he came across, the armed and the unarmed, the neutrals and the Unionist. He drove off horses and cattle, he burned hay and barns and wagons, he killed men, he slaughtered pigs and Pins and left them to rot.

The inhuman heat and hatred hung over the Territory all the summer and into the autumn of 1861. On November 19, a Territory-wide lightning flash broke open the building storm, and it began to rain blood. This was at the horrifying Battle (Massacre) of Round Mountains, that avowed attempt to extinguish the neutralist and peaceful Upper Creek Indians to the last person of them. The sticky red rain continued for four years.

After Round Mountains, the Territory Indians died at Bird Creek, Shoal Creek, Locust Grove, Spavinaw Creek, Fort Davis, Sugar Creek, Fort Gibson (three actions there), Honey Springs, Fort Wayne, Hitchiti Ford, Oktaha, Tuchi Town, Elk Creek, Perryville, Backbone Mountain, Tahlequah, Park Hill, Edward's Post, Wilson's Creek (Oak Hill), Cowskin Prairie, Lee's Creek, Salina, Sallisaw, Gray Horse, Wolf Creek, Bayou Bernard, Carthage, Cane Hill, Shirley's Ford, Newtonia, Bird Springs, Webbers Falls, Poison Creek, Dwight's Mission, Dutch Mills, Prairie Grove, Manus, Wichitaw Agency, Barren Fork, Poteau Bottom, Middle Boggy, Tonkawa Encampment, Tulasie Burying Grounds, North Fork Town, Huff's Mills, Pleasant Bluff, Massard Prairie, Flat Rock. And there were the skirmishes and raids that are not given the name of battles.

So? There was slaughter in the Territory? Was there not greater slaughter in the states? Was there something special about this?

Yes. There was something discrete, unique, and special about the affair in the Territory. There was the main Civil War that God allowed, and the twelve Indian civil wars that Albert Pike created. In the hardest hit of the states, one tenth of the women were left widows. In the hardest hit of the tribes, three quarters of the women were left widows. The fractions would have been larger had not so many women been butchered in the Territory, a thing that had no parallel in the states. We have an estimate that half of the Territory Indians died in those four years, but we have statistics only for the Choctaws—and those rough ones. An estimate of their numbers for two different years by the U. S. Indian Office gives an idea:

In the year 1861, 18,000 Territory Choctaws.

In the year 1865, 12,500 Territory Choctaws.

The more fortunate Choctaws lost only one third of their people killed in the war years. But the Choctaws avoided their own internal civil war, and their Territory (farthest South and under the Confederate shield) was less subject to raiding than any other. Generally only their men died and in regular battle only. But it bit them deep.

And after it was over with, and when all the blood had been let out of them, such Indians as were left had been turned into white men. Hannali Innominee had once said that an Indian is only a white man with more blood in him.

CHAPTER FOURTEEN

1.

Shave by candle. It does smell good burning in the field. By and by I build another boat.

Hannali Innominee was shaving by candle—not by candlelight—by candle. Like most full bloods of whatever tribe, Hannali was lightly whiskered. Once a month or so he ran a flame over his face to singe off the paltry growth.

Well, didn't that burn the very rind off him? Not very often. He handled the flame well, he was weathered and tough, and many Indians did it that way. I know an Indian who still does it with a flame, and this is more than a hundred years later.

It was still early autumn of 1861, following the summer that had simmered with heat and hatred. When Hannali had shaved, he would put on a frock coat and sit at a full dinner with New Orleans wine on the table. One of Hannali's sons was riding away that night, perhaps to be gone forever, and they would see him off in quiet style.

Hannali had sat up in his watch tower for most of that day, dropping rifle shots singing at the feet of trespassers half a mile distant. He scared them liverless with his shots; they weren't sure he was as good a shot as all that.

Hannali had had a hundred cattle stolen, and knew that he would lose most of the remainder. A neutral Indian was now fair game for anybody. There was no use getting excited about it. Albert Horse had gotten excited about his own livestock being stolen, and Albert had been killed for it. Hannali missed him.

And also during the day Hannali had watched his own cornfields burning in three directions. It would have been a good crop. No matter. He had enough in his granaries to last. Corn nearly ripe for picking burns with a pleasant odor. Holy Mother of Corn, but it does smell good burning in a field! No oven gives that aroma.

Men had burned Hannali's boats and his ferryboat; they had sent them drifting downstream aflame to great shouting. Next day, the same men who had burned the boats came to Hannali and asked how they were going to get across the river to North Fork Town when there was no ferry.

"By and by I build another boat," Hannali told them.

"If that you could hurry," they said, "this is inconvenience."

Men had kidnapped five freeborn Negroes from the settlement at the foot of the hill and taken them off to slavery in Oklafalaya. Some then signed work contracts that were the equivalent of slavery and started off south. Others slipped off by night north to Kansas.

There were many things going on to fret a Freedom Indian and make him rue his neutral stand. Now the son Travis and one son-in-law would be riding off to the aid of a fox named Yahola.

2.

The Laughing Fox. Were Billy Bow-Legs and Alligator comic strip characters? The panoramic God raises fifty-five or sixty men.

A hundred miles west, Opothle Yahola was gathering his people into camp to move them he knew not where. These neutral troops had received three warnings to sign with the Confederacy and contribute troops. There would be no more warnings. The neutral Creeks were marked for total extinction, to be an example to any other tribe or faction that remained neutral.

These Upper Creeks were the least warlike of the Territory Indians. They were a simple people and had a childlike dependence on their leaders. This dependence would not be a weakness if they had strong leaders or one very strong leader. And in Opothle Yahola they had a man who had been one of the strongest leaders ever.

Yahola was still vigorous in the council and in the saddle. He was the Laughing Fox who used to slip out of traps in the old Georgia-Florida days.

Had the man changed? No, not as some other men changed in that period. He had only changed naturally. The closest I can come to it is one early reference that he was born about 1778, so he was about eighty-three years old. He was still an inspiring leader, but he might not be able to cope with the massive attack that was being launched against his people. Who else was there?

The second man of the Upper Creeks was Oktarharsars Harjo (called Sands by the white men). Harjo had now become number one man in name, declared chief by Opothleyahola, and immediately the Confederacy had put a five-thousand-dollar price on his head. He was a good man but not a great man. And who else was there?

Nothing but a bunch of comic strip characters, it seems. There was Alligator, a Seminole renegade with a mouth as big as an alligator's and with a skin scaled and mottled green with disease. There was Billy Bow-Legs, a waddling dwarf whose legs made a complete capital O. There was Jim Ned, "a person half Delaware and half Negro," a mouthy coward whose eyes bugged clear out of his head with fright whenever a real man approached him. There was Halleck Tustennuggee, another Seminole who lived so far back in the tangled country that he had to wipe the owl dirt out of his eyes to see daylight. They were all clowns, cowards, and crud.

Were they really like that, or was this only a part of that defamation that had been sent across the Territory in a calculated wave of hatred? The names of these men, but not the descriptions, are familiar if we rack our brains. There were men of these very names, thirty years before, who had saved the Creek and Seminole nations from complete extinction by their fantastic resistance. Neither the whiteman Indians nor the full bloods of the two tribes would be alive had it not been for men of those names.

145

They were the same men grown older. There were the two great Seminole brothers who had joined these refugee Creeks: Alligator (hereditary king of that clan), and Billy Bolek (Bowlegs to the white men), the sons of the first Bolek who was the son of Cow-Catcher who was the last of the real Seminole kings. Alligator did not have a grotesque large mouth, nor was he mottled green. In that earlier generation he had been described by a U. S. Army officer, "Alligator is a most sensible, shrewd, active, and jocose man, worth all the Indians I have seen." And Billy Bolek was not a waddling dwarf, but a fine tall man.

The half-Delaware half-Negro Jim Ned was not a mouthy coward. The descendant of two persecuted peoples, he had become a soldier of fortune who threw in with the underdogs in every conflict. He was said to be the best rifle soldier in the Territory bar none, and he would give a spirit to any defense.

Halleck Tustennuggee, however far back in the tangled country he lived, had fought in deeper country. He was one of the old Seminole battlers of Florida who had held out so long and so valiantly that the tide of public opinion in the states finally turned and the total murder of the Seminole Nation was not permitted. Halleck had made many last stands. Of course he had lost them all, but the Seminoles would not have survived if he and men like him had not made them.

But the leaders were old, and such arms as they had were equally antiquated. Against them were coming all the Confederate Lower Creek Indians, all the Seminoles of the Confederate Faction, the Confederate Creek and Choctaw nations, several units of the regular Confederate Army headed by the Fourth Texas Cavalry. They were going fox hunting in a big way.

Opothleyahola sent up an appeal for men of the sort he did not have, to an old acquaintance and sometimes friend.

"It is myself, Yahola. Plead ye not ignorance, you know who I am. The Laughing Fox! I recall that you always had trouble with Indian names. I ask a favor, not for myself, for my cows and calves. Twice before you granted me peculiar favor when I was in death need, and once I aided yourself when you knew not where to turn to find a defender. I ask for one thousand men, such men as was I in my youth, and with the guns that were not made then.

"You laugh! Yes, it is a joke. I have my humor and you have

146

yours. In all the world there have never been one thousand men such as I was then. But give me a hundred! This is not a joke. Give them to me now, or I will be at the doorway of your lodge within one week—that much against my will—and we will settle this with more than words."

Opothle Yahola was not a Christian Indian. He was a sort of panoramic deist. But where could even the God of a panoramic deist find one hundred such men? As a matter of fact, He could not find that many, and He tried. He called on His every resource, and finally he came up with fifty-five or sixty. He summoned them to the aid of Opothleyahola the Laughing Fox.

There were no better men anywhere; there was something special about every one of them. They were smart as steel, swift, strong, intelligent, with the best rifles and horses anywhere; knowing men and motives, belligerent as bulls, crafty as coyotes, they were the best. It bothered those men that the most peaceful and pleasant nation in the Territory, the Upper Creek Indians, had been sentenced to death.

Some few of them were out of Stand Watie's own killer Cherokees. Some were from the pledged Confederate Choctaws of Oklafalaya. There were young men from the Chickasaws, those most stylish fighters.

There was a young man of the Colbert family whose father would squeal like a stuck shoat at the news; there was even a McIntosh. There were Comanches and Caddoes and Anadarkos of the plains, the elite of their young men, five white-man buffalo hunters, a handful of intelligent freeman Negroes, two white-man gamblers, Quapaw Indians, Mexican-blood men from the Santa Fe run, men who simply could not be classified at all.

There would be a capable young man named Travis Innominee and his brother-in-law Jemmy Buster. And four other men would be riding with those two when they arrived.

3.

Who eats Comanche potatoes? From Tukabatchee Town to Round Mountains. Kiowas smell like mares' milk. What do white men smell like?

"It is understood that you cease to be my son for the while of it," Hannali Innominee told his son Travis, "you now take sides in a conflict you cannot return to this house while there is still war."

"I do not cease to be your son or the son of my mothers," said Travis. "If you say that I may not return then I may not, but I believe you are wrong. These are Freedom Indians like ourselves. They wish to remain neutral, and they are besieged."

"They are not quite Freedom Indians," said Hannali, "they are combat Indians when they gather together and arm if each man remain on his stead and armed he may be neutral if they gather together they are not it is a hard distinction when you go from here you join the northern faction."

"They do not even know what the North is," said Travis, "they have never seen northern men."

"Never mind they will see them," said Hannali, "it is your last evening here and we will not argue you have decided and I have decided but there cannot be divided feelings here at the table what am I a white man that I should play the heavy father nevertheless you cannot return here while there is war."

"Maybe Travis will return, and your eyes be dimmed so that you cannot see him," said the voice of Robert Pike.

"The ghost is talking the man we cannot see," said Hannali, "no we will not play the spook trick twice we are not so shallow as that Travis goes and Jemmy and they can not return all pretend we are merry now pass pig mush pass buffalo rib pass hot bread pass sand plum pass wine pass whiskey pass snuff and cigars somebody make joke make merry you ghost voice make joke."

"Maybeso ghost Robert will tell us a funny ghost story," said Natchez. She glowed like a lantern from the wine and whiskey, and seemed younger than her daughters, almost younger than her granddaughters. She was a Territory beauty with a difference.

"I'm only a second-rate ghost," said Robert Pike. "I'm bodied,

148

though I have, in this house, the gift of invisibility. Maybe Alinton can tell a ghost story from his wander year."

"Pickens the green Indian bought a ghost skin once," said Alinton. "He had had a good year out with the Skin Indians. He had bought a snow-white buffalo skin. He bought a green panther skin. It was a fake and the green came off when it got wet in the rain, but he got it cheap. Then a Skin Indian told Pickens that he would sell him the most rare skin in the world for nine dollars American.

" 'If it is really the rarest skin in the world, then I will buy it,' said Pickens. 'I can double my money on it.' "

"So the Skin Indian brought him a skin and said 'Here it is, it's a ghost skin.' 'But I cannot see a ghost skin. I can't see anything at all,' Pickens told him. 'A real ghost skin, would one be able to see it?' the Indian asked. Pickens agreed that one would not be able to see a real one, so he bought the ghost skin and took it home with him."

"What did he do with it?" asked Philip-Nitakechi.

"Nailed it up on his wall," said Alinton, "since it was so valuable, he decided to keep it for himself."

"Can he see it on his wall?" asked Charles-Mexico.

"No. But he can see the nails. That way he knows it's there."

"I tell you a story about Creek Indians," said Hannali, "when first the Creeks came to the Territory the Plains Indians took them out and showed them the buffalo hokeys lying around on the ground they told them that those things were Comanche Potatoes Man the Creeks have it made then they live on those things for years they pick them up right off the ground no people ever had it so made then they find out what those things really are and they won't eat them any more that is when the Creeks go into their decline those things were nourishing."

"Where is ghost story in buffalo hokey?" asked Martha-Child.

"Was I say it was ghost story," protested Hannali, "I was only say it was story."

"Besides is not nice to tell buffalo hokey story to children," chided Mama Natchez, "Papa Hannali knows better."

"Is nobody know a real ghost story?" asked Charles-Mexico.

They pretended they were merry, passed the whiskey, and told jokes and supper stories. It was the last time they would all be together in this world. But they were serious too.

149

"How has the Fox called for you, a man he doesn't even know?" Famous Innominee asked his brother Travis.

"Yahola didn't call me. Another did it for him," said Travis. "It was a summons dream like our father once had. Ride to the aid of the Laughing Fox, he said in the dream."

"Did the dream come to you too, Jemmy?" Famous asked.

"No. I'm not Indian enough to receive a summons dream. The cattle aren't driven north this year, but we drovers still have our telegraph. We know what is happening."

Robert Pike wished to ride out with Travis and Jemmy, but Hannali wouldn't permit it. Ghost or no ghost, Hannali would kill Robert if he attempted to leave. Hannali could dim his eyes to one thing to save a life, but a truly neutral Indian couldn't harbor a man and than allow him to rejoin the fray. So Robert Pike must stay on— frustrated and invisible and with his parole given—in Hannali House.

A little after dark, Travis Innominee and Jemmy Buster rode away from the House, swam their horses across the river, and rode right through the Confederate Indians posted in North Fork Town. They rode as invisible as the ghosts themselves.

At about half-dawn they met four white men. Travis was startled, and Jemmy was not. These four men, Texas by their talk, were waiting for Jemmy and his brother-in-law. They also were riding to the aid of Opothle Yahola.

The panoramic God to whom Yahola had appealed had not been able to find one hundred men equal to the Laughing Fox in his youth, but he had found more than half that number, and some of them in unlikely places. These four were such men as other Texans only boasted of being: Jeff Merriwether, Sudden Scott (Scioto), Eneas Evans, Charles Bethany. They weren't riding just for the trip.

They rode carefully that day and the night, avoiding Confederate patrols. They came to the hidden buffalo camp of the Upper Creek Indians at second dawn. It was the entire nation of the Upper Creeks, men, women, children, dogs, horses, and cattle. It was a busy camp, staging for a great march to safety somewhere. There were the dissident Seminole men there too, and the more than half hundred of the elites of every sort, men whose consciences would not allow them to stand aside and allow a nation to be murdered. It was only a wayside camp set up by the Creeks who had fled in terror from their own Tukabatchee Town, and were on their way—though they did not know it—to Round Mountains.

Hey, do you get the smell of that old camp? An old Territory trader and plainsman has written what the Indians smelled like to him. The Osages smelled of pig weeds, the odor always clinging to their legs and persons as though they had run through a thousand miles of weed patches. The Choctaws smelled of fat ponies fed on big bluestem and run till they lathered. The Seminoles smelled like embattled badgers, musky with anger. The Poncas smelled like butchered beaver, and the green skins of those animals pegged out. The Comanches smelled like the tea they made of mesquite pods. The Kiowas smelled of alkali dust and mares' milk. Lower Creeks smelled like last year's wheat in an unventilated granary. The Upper Creeks smelled like the glue made from buffalo hoofs. All those Indians were present, so it was a pleasantly smelly camp.

What did the white men smell like to the Indians? The Plainsman becomes coy here, but leaves the impression that it was an obscenity word.

4.

Take a Snake Indian as old as the rocks.
Cross with Coyote—and he is the Fox!

This was foreign country to Travis Innominee and Jemmy Buster, to almost all the men who had joined the Upper Creeks. It was even foreign country to the Lower Creek Indians.

> Take half a man with an empty head,
> Cross with a blind wolf, and get you a Red.
> Take a Horse Indian with mud on his beak,
> Cross with a polecat, and get you a Creek.
> Take a Creek Indian about half awake,
> Cross with a buzzard, and get you a snake.

That was a jingle that the men of the Texas Fourth Cavalry made up about the Upper Creek Snake Indians and their leader Opothleyahola, the Laughing Fox. The various Confederate Indians who rode with them may not have appreciated the first stanza, and the Lower Creeks may not have liked the second.

But the Snake Creek Indians were not really a low people. It is said that they were the least civilized and the most civil of all the Territory Indians. They have been called the Puritan Indians, but they had none of the fanaticism that belonged to the Puritan whites. They were absolutely honest and could not abide vulgarity of any sort. When they were under siege at Round Mountains, the thing that wounded them more than rifleshot was the shouted obscenities of the attackers. That the women should hear such things!

They were still bow and arrow and lance Indians. Not one man in a dozen had a rifle, and not one rifle in a dozen was a good one. The Snake Creeks had big fires going in their buffalo camp now, so it could no longer be considered as hidden. They were drying and jerking beef and buffalo meat to carry on their journey, making wheat flour and corn flour and hominy, roasting and eating carcasses so they would be fat Indians when they began their hunger march, cobbling up their wagons and equipment, preparing new buffalo robes and blankets.

The elites set up a gun shop and did what they could for the ancient weapons of the Snakes, and gave them instruction in rifle fire. But it was Opothle Yahola himself who gave them all instruction, elites, Snakes, Seminoles, Chocs and Chics, and Plains Indians, in tactics. The Fox had defeated regular army units of overwhelming numbers before most of those present were born. He knew about the siege-town camp, the feint, the breakaway, the running fight.

But always the defense must be a circle one, the cows and calves in the center, the bulls on the outer ring. It would restrict their mobility; but if the men had wished to abandon their families, they could have been away and to safety long ago, and nobody ever could have caught them.

It is said in some sources that Opothleyahola had three thousand men when he made his break to the North. He did not; he had three thousand people, men, women, children. He had about a thousand men, counting half-grown boys and old men, who could be counted as a fighting force. So he would be outnumbered about two to one by the regular Confederate forces, white and Indian, brought against him. He would be outnumbered at least ten to one in weapons.

On this afternoon, the Upper Creek Indians built their roasting fires larger than ever and spread out the new carcasses. They outlined their sundown camp with the rows of fires, and made more noise than was common to them. The time was overripe. They had learned that the head of the Confederate columns was only a day's ride away. So the wagons began to rattle north as soon as it was dark, and the livestock herds to move along driven by women and children and old men.

5.

Gentlemen, that is shooting and that is talking.
My brother is the wind.

The old Fox Yahola held his last peace court at a big campfire with a hundred men around him. It was a loud-talking thing. They had to make noise to make it seem that there were more of them, to cover the fact that the women and children had stolen away and there was only the men left. You might, if you spent a life in looking, find one hundred men as good; but you would not find one hundred men as colorful as those around the fire that night.

There was Oktarharsars Harjo (Sands), the acting chief. You think he wasn't a good man just because he didn't know all about shuffling troops? All right, you ask him to wrestle. There was the man Tracks—the finest scout ever and a fabulous rifleshot. There was a German man named Blau from St. Louis who had been traveling to find whether buffalo hides might not make as good shoe leather as cowhides. He was a strong man both in body and opinion, and he had a gold medal he had won for rifle shooting at a St. Louis club. "It's big enough," joshed Alligator. "I could shoot one of them too if I knew where they roosted." There was Jeremiah Judd, a mighty, black-bearded white man who spoke bitter and who spat green. But it is always the children who first dive below such surface appearances. The small Snake children had known him as theirs, and climbed all over him as though he were a mountain.

There was Alligator himself and his brother Bolek who now accepted the name Billy Bow-Legs with complete good nature. There was Jim Ned. Jim Ned could pick out a duck high overhead, clip off its wings and tail feathers with rapid shots, pluck even its pinfeathers with closer approaches, decapitate and draw the bird with accurate angle shots, and then shoot so rapidly and hot as to roast the duck perfectly brown, and catch it as it came to earth. He had a new roasted duck in his hand for proof that he had just done it, and he tore off duck pieces and passed them around.

The man Tracks said that he could do the same trick with a refinement. While he so treated the duck with the rifle in his right hand, Tracks would load the bird with salt and pepper with a shotgun in his left hand. Moreover, he'd hold a trencher plate in his mouth and would catch the bird so deftly on the plate in its own gravy as not to spill a drop. Gentlemen, that is shooting and that is talking!

Halleck Tustennuggee stated that he was a better shot than either of them, but that he was a modest man and not given to boasting. He believed, however, that he could do the same thing, and that he could at the same time—with his third hand—bake up a batch of corn bread and have it hot before the bird came to earth.

Travis Innominee was there. Travis, as Hannali used to say, could shoot a rifle and tell a story better than most boys and as good as some men. When Travis had first appeared in the camp, Opothle—mindless of the years—had first believed him to be Hannali whom he knew long before. He had cried when he saw that it was not Hannali; he believed Hannali to be invincible. Then he had cried no more. "It is the same thing," he said. "He has sent his son, his spirit."

Charles Checote was there. Not all of that family were sworn to the Confederates. There was a big Negro man known only as Saint Peter—a man to have beside you in a scrap. There was Silver Saddle —a blue-eyed, dark-brown man who could translate for all the Plains Indians and who might have been anything. These new men who had come to the aid of the Snake Creeks were all jocose and loose, and they had the finest rifles that God ever made.

"An old friend will be coming to visit me tomorrow," said

Opothleyahola, "but he will not be coming very close. He is a valiant man, so he will be riding in a buggy far behind the fray."

"Who will come in a buggy, father-cousin?" Alligator asked.

"Chilly McIntosh, may he have his eternal rest and that damned soon. He is so fine, even his spit is sweet."

"It is the white man McIntosh I worry about," said Alligator.

"So odd that a white man should be better than an Indian man of the same name," said Yahola. "But the white man McIntosh will be coming on the next month's road, not on the tomorrow road."

They were talking about Chilly McIntosh, a Creek chief by the grace of Albert Pike; and about Colonel (soon General) James McIntosh in command of Confederate forces at Van Buren, Arkansas—so good a fighting man that fighting men everywhere had intuitive knowledge of him.

"It is time; it will have to be time now," said Oktarharsars Harjo (Sands) when they began to smell the coming morning.

"Not yet," said old Yahola. "I know the wind. He is my brother."

The wind there is almost always out of the Southwest. But sometimes, just before dawn, there is a great carrying blast of it out of the North, and Yahola said that it would be coming now.

"Their advance guard, and we do not know how many others, have ridden all night instead of sleeping up. I hold my breath that we will hear the bugle to sound their charge."

"Breathe easy, Harjo. Soon there will be times when you must hold your breath indeed. My brother the wind—does not an old man speak flowery, Harjo?—will also hear the bugle. He waits for it."

It came, the bugle call to sound the charge of the Confederates who had ridden all night to surprise the camp of the Snake Creeks. The wind heard it, and gave out the great carrying blast from the North. The Snakes and the Elites were on their feet like jumped deer, bringing brands from their half-mile-long row of fires to a brushworks they had prepared. And instantly there was a grass fire and a brush fire sweeping like a blade at thirty miles an hour and setting off the dry November plains like an explosion.

The bugle call changed to a retreat, and now the Confederate Indians and whites must ride out of reach of the holocaust. The Snakes and their Elites vanished north behind the smoke screen. They would overtake their main body within four hours. They had gained a day of grace by their trick. They would have time to make a river-crossing ambush in the North, and to erect earthworks where they could make a stand.

6.

A ring of bulls. A nation was being murdered that afternoon. Who knows the snake-hair plant?

It was the afternoon of the following day (November 19, 1861) that the Snake Creeks made their stand at Round Mountains. The marker of the battle is set up a little southeast of Stillwater, Oklahoma, probably four miles too far north, but close enough. It was north of the Cimarron and south of the Arkansas River, in easy rolling country, and was surely more wooded then than now. There were no Round Mountains at Round Mountains; there are several theories of the name, none of them very good.

The Snake Creek Indians crossed the Cimarron River on the afternoon and evening of November 18. This was near Perkins, Oklahoma. The Cimarron (then called the Red Fork of the Arkansas) is not a great river, but it cannot be crossed just anywhere. A river-crossing ambush was set up, and positions dug in several miles to the north of this.

By this river-crossing ambush, Opothleyahola set the time of the battle itself (late afternoon of November 19), and bet on the Confederates trying to wind it up before dark. He meant that they should be hurried. He knew how they would act when they were short of time—with a great white man charge, not with an Indian infiltration. The Fox knew that he must shatter that charge when it came; there would be none of them left alive if he did not.

The Confederates came to the Cimarron Crossing about noon and ran into the sniping, delaying action. The attacking force was a sound one, and they forced the crossing vigorously. They crossed into a mild sort of trap which they did not recognize. The defenders could have held them up longer and punished them more, but if so the battle itself might have been postponed till the following dawn. This the Fox did not want. He had no chance at all against an unhurried day-long attack. So the attack on the dug-in positions came in the late afternoon.

And it went badly for the defending Snakes from the first. The Confederate Chickasaws, working the wings, were flashy and valiant. The Confederate Choctaws, ramming the center, were relentless. The men of the Texas Fourth Cavalry were not gun-shy, but most of them were held back from the early fighting. Groups of them were picked to follow through on any real penetration. The rifle fire coming from the Snake Creeks was stronger than the Confederates had expected, but it was not of any great depth.

The Snake Creek defense was of necessity the ring of bulls—with the cows and calves shielded by it. As such, it was not maneuverable. The attackers wore down the flanks and breached them, opening pocket after pocket of slaughter for the Texas men who liked that kind of stuff. There were not enough old Creek bulls to maintain everywhere the ring around their dependents. There was merciless massacre of women and children at the break-through points.

A nation was being murdered that afternoon. The intent was to murder it to the last individual. And something happened during the easy slaughter that had become only a memory to the Territory Indians: scalping, shocking clumsy scalpings, not at all in the old Indian manner, and not done by Indians.

In certain Texas homes there are still curious relics to be found. They are darkened plantlike things of long fine filaments, and with a dark clot at the roots of them. They are the rare snake-hair plant, and they were taken at Round Mountains.

CHAPTER FIFTEEN

1.

*The withering fire. Was it the father of Travis
Innominee or was it his other body beside him in
the dusk? I thought we broke them of that boy's
trick thirty years ago.*

It was late when the Confederate Texas Cavalry assembled to finish
the affair. Colonel Douglas Cooper, the white-bearded old Indian
agent and new colonel, decreed that the white troops should attack
with a massed cavalry charge; and the Indians were aghast at the
idea. "It were better to hold up the parade stuff till we finish off the
Snakes," they protested, "men you bunch up like that they cut you
down like cane." But the Colonel insisted on his all-sweeping cavalry
charge.

The regular white cavalry would form the center, backed closely
by the fearless Choctaw horsemen, and with the intrepid Chickasaws
sweeping on the flanks. The charge should break the desperate ring
of the defending Snakes who were now shredded to pieces and
hardly able to maintain their lines or close their gaps. The ring had
already been broken, in fact, unbeknownst to the attackers. The
Elite fighters in particular, who had been ranging everywhere to

close up gaps, had now moved to one central spot by the orders of the Fox, and the gaps were allowed to go unplugged.

The attackers drew up in massed formation just out of rifle range. Just out of rifle range? How did they know the effective range of rifles in the hands of the Elite? The men and horses tensed, and then broke forward—to run into a wall before they had completed that first lunge.

It all happened within a minute, one has said. Within thirty seconds, another. For the charge began from open ground, supposedly out of effective range. Then it came in a simultaneous blast like an explosion, the most withering, murderous, unerring, concentrated rifle fire ever seen or heard in the Territory. Three hundred of the attackers fell within a minute. There had never been such shattering volleys.

Were the Elites really that good? They were as good as men could get with the rifles of the day. Whether or not Jim Ned could sear the pinfeathers off a high-flying duck, he could hit those Texas boys in the middle. Saint Peter, the man Tracks, Alligator, Billy Bow-Legs, Jeremiah Judd, Sudden Scott, Travis Innominee, Halleck and Harjo, Jemmy Buster and Charles Bethany, something over half a hundred of the Elites, something over two hundred of the sharpest striking Snakes, they broke that thing as it started its surge. And in the middle of them was a form so sudden, so giant, so thunderous, that it seemed to be one of those sky heroes who often came down and took part in Indian battles.

What was the great form that was seen at the time of the volleys, and then was seen no more? Who was it who grinned so garishly that it flashed the whole evening sky with November lightning? What old Mingo form with a repeating rifle three times as long as any rifle ever seen? What fearsome whooping thing who toppled men from their horses with the mere blast of his voice? Of whom did the Fox laugh out, "It is himself and not the cub who is here now?" Had Hannali Innominee broken his parole and come with the incredible repeating rifle that he had made with his own hands?

More likely—the men said much later—it was the fetch or double of Travis Innominee which had taken the form of his father. The fetches or other bodies of Choctaws could often be seen fighting beside them in battle. The men of the Snake Creeks would set up the fiction that they had not really seen Hannali—just as Hannali had set up the fiction that he could not see Robert Pike—for Hannali was known as a sworn neutral; and who would doubt a man's oath because of something that fooled the eyes when the light was failing? Later they would set up the fiction—but it was still right now with the attacking cavalry going down like sickled barley.

Charles Checote and Silver Saddle, Jeff Merriwether and Eneas Evans, the kraut named Blau and the old Fox himself, they cut down that Fourth Cavalry with their murderous blast. The attackers never recovered from that furious fire or from the pall that came down over them.

There are days all through the summer and into autumn when the twilight lingers forever. Then there will be a day—and the number of it is November 19—when the winter is coming with a rush and there is hardly any twilight. Sundown, then darkness. The attackers had waited too long, and then moved too hurriedly to wind it up before dark. Opothleyahola had timed it all perfectly. The November night was his brother as well as the wind.

"A massed cavalry charge, and some of them twirling sabers!" exclaimed Alligator in wonder. "I thought we broke them of that boys' trick thirty years ago."

2.

The battle everybody lost. Banter of bugles. The Gibson Road.

There are many battles in history which both sides claim to have won. Round Mountains was the battle that everybody lost. Both sides retreated with panic speed.

The Snake Creeks had lost a thousand dead. Many of these were their women and children slaughtered at the break-through points, but several hundred of their fighting men had been killed also.

The Confederates had lost one hundred killed and two hundred hurt from the withering rifle volley that had caught them gathered brainlessly in the open for a charge, the volley which actually finished the fighting. About a hundred other men, mostly the Choctaw and

Chickasaw Indian Confederates, had been killed in the tangled afternoon fighting in the woods and thickets, the only real fighting of the day.

The count would show the Snake Indians badly beaten. But they had held the field and driven off the attackers so decisively that the attack could not be renewed.

Both retreats began at dark. Opothleyahola ordered everything loaded up, the wounded stacked into wagons or slung over horses, everything unessential left behind, and the dead abandoned unburied. They started north in disarray, and a strong pursuit would have annihilated them. The old Fox had gambled, by his shrewd insight of men and of a man, that there would not be a pursuit. And there wasn't.

Opothleyahola could not know, of course, just what justification Colonel Cooper would seize upon, but he knew what it would amount to. For it was just at the time of the night panic following the breaking of the cavalry charge, that Colonel Cooper began to worry that he was needed elsewhere. It was an unaccountable worry, for his superiors had not seen fit to worry about it; and Colonel Cooper had not worried about it ten minutes before.

Now he worried that he might be needed back at Fort Gibson. What if General Hunter should invade the Territory with U.S. troops? Rationally the thing could not happen till the following spring, but night panic isn't rational. Colonel ordered an immediate forced march back to Fort Gibson, and already hundreds of Texans were strewn out far ahead of him on the Gibson Road.

The Confederate Indians could not comprehend the decision to withdraw. Many of them would have given it up and ridden off home in disgust had they not been held in line by the "Blue-Eyed Company"—the white-blood Choctaws. They were all soldier Indians, they said, and they would obey orders. They joined the withdrawal to Gibson. Only a small group was put on the tail of the Snake Creeks, not to give battle to them, but to harry them a little and to give an account of their movements.

• • •

Jeremiah Judd and Sudden Scott rode the tail end of the last of the Creek wagons, and with them was a small Snake girl—happy in the morning and already forgetful that her parents had been killed. Sudden Scott had a bugle which he had taken from a dead Confederate, and with this he mocked the bugling of the following party. They bantered each other, and said some defiant hard things back and forth by bugle.

"What does the other buggle say?" asked the Snake girl who had learned camp English in a week from Jeremiah Judd, "does he say he is our friend come to help us?"

"I will be kicked by a grasshopper with a wooden leg if he says that," growled Jeremiah. "He is no friend of ours."

"Is the other one a real buggle animal, or is he only a little brass horn like ours?" asked the Snake girl.

"Oh, he's a regular bugle animal that they have," said Jeremiah. "Sounds like about a nineteen-year-old male. A real big one."

"And we have only a little horn to make the buggle sound," said the girl. "They think we got a buggle animal too. We fool them."

"We fool them, Snake Girl," said Sudden Scott, but they fooled nobody. Their every action was noted and followed. They could not travel any great distance before they would have to lay up and treat the wounded, and any camp they made would be known. Nevertheless, they had a respite, even though it was a forced flight with many of them dying on the way.

3.

Almost to bitter words. House divided. Famous Innominee and the Cherokee Pins.

Opothle Yahola had won twenty days of grace—November 19 to December 9. He went into another camp to try to restore his stricken people to life. He also reached out in diplomatic attempts; and there was much unofficial scurrying about the Territory. The Innominee family was involved in some of this scurrying.

Hannali—for all that he fought to remain a complete neutral— was in bleeding sympathy with Yahola. He knew the man well from early days. Twice Hannali had been to Tukabatchee Town, that closed mecca of the Snake Creeks which none but Snakes could enter. Hannali entered as special brother of Yahola. He believed Yahola to be as great a man as Pushmataha or Moshulatubbee. Though not a Choctaw, the Fox had the aleika magic on him. He was somehow the Fox-Hard-to-Kill of the Choctaw fables. He was the Fox-Know-the-Way, the Fox-Come-Again, the Fox-Laugh-in-the Sun from which he had his modifier name. It was full blood calling to full blood, for all that Hannali still swore to remain the most neutral Indian who ever lived.

It was for this reason that Hannali did not go into a fury when Rachel Perry said that she was going to ride to find her husband Travis among the Snake Creeks. She was indeed a Creek girl, but of the lower white-blood-mixed Creeks, of the Checote kindred.

"So I will no longer be your daughter-in-law, Papa Hannali, since my Travis may not be your son for the while. But I go tonight."

"No you go tomorrow and not tonight," said Hannali. "I let you not ride off unguarded like a night witch you were never my daughter-in-law do not use white-people phrases to me you are my own daughter and forever you will not go alone and in danger I have other great sons to see after you."

Hannali knew that all the rising sympathy in his household was not for the Snake Creeks nor for the North to which they were fleeing for their lives. The news of the massacre of Round Mountains had an unusual effect on Alinton Innominee. Alinton felt that—as they were Choctaws—they should stand with the majority of the Choctaws, for the South. He had ridden up and talked to many of the Chocs on their withdrawal from Round Mountains to Fort Gibson, and he had come to their rough way of thinking. If you are given the task of hunting down the things, they said, you do not inquire whether they are good foxes or bad foxes, good snakes or bad snakes. The Choctaw soldiers believed their officers that all the Indian troubles were due to the government of the North, and that the South would deal benignly with the Indians after the war was over with.

Famous was contemptuous of this theory as Alinton tried to put it in all its catchwords. Famous paraphrased a saying of their uncle Pass Christian, that from Grandfather Barua, Pass Christian had received the intelligence, Hannali the vigor, and Biloxi the pot. Famous said that from Papa Hannali, he Famous had inherited the brains, Travis the bravery, and Alinton the bluff and bluster. They came near to blows, and Hannali had to interpose his bulk.

"I remember three brothers who were very different," he said, "and their names were Hannali myself and Pass Christian and Biloxi these three never in their lives had quarrel of any sort nor ever one angry word I doubt if it can be said of any other set of brothers since the first two sons of Adam had their misunderstanding I will enforce that you love one another if you will not do it in a willing manner."

And yet they had come almost to bitter words in that morning argument. Then they parted, never to meet again in life. Famous took his sister-in-law (no, his sister) Rachel Perry in his fancy buggy to find Travis with the Snake Creeks.

Could they find the hidden Snake camp? In the upper Territory country, they always said that the news traveled by Cherokee creeper—a ground-growing vine—and Famous was Cherokee as well as Choctaw. It was no secret where the old Fox had gone. He had crossed the Arkansas near the mouth of the Cimarron (the Red Fork) River. The country north was full of Confederate-allied Big Osages, and the Fox veered east to avoid them. He made camp where his people were unable to travel farther. He buried two hundred who had died on the way. Some had held off dying till they came to a peaceful place for it. Here he found good grass and water. And here he found friendly Indians where he expected enemies—among the Cherokees.

These were the Pin Indians, the full-blood faction of the Cherokees. The Pins befriended the Snakes and saved the lives of many of them before the issue was joined again. For this, more than half the Pins would be killed by the white-man faction of their own tribe. The controversial Stand Watie would hunt them down like rats. The Snake recovery camp was on the south bank of Bird Creek, just northeast of present Tulsa. Famous brought Rachel Perry to Travis there.

Famous was often threatened on his two-day drive, but nobody risked trying to take him. Famous had not more steel in him than Travis, likely not more than Alinton. But he was better known up through the Creek and Cherokee country, and he was known as a man and not a boy. He had the voice and the command that his brothers lacked; he scared men.

Famous and Travis did not speak at their meeting. Travis was a combatant; Famous was a flaming neutral who would not be compromised. But Famous spoke to the old Fox Opothleyahola—for some time, and privately. Famous undertook a commission for the old man, and among the Cherokees it would be partly successful, as would be seen later. Of course, Yahola had other ambassadors working for him.

Famous undertook a rambling journey in behalf of the Fox, and of his own neutrality. He visited big men of the Cherokees, the Lower Creeks, his own Choctaws. He even rode into Fort Gibson (now the Confederate stronghold), spent half a day, and rode again free—although there were orders out for the arrest of himself and his father Hannali. The pleading of Famous and others for the Fox and his people did have some effect with the Cherokees, and probably with the Choctaws.

4.

Chusto Talasah and Chuste Nahlah. Fox is still fox.

General McCulloch of the Confederates had Colonel Douglas Cooper and his Texans and Indians readied for further assault against the Snake Creeks. He didn't need any help from them in watching the Union General Hunter do nothing. But he did give Cooper more help, though Cooper already had the edge of more than two to one in fighting men, and his regulars and the Fox's irregulars. McCulloch gave Cooper a substantial force of Cherokee Confederates under Colonel John Drew. By the conduct of a few of the Cherokees of Drew (and only a few of them, though the number and impression has been magnified) this second assault against the Fox would fail.

There is confusion—due to the names of the actions—about the second and third stand of Opothleyahola and his Creeks against the Confederates, and some histories make one battle of them. The two latter battles were fought four miles and seventeen days apart. The first of them, Chusto Talasah, also called the Battle of Cav-

165

ing Banks, was fought on December 9 at Little High Shoals on Bird Creek. This is the *Battle of Bird Creek*.

The second of them, Chuste Nahlah, was fought on December 26 on Shoal Creek, *not* on Little High Shoals of Bird Creek. This is the *Battle of Shoal Creek*.

It isn't known to what extent the forces of Opothle Yahola recovered in physical and military health at the camp on Bird Creek. It had come on an early winter, and dozens of the Snakes were dying every day. The Pin Cherokees contributed food and skins to these refugees. For medicine and doctoring, the Creeks had the Seminoles among them. In all the five tribes, the profession of medicine had been carried on by the Seminole Indians only—and by Seminole families in other ways the most backward. They were the herbalists, the fever breakers, the bone setters, the psycho-healers, the curers generally. They understood about infection, they could probe and remove arrowheads and bullets, and could amputate expertly; and their herbals were good ones. Most of the "old Indian remedies" peddled by white men medicine wagon operators in the following decades were Seminole remedies. Opothleyahola's camp had doctoring near as good as that of the Union and Confederate camps of that same Civil War time.

Then the Confederates of Cooper came to the attack once more. They were reinforced by more white companies out of Fort Gibson, by further Choctaw forces, and by the Cherokee forces of Major Pegg and Colonel Drew. Cooper now had an advantage of more than two and a half to one in fighting men. It should have been enough. It wasn't.

The first Confederate troops to reach the Bird Creek camp were men of the portion of the Cherokee regiment that was under the command of Major Pegg. But they did not attack. They asked to parley instead, and they walked into camp.

The news that had traveled by Cherokee creeper, the tendrils of which had been Famous Innominee and many others, was not the same as the official news. These Cherokees now insisted on finding for themselves whether the official version was true; they discovered it to be a complete lie.

These Snake Creeks were *not* Unionist Indians commanded by Unionist officers and built into a giant force to smash their brother Territory Indians. They did *not* have a camp filled with booty; theirs was a starvation camp. They owned no great guns nor cannon the capture of which was essential. They hadn't wagons laden with gold. They hadn't white men followers with measuring chains to measure and divide and steal the land of the Territorials. Most of the Snake Creeks were bow-and-arrow full bloods driven to the last extremity.

About a third of this Cherokee band—some hundred and fifty men of them—declared for Opothleyahola at once and announced that they would remain with his forces and fight with him. The other Cherokees withdrew from the parley and returned to meet the Confederate Army of which they were the advance guard; but they were full of doubt now, and they spread that doubt.

The Cherokees were a little naïve about dissuading the main Confederate force from the battle, however. Almost every man of the advancing Confederates, and certainly every officer, knew the true state of affairs. All who had been at Round Mountains knew it. They had maintained the lie for their own amusement and for the public consumption, but they knew what sort of people were the Snake Creeks whom they were returning again to murder.

Nevertheless, a portion of the Cherokees did refrain from the battle, and there was no time to compel them to it. They would be punished later. This Cherokee defection was not important in numbers, but it would be used as an excuse for the failure of the Confederate assault.

And the assault did fail. For four hours on that December 9, the Confederates charged the Snake Creek camp, and every time they were thrown back. Opothleyahola had established strong position here. He could maintain a solid front, and Colonel Cooper seemed committed to the same massing tactics that had ruined him at Round Mountains. If Colonel Cooper had learned anything at Round Mountains, it was only how to lose more decisively. The murderous flanking raids of the Confederate Indians at Round Mountains were not repeated; it is suspected that they were malingering and saw no reason to argue with Cooper's policy. It was all frontal assault—mostly with white troops—and the Confederates could not break the front at all.

There were some signs of Snake exhaustion; some sectors of the front that had first answered with rifle fire, now answered with arrow. They were running out of ammunition, and holding what they had left for the climax.

It has been charged against the Choctaw and Chickasaw Confederates—the only time this charge was ever brought against them— that at Bird Creek they didn't press the issue as vigorously as they might have. They had been shamed by the Cherokee band naïvely blurting out the truth of the affair, and they saw that the ordered tactic was suicidal. They could have raided around and cut the old Fox's forces to pieces. The tactic of the open charge which had failed at Round Mountains was repeated at Bird Creek for the entire battle, though at Bird Creek there was always some cover and the charges could not be completely open.

Then the Confederate error was compounded in one massive incredibility. Cooper drew his entire force up for one massed charge in extreme depth, and ordered them onward so closely grouped that they could not maneuver.

Like a nightmare that has been dreamed before and must be dreamed again, came the great withering volley from the Snake Creek lines, and the Confederates broke in total panic. They didn't stop till they had reached Fort Gibson sixty-five miles away, though the Fox couldn't have followed them with a single man. There had, indeed, been a difference between this volley and that at Round Mountains. This had the same initial roar; but just as the attacking mass broke, the volley choked down, coughed, and turned into a whispering slither of arrows. The Snakes had shot their wad, had almost no ammunition, and could have been taken easily if the charge had held for another fifteen seconds.

5.

The skeleton force. There were no ordinary persons there. The sick lion hunts down the mice. Oh the smoke that will not rise again!

Opothleyahola had seventeen days of grace, but he had no illusions. He knew that the assault would now be put into the hands of a competent man, and in that case he was lost. He knew that at Bird Creek he had been defeated forever, regardless of the apparent outcome.

He began to send his people off to the free country of the North whether they were able to travel or not. Several hundred of the women and children would literally freeze to death on the journey, but other hundreds would get to Kansas.

There was real fury among the Confederate commanders at the news of the disgraceful retreat from Bird Creek. The man selected to wipe out the disgrace was Colonel James McIntosh ("It is the white man McIntosh I worry about," Alligator had said before Round Mountains. "He will come on the next month's road," said the Laughing Fox) brought from his command at Van Buren, Arkansas. It was all up with the Snake Creeks now.

. . .

They smoke and they talk. The pipe goes from last lips to last lips of all the men who will be dead tomorrow. The only women left in the Creek camp were frenzied harpies who refused to leave, or certain cool ladies (as Rachel Perry) who were mistresses of their own fate. The only children left were the children of these. Actually Opothleyahola had won one battle. He had fought two delaying actions and near half his cows and calves had arrived or would arrive in free country. It was something. Rachel was with her husband Travis on the last night, but the brother (brother-in-law as the White Eyes call it) Jemmy Buster was dead. So many good men had been killed!

It was now one of those end-of-the-world affairs, and there were no ordinary persons in the camp. There were old men still fighting this peculiar war after they were dead, for the great wars of their lives had been fought thirty or forty years before. There were the allies of all nations, but their ranks now so thinned that they were no more than symbolic. It was a skeleton camp, a shell camp, near empty on the inside. It had been moved about four miles, the old camp standing with dead men propped on the rim rocks as though still guarding to serve as a decoy.

The white man McIntosh came up the Verdigris River from Fort Gibson with sixteen hundred white troopers—the South Arkansas Mounted Riflemen, the South Kansas Regiment, and large bodies of Texas Cavalry. The Confederate Indians were still under the nominal command of Colonel Cooper who was no soldier, but under the actual command of Stand Watie who was one.

"Can you keep up?" white man McIntosh asked Stand Watie, and Watie laughed without humor. With his "big-man" Indians, the best mounted and finest man in the Territory, he could keep up with anybody, he said.

But he couldn't, though he moved rapidly. McIntosh drove his own men hard over the snow and ice; they were superior men and they moved steadily up the Verdigris and up Bird Creek from its Verdigris mouth. The Indians of Watie meanwhile came up the Arkansas River to its Big Bend, left the river at Lutchapoga (this is the Lokar-Poker town of later Territory days, it's within present Tulsa), and raced to be behind the Snakes at Bird Creek and cut them off. But Watie didn't come behind the Snakes; he blundered face-on into what had been their camp and was greeted by white man laughter. The battle was over with. The last Snake and allied remnant had been wiped out.

They didn't catch Yahola the Fox. An apocryphal story (and most of these apocryphal stories were true) has it that Alligator ordered the Fox bound, loaded in a wagon, and carted off to Kansas against his will. He did arrive in Kansas, where he died the following spring. The Seminole warrior Halleck Tustennuggee was in command of the skeleton force that made the brief stand at Shoal Creek, and most of the others present were die-hard Seminoles. They covered the retreat of the remnant, the last of the Snake Creeks who made the break through the snow to Kansas.

These Seminoles were astute men in their own way, but there was one aspect to them that was incredibly childlike. Most were still under sentence of death by the United States for their leading outlaw resistance bands in the Florida wars more than thirty years before. They imagined that they would be remembered, that the Union officers to be met in Kansas would be the same Union officers they had fought in an earlier generation, that they would be shot immediately under the old order. They would as soon die where they were.

There was only a handful of prisoners taken at this battle that was hardly a battle. It may not be true that McIntosh ordered them exterminated; it was the nature of these men that made this necessary.

Alligator was trapped alone in a draw, bareheaded and barefoot in the snow, and holding an empty rifle like a club.

"Surrender or die!" they told him.

"I die," the graying Alligator said simply, so they killed him there.

. . .

Stand Watie was furious that there had not been a pursuit of the final Snake Creeks who had escaped under cover of the "battle." He set out with his killers, "big-man" Cherokees on that pursuit. His racing forces caught and cut down hundreds of the fleeing Snake Creeks. Seven hundred Creeks died on this last flight, but likely more of them died of cold than were killed by the hunters of Watie and Cooper. About seven hundred all told (most of them from the earlier flights) got to Kansas safely; this was out of the original three thousand of them before Round Mountains. But the able-bodied men of them swore that they would take retribution ten times over for the murders, and they would do so.

. . .

"The Snake is dead on the Mountain, and who will care for her children? The calf tries to suckle at the dead cow. My enemy has counted coup upon me, and the White Eyes have murdered my mother.

"The parfleche is empty, the lodges are burned, it is dismal to die this way. Who will set up the poles for us? Who will know the right way to tassel the lance?

"Oh the lips that are cold! Oh the fine bodies that come to stink! Oh the smoke that will not rise again!"

CHAPTER SIXTEEN

1.

*Why have God punished us so grievously? Sundown
Day for us. With the principality.*

Some months had gone by, and the Territory had been bleeding
to death from its thirteen civil wars. Every settlement in the
Territory had been under attack. Every town had been destroyed.
All but one of the strong houses of the Choctaw North had fallen.

One day Hannali Innominee awoke—not knowing that he had
slept—absolutely shaking with horror. He had been napping in the
daytime when it came to him. He'd had these horrifying intuitions
in his life several times before, and they had never been mistaken.

He broke out of the house and ran to a ravine hardly a hundred
yards away, for his black intuitions always carried complete details.

"Why have God punished us so grievously who try so hard to
be good," he cried as he ran, "it is because I have broken my word
my parole." What did he mean by that? He didn't doubt what he
would find. He had seen it in every detail when he wakened in
horror.

Salina Innominee was done to death in the little ravine. It was a
stark, bloody thing. We will not linger on it.

That was the earthly end of Sally—a very good girl who was possessed by a Devil. But there is something about her ending that we miss, that we would still miss if we examined her closely. But Hannali caught it, not at his first intuitive vision of the horror, not at his actual coming to the site of the murder, but as he tried to compose himself. There was a mystery in the middle of the bloody business.

The murder of Sally Innominee was a stark bloody thing, but there was something peculiar about it. She had been struck dead with a single stroke—suddenly, painlessly, almost compassionately. The brutal and bloody business had all been done to her body after she was dead. Hannali—due to a lifetime's experience in which violence had a part—was able to sort out these effects with half his mind. Even the bloody business after she was dead was less than it appeared. The blood from the one wound had been spread to make it appear that she had been wounded many times. It was as though someone had staged and disarrayed the body after the killer had left.

But she was dead, and the Devil had killed her. That she had died suddenly and painlessly was small solace.

. . .

Ten minutes are gone—all that we can allow Hannali to recover from the shock. He has lived back through thirty years in those ten minutes, and he is back in the house. He stands silently with a coarse paper in his hand, the screed he knew he would find.

Perhaps the man wrote in his own hand this time. He may have picked up the writing art during his irregular soldier life; and this was the longest missive he ever wrote.

"Fat man I draw you out I warn you dou not come this is the only time I ever warn you I have kill your heffer calf it was not easy for mixed reasons for me to dou this thing You want find me? I tell you where in Hitchiti Meadow I wait for you—"

The writing did not trail off, but the mind of Hannali did. There was more here than simple outrage; this was a trick within a trick. Hannali's passion over this would never be spent; the Devil had killed his daughter; it was the final lightning stroke out of the horrifying cloud that had hung over his family for a generation.

Sally—Salina—was gone, the best girl ever, but for a long time she had been defective in her mind. But there was a second prong to the present attack, and Hannali analyzed it as he read.

"In Hitchiti Meadow I wait for you," ran on the screed of the Devil, "and at the Nourth rim I take one free shot at you from four hundred yards but no outher advantage then you will know where I am then one of us will kill the outher—"

Hannali's mind broke off again. He was an old badger who scented every trap, and this one was so strong that it stank. But a badger won't avoid a dog trap in any case. Hannali raised his hackles to the taunt of the Devil-Dog, knowing all the time that it was bait and that it might be fatal.

Hannali's great son Famous had gone from the house for several days, and someone had known that he was gone. It was their rule now that one of those strong men, Hannali or Famous, should always be at the house. The raiders would not try it if even one of them was there; they were much afraid of the Innominee men.

Oh, this was a double attack! But how to handle it.

"This is sun-down day for us fat man," the letter ran on, "there is one thing you dou not know about Whiteman Falaya I want tell you he is not one all pece man like you think he is many pece man it was our father Poushmataha said even the buzzart sometime gag but what he dou when he have gag it out is he not still buzzart come get me fat man I taunt you out I tell you one thing thou there are worse men loose than is Whiteman Falaya you think that is not pospel there are men in this so bad they scare me as I scare outhers there four I dou not care which of us it be let it be bouth and I am end in every way come shooting fat man I wait for you alone this much is true Whiteman Falaya."

Besides Hannali, there were two men in the house; Forbis Agent, the bookman and dreamer, and Robert Pike, the invisible Unionist soldier. The women were there: Natchez, Marie DuShane, Martha Louisiana, the three mothers; Luvinia, Hazel, Helen Miller, and Marie Calles. And the children, the biggest of them no more than half-grown—the smallest still infants.

Two men, good men but not strong men in the sense that Hannali and Famous were; seven women; twenty-four children. Hannali gave them rapid instructions. Then he took his rifle, looked again at his dead daughter, and went out afoot on the manhunt.

174

"I cannot let one thing go I cannot let the other go," he said, "I would have to be two different men in two places God give me strength for it You owe me this God how have I sinned that this should happen to us?"

Hannali walked rapidly to Hitchiti Meadow. He would have to deal with the double menace one prong at a time. He dimly concurred that there were worse men loose than Whiteman Falaya; he caught a whiff of those men now. Whiteman Falaya was only the Devil—a Devil who was scared when he learned that there were men so much worse than himself. He wanted it over with, he wanted the sundown day for himself. Well, he would get it, or Hannali would get it.

A cloud purled out of the southwest. Within a very few minutes it would cover the sun, and by that time one of two men would be dead.

The mind of Hannali Innominee was cleared somewhat when the "free" shot of Whiteman Falaya caught him in the fat loin.

It was now battle with the principality.

2.

In Hitchiti Meadow I wait for you. Perfect shooting on the edge. The ghost is fleshed. Time run out.

Whiteman Falaya had tricked him, of course, but Hannali had expected the trick. The "free" shot had not been from four hundred yards but from less than twenty. The ghost killer was behind Hannali.

Whiteman Falaya had not been in the meadow, but in a clump before its entrance. He indicated his position—more than by his shot—by his laughing, chuckling, barking, gobbling cry. This was the Indian gobble—the most eerie death challenge of all.

In the thinnest strip that one can slice from a second, Hannali rolled to shallow cover and caught the whole background with his eye. He knew every tuft here, every jag of turf, every reed, cedar snag, bush, clump of grass; and he knew which had been disarrayed.

It was his own land, the same to him as the inside of his house or head. Here he would not be had by anyone.

Hannali scented his man strongly; he caught the excitement and arrogance in the scent, and also a touch of fear. Every man who had ever heard of him was afraid of Whiteman Falaya; but Whiteman himself—and Hannali could sort out the emotions that made up that body scent—was exhilaratingly afraid of Hannali.

Hannali knew—probably he had always known—that he himself was better at this stalker-killer game than was Whiteman, possibly better than any man whatsoever. But he was shot painfully, and time would run out on him as he would weaken from loss of blood. He had known that the shot would be close and in the back; he had been waiting for it. He also knew that the shot was not meant to kill. Whiteman did not miss at fifty yards, nor did Hannali himself. Either of them could drill a turkey in the eye at that distance.

Whiteman Falaya was moving rapidly and silently, in deep cover, along the fringe of the meadow. The good ears of Hannali could not hear him, and the sharp eyes could not catch any movement; moreover, Whiteman was circling in the direction opposite that which Hannali at first guessed. Even the scent was lost by the shifting of the wind. But there are secondaries by which even a ghost may be tracked.

The Kiowas can tell you the flight of a hawk in the sky yesterday afternoon, going only by the marks of rodents on the ground. And by such secondary means Hannali was able to track the ghost in the bush.

A kingbird set up a slight squabble some distance away. A nighthawk, farther away and in another direction, grunted and flopped up off a stump—and Hannali had a triangulation. There was the click-click of grasshoppers rising, some distant and some near. There was the snick of a field rat going through the roots of the grass. These disturbances could be charted.

There was nothing supernatural about the ghostly-moving Whiteman Falaya, but there was something very near to it in the sharp sensing of Hannali. It was as though a giant traveling finger pointed out the whereabouts of Whiteman Falaya as he skirted the meadow silently.

Hannali fired!

He fired even before he saw the fractional movement; had he waited for it, he would have missed. He fired at where the adversary—a shallow slice of him—would have to be. He hit.

The only sound was a sharp intake of breath forty yards away, and Hannali knew that he had creased Whiteman in the buttocks. The cover there was too shallow by an inch or so. Whiteman would have been by there in less time than a hummingbird's blink, but Hannali caught him at his instant of transit.

The shot both lifted dust and skinned Whiteman. Lower by its own diameter it would have ricocheted. Higher, it would have missed or cut the man less painfully. This was better shooting than drilling a turkey in the eye. It was perfect shooting on the edge.

"The ghost is fleshed," said Hannali to himself. He meant that Whiteman could no longer move in absolute silence. No man, tensed and in pain, can do so. By his wound, Whiteman had taken on the heaviness of the flesh.

Hannali stood erect—in the open—and he had the advantage. He was out in a meadow four hundred yards across, with no real cover, and he disdained what slight cover there was. It was his opponent, in the lush tangled cover that fringed the meadow, who was pinned down. Whiteman could not show even an eyeball for an instant without having it pierced to the brain. Hannali had simply settled his dominance in this by his calm and sure presence.

Try it, Whiteman, try it!

Whiteman Falaya flicked up a finger. And lost a nail. But Hannali's shot had not now come from fifty or forty yards out. It had come from eight. He was right on top of Whiteman. It was heavy Hannali, wounded and tightened up, who was able to move noiselessly when they came to the showdown call. Hannali was the ghost now.

He had Whiteman pinned down in the too-shallow cover, unable to move at all, and was almost standing over him. Hannali was a sure man and he had a sure thing. Whiteman had never played at murder with a complete man before. He had only played with ordinary men.

But was time running against Hannali? Not in the immediate case. Whiteman would be losing almost as much blood as Hannali, and Hannali had more blood to lose.

But the other time was running out. The second prong of the

threat stampeded back into Hannali's mind. Hannali sniffed the air. Nothing. Nothing yet. It was three-quarters of a mile.

"Finish it fat man," Whiteman Falaya called out, "come crash in you kill me but I kill you too we go together to die is all I got left."

"I've a duty to live till another day," said Hannali evenly.

There were flat rocks there of five to eight pounds heft. Hannali began to toss them over the ledge cover onto Whiteman. There was the sound of a heavy fall on the rib cage, of a mean glancing blow off the skull. Hannali had Whiteman's body outlined behind the edge.

"You hurt me," called Whiteman. "Fat man you will learn that there are worse men loose than Whiteman Falaya."

"I learn it now," said Hannali. He sniffed again, and it was there. All doubt vanished with the first rifle shots three-quarters of a mile away. Time had run out.

Hannali crashed in shooting. He had not the time to kill carefully. He killed Falaya, but Whiteman got in his second shot. Whiteman had a pleasantly dark dead face, seeming younger than it could have been. And Hannali's own face was horribly ashen. He'd have died from that second shot if he hadn't another duty unfulfilled.

3.

Great Red Flowering. Dead with her hair still on fire. The end of the world of Hannali Innominee.

Hannali was running back to his house. He was bleeding out through his ribs now, and a man has no business running when he is shot there. Three-quarters of a mile, and already the hot-smoke scent of it came to him.

How fast can a twice-shot man run three-quarters of a mile? How fast can an old heavy man do it even when the raiders are putting the torch to his house and his family? The worse men than Whiteman Falaya had set fire to Hannali's house, and they would shoot down anybody who ran out from the flames. In the house were two men—good men but not great men, seven women, twenty-four children.

"It is sundown day for us Fat Man," Falaya had written.

"It is no sundown day for me and mine yet," Hannali groaned furiously. But the second shot into the rib cage had robbed him of breath and strength. A bear can charge thirty yards after he is killed by such a shot. Hannali was more bear than a bear, but could he charge three-quarters of a mile?

Hannali had planted red roses in front of his Big House, even though they were a white man thing. He enjoyed that flick of red splendor whenever he came onto the house from the front. But he did not enjoy the great red flowering that engulfed the house now.

Both the low-flopping wings of the house were on fire. They burned so hot that they exploded outward here and there, but the whole house would not go so quickly. There were stone rooms with flagstone floors that would not burn completely; there were strong rooms in the house.

The defenders and raiders were dueling it out. The guns spoke sharply, and Hannali understood every one of them. He knew the voice of every firearm in his establishment, and he could catalogue the guns of the raiders—the Sharp's Carbines, 52 Spencers, 44 Henrys. They were not the indifferent Indian trade rifles, and they were not shot by unorganized raiders.

From the house, someone was shooting with a very sweet little rifle of Hannali's, but the shots were going too high—singing away in the air like hornets. That was Forbis Agent trying to repel the raiders and make his own broadsides meaningful, but he hadn't the knack.

"That son how have I neglect to teach him to shoot proper," moaned Hannali, "how have I so bungle a thing."

A cranky old shooting piece was speaking at longer intervals. This was handled by a man who tried to make every shot count; he was but a fair shot, yet it was something. There had been a boy with watery eyes who wanted to see wild Indians; now he faced coldly savage Indians and white men. It was Robert Pike, the spook who took on flesh when the sanctuary of the house was violated and he was released from his parole.

The light squirrel rifle of Marie DuShane was talking in breed

Indian, but it was a short-range piece and the raiders were right on the limit of her effective range.

Three defenders dueling it out with fifty raiders who held back a little to let the fire do their work for them.

Hannali sat down heavily when he was within his own range of the thing. He was sick to death, but he could not allow himself to die. He began to kill raiders from four hundred yards out.

Hannali's return finished the raiders. The Indians among them were superstitious, and the white men more so. It was as though Hannali, having killed Whiteman Falaya who was a ghost and unkillable, was a man returned from the dead or the inheritor of a charmed life. The big Choctaw was a Territory legend, really more feared by his enemies than Whiteman had ever been. Hannali stunned them all by his return, and he killed half a dozen of them before they knew what he was about. They broke away, took to horse, and raced around the burning wings and behind the house. But they could still kill as they went.

Hannali arose again, though it would be pleasant to stretch out and die. He staggered toward the house as though falling uphill. Like a worn-out mule, he lunged and ran because he was too far gone to walk. He felt the hot blast of the house and the crowning glow before the high gable crashed down.

He was through his big front door and into the flaming room. Fire could not instantly fell a man as full of juice as he; he could live for a little while in fire. Forbis Agent was dead under a burning beam. Nobody else was there either in life or death.

Hannali fought through the house and to a little plot behind. The raiders were going over the hill, and Hannali dropped the last one of them dead from the saddle. There was something artificial about the act—it was like one of the outré stories that his father Barua used to tell. He had upped with the gun and fired in sheer weariness, and seven hundred yards away a man had tumbled from his horse. It was almost a white-man story thing. Then Hannali saw something too ultimate to be a white-people affair.

Marie DuShane was dead with her hair still on fire. The snout of her light rifle had plowed into the ground where she had fallen with it.

If Marie DuShane was dead, then the family was dead. She had been everything to them all. She was more soaring than the little bird Natchez, and of a darker passion than Martha Louisiana. She had been, after she discovered her own person, one of incredible kindness and complete competence. Hannali had seemed to be, but Marie DuShane was the family.

Hannali called out in a cracked voice. He got no answer from anyone. He started back through the still-standing rooms of the house. He lost his senses and fell to the hot stone floor.

. . .

Here is hiatus. How insufficient the word for the end of the world! The world of Hannali Innominee was ended.

. . .

When the world should start again—jerkily and without real authority—it would not be the same world nor would they be the same people in it. It would be a shadow world of shadow people. Later they would gain some substance, but they would be of another sort—of another nature.

It had ended there. And something else had ended unnoticed at the same time. For perhaps the Five Tribes Territory civilization came to an end with the fall of that last strong house of the Choctaw North.

. . .

The smoke rises, but foully, and high above the roof hole.
The talk is gone. The people are gone.
The world is gone in the reek.

4.

Of another part, and in the latter days. Bull blare. Dead family come back to me. Is God silent is there no voice?

Hannali did not know if he were in the same world or another, if he were alive or dead; but he did know that about three hours had gone by. His sense of time was something that even death couldn't distort.

He was in his own strong room, and he had not got there by himself. He had been patched up and his bleeding stanched; but he was crawling with fever, and in great agony and stiffness from his wounds.

He arose to see what could be done in the new desolate world into which he had just been born. It was Robert Pike who had brought him there. Hannali could sense a man three hours gone, in this world as well as in the previous one. But that waiting man had not waited to take farewell. He had, however, left a note on the table.

"Papa Hannali, I have fixed you up as well as I might, and now is the time to make my break. They will be scouting back in sight of the house before dark. I am no longer afraid of them, nor of anything, but I do not wish to forfeit my life. I believe you will not die.

"I will be back again, from the North. Their attack breaks my parole. They think they are raiders! Those Devil Cherokees have never seen raiders till I come back.

"I scouted for an hour. I can't find any of the family alive. Helen Miller is in the little canyon a half mile behind the house. You call it Choke-Cherry Canyon. She took some of the children there, but they killed her and them. Marie is behind the horse lot. She tried to hide the smallest ones in the feed lot; they found them. I know you have seen Marie DuShane dead. The first bunch caught Martha Louisiana outside. They hooted that they would sell her for black in Oklafalaya. Natchez took others of the children somewhere, I cannot find them or her, tomorrow you will find them dead in some draw.

"I was member of your family, the most odd family ever. I will repay what you have done for me, and revenge what has been done to you. I know the big men of the raiders, their names and their faces. I count me twenty houses of them that will be fired by me before I am finished with it.

"Robert Pike, Sergeant."

Hannali moved out of the room with terrible stiffness. He called aloud, but he could not be sure that his voice made any sound. It was a feeble thing that was like a joke of his old voice. He went out of the house.

The house was still burning in several parts. It would continue to smolder and smoke for several days, but it had already divided itself. The good stone parts had been burned clear of their attachments and stood firm. They would need only beams and rafters and roofs and refitting—if ever a man should decide to live again.

Hannali made a bugle with his hands and gave a loud mournful call. It was a sick cow call. Had two bullets, smaller than the end of a finger, turned Hannali into a cow? No. Now he put the bull into his blare and sounded powerfully. There were none of them alive to answer him. Very well. Then he would call them up dead. He sounded a final great blast. "Dead family, come back to me!" was the burden of it.

A dead grandson appeared. It was Famous-George—a son of Famous Innominee and Helen Miller. "Is it safe we come back, Papa Hannali?" the grandson asked fearfully. Hannali nodded, for he couldn't speak. Then he sat down suddenly and heavily, bear-fashion on the ground, to wait what other apparitions might be. He was confused for almost the only time in his life, and hope came to him but gradually. Some of his people were still alive. Famous-George had gone to bring others from whatever limbo they were hidden in.

The daughter Hazel came with Peter-Barua (of Travis Innominee and Rachel Perry) and with Martha-Child (of Forbis Agent and Luvinia Innominee).

"Are there no more my daughter," Hannali asked her with faint voice.

"We will see. Natchez and her clutch, I think. Can you get up?"

"Always I can get up once more after I am dead where do we look."

Natchez was down in a pit that had been used variously for a cistern and an underground silo. It was covered over with brush which Hazel removed. Natchez had not answered the bugling of Hannali, and would not have answered any call by anyone. She had been told to remain completely silent until the brush had been pulled back and she was able to see the faces of those who came for her. And she had kept the children quiet through it all.

Natchez handed up the four children she had with her: Helena, the small daughter of Alinton Innominee and Marie Calles; and the three infants, Thomas-Academy (of Forbis Agent and Luvinia

183

Innominee), Charles-Chitoh (of Travis Innominee and Rachel Perry), Anna-Hata, the blue-eyed daughter of Jemmy Buster and Hazel Innominee.

"Are there no more my daughters," Hannali asked again.

"Not unless Martha Louisiana is still alive with them," said Hazel.

"I have to be sure," said Hannali, "have they taken all the ponies."

"They are not take any of them," said Famous-George. "I was let all the ponies loose and tell them to stay clear of those men the men was not able to catch or find our ponies."

Hannali again made a bugle with his hands, and gave out with a weird pony call that nobody had ever heard before.

"One of them will come," he said then; and a heavy pony did come with a scurry of broad hoofs.

"It's on to dark, Papa Hannali," Hazel told him. "They'll kill you on the way, and we will all die without you."

"Nobody will kill me daughter I owe death too much grudge this day he will be afraid of me for what he has done he will hide his face and slink away."

Hannali found Martha Louisiana about three miles down country. Apparently she had become too battlesome and they had killed her. Hannali brought her back slung across the pony. He walked painfully, and the animal followed. No pony could have carried the two of them.

Nine were still alive: Natchez, Hazel, Famous-George, Peter-Barua, Charles-Chitoh, Martha-Child, Thomas-Academy, Anna-Hata.

Twenty-three were killed by the raiders: Marie DuShane, Martha Louisiana, Luvinia, Helen Miller, Marie Calles, James, Marie-Therese, Henry-Pushmataha, Philip-Nitakechi, John-Durham, Francis-Mingo, Strange-Joseph, Nicholas-Nakni, Louis-Hannali, Jude, Matthew-Moshulatubbee, Mary-Luvinia, Gregory-Pitchlynn, Anne-Chapponia, Charles-Mexico, Pablo-Nieto, Forbis Agent, Bartholome.

One had escaped—Robert Pike.

Salina had been killed by Whiteman Falaya to bait Hannali away from the house. Twenty-four of them dead in one day!

"My son Famous may yet return," said Hannali. "If he do then he must become head of the family."

"No. My father will not ever come back," said Famous-George.

"Are you Alikchi-man that you know this?" Natchez asked.

184

"Yes. I know about my father that way," he said. Famous-George was ten years old.

"Is my son Famous dead," Hannali asked him.

"My father is another man now," said Famous-George. "He will die soon as that other man."

Famous Innominee did not come back. They would receive a writing in his hand saying that he became dead for his own reasons, that they might possibly hear of a man who reminded them of him, that perhaps he could turn again and come alive to them after it was all over with.

We have our own theory about the man that Famous became—one of the sudden new Union captains, a man of shocking force. He had a short and incandescent career, and died under a name that was not Famous Innominee.

. . .

Hannali sawed boards in the morning. Famous-George and Peter-Barua sawed and hammered them to make twenty-four coffins. Hannali picked a soft-bottomed meadow for the burial plot. He would dig till he bled too badly. Then he would rest till stanched, and dig again. Natchez and Hazel dug tirelessly. They buried their dead.

"Who will know the Latin to say now that Marie DuShane is gone," Hannali worried.

"Who was you think would know the Latin," said Famous-George, "who have inherit the brains of this family anyhow?"

Famous-George read it out of the book from the *Subvenite sancti* down to the last *lux perpetua*.

Everything that follows is epilogue. Yet the contingent latter life does have advantages. A man already dead is spared many worries. He sees things in a truer aspect, and he will soon be able to develop a pleasure in it all.

"Our faith constrains us to believe that Death is only an incident," said Hannali, "a good man will not fear it and a busy man will hardly notice that it has come and gone it is the same with my foredeath here I doubt that it is extraordinary to me it must come to many men."

185

CHAPTER SEVENTEEN

1.

*From Cowskin Prairie to Edward's Post. A tired
horse and a dry cigar. It ended on July 14.*

In all those years, the warfare in the Territory seemed random, but
it followed a certain pattern. The intent of the South was to use the
confused Territory as a screen against northern attack on Texas, and
to employ in this Indian troops only, and the veriest sweepings of
misfit white Texas units. It was by accident that some very good
Texas soldiers were swept into the Territory action; had they been
correctly classified as first-rate they would have been used elsewhere.
The South was generally successful in this tactic. Texas became a
great reservoir of soldiers for use in the conflict in the states, and
Texas herself was defended by the hodgepodge.

At the same time, the South disguised this holding action by a
series of really showy raids. They were not intended to result in
the permanent occupation of northern Territory, so they could be
shallow and swift. From the southern viewpoint, it did not matter
whether the raids succeeded or failed. They were intended as a
diversion; they would punish the Kansas and Missouri regions and

keep them in a turmoil; and the raiders killed would be mostly Indians.

The object of the North was to prevent any dangerous build-up of Confederate forces in the Territory—anything that could be used as a serious flank threat. The North could have conquered the Territory, but to hold it they would have to borrow manpower badly needed elsewhere. Five times the Unionists came down into the Territory in superior force, scattered the opposition, occupied most of the area, and then withdrew again. And five times the Confederates reoccupied and destroyed. These ten total sweepings of the Territory were very bloody affairs, but most of the blood spilled on both sides was Indian.

The name men among the Confederate raiders were the splendid Jo Shelby who used regular troops; the devil Charles Quantrill who had been on both sides and who now had a new Confederate license to murder—with such men as Frank James and Jesse in his following, and others who were killers from the cradle; and the double-devil Stand Watie and his killer Cherokees.

And whenever the raiders had ruled for a few months, the Unionists would come down and break up their nests. Five times they did it with expeditions that were total war, but the Confederate resistance was always a stubborn thing. Stand Watie was a real military genius, whatever else he was. Tandy Walker of the Choctaws was another. He had been chief of all the Choctaws in 1858 and 1859, or at least the chief of the Skullyville Convention party. He was a boy-faced beardless man whose Choctaw and Chickasaw troops stood up to white troops, all sorts of Indian troops, and inextricably mixed white, Negro, and Indian troops; and in one sense they were never beaten. He fought twenty battles, and he was never *driven* from a field. It is true that his men usually disappeared from the field in the night following the battle, but that was his strategy: to inflict terrible losses, and then to melt away. He hadn't the means to fight two- and three-day battles.

Tandy Walker commanded the Second Confederate Indian Brigade which was made up of the First Chickasaw Battalion, the First Choctaw Battalion, the First Choctaw and Chickasaw Battalion (Alinton Innominee rode with this group), the Second Choctaw Battalion, and the Reserve Squadron which was led by Captain

George Washington—the Caddo Indian chief who was friend of Hannali.

They would be fighting yet, if the Unionists had not ceased to come down into that country, and if the Confederates had not weakened and surrendered elsewhere and called on them no more.

At first there had been the universal assumption that the South would win. There had then been a year of doubt, followed by the years when it was clear to any man of any hue that the North would prevail. But nobody in the Territory switched sides when fortune turned. All were as stubborn in their allegiance on the last day as on the first.

When did the main Civil War end anyhow? Do not be insulted, but it is possible that you are mistaken in your answer.

Robert E. Lee surrendered on April 9, 1865, but that was not the end. There were numerous leaders left who swore that they would never surrender; and yet, one by one, they did so.

On April 26, Joe E. Johnson surrendered the Army of Georgia.

On May 10, President Jefferson Davis was captured by the Unionists.

On May 24, General Kirby-Smith, the last of the die-hard Confederate generals in the southern states, surrendered. This date is usually given as the end of the Civil War; but there was still fighting in the Territory, and the Confederate Indian armies were intact.

Peter Pitchlynn broke the first deadlock. As new chief, he took over from the military leaders and announced that it was finished as far as the Choctaws were concerned. He surrendered, not to an army force, but to a federal commission.

What would the mad-man raider of the Cherokees do? Stand Watie was a full Confederate general. He was an end-of-the-line man, but he knew when the party was over. He surrendered on June 23, the last Confederate general to surrender.

But it wasn't over with yet. The Chickasaws were still in the field, unbroken and expert. They were howling for somebody to come down and fight them. They had been the magnificent fighters all through the fray.

As Peter Pitchlynn had done with the Choctaws, Winchester Colbert now dealt with his Chickasaws. Chief (Governor) Colbert dismissed the military leaders, and he told his men that the wars were over. The Chickasaw army began to melt away, most of the men riding off to find what was left of their homes. Governor Colbert barely held enough of them to have a token force left to surrender—about a hundred men.

On July 14, 1865, with only two followers, a Union major walked a tired horse into the Chickasaw encampment. The major mouthed a dry cigar, and he seemed to be a very dry man himself. Governor Colbert identified himself. The major presented the papers of surrender, and rudely asked Colbert if he could read.

"I can," said Colbert. He read the papers and then signed them, and the major put them back in his pocket. He lit his cigar with one of the new sulphur matches, and walked his horse out of the camp again.

The Civil War was over, and the date was July 14, 1865.

The Civil War itself was over, and yet its last battle was not fought till seventeen years later, in 1882, near Okemah in Indian Territory. The Indian Civil Wars did not end with the white man peace; in all those seventeen years there was desultory fighting. The last phase of it was called the Green Peach War, between two Creek factions: the full-blood group led by Isparhecher (in whom the ghost of Opothleyahola walked); and the mixed-blood group of Chief Checote. The bitterness did not die until the last Snake Creek with childhood memories of Round Mountains and Bird Creek and Shoal Creek was dead.

2.

They drove the nails they had forgotten. Apache to Waco. To reward enemies and punish friends.

The Indian Territory was in very bad shape at the formal end of the Civil War in 1865. Twelve thousand homes—80 per cent of those in the Territory—had been burned and destroyed. *Every town and settlement* had been destroyed. Somewhere between one third and one half of the Territory Indians had been killed—this before the disease epidemics hit in late 1865.

Almost all livestock was gone from the Territory; seed corn and seed wheat were not to be had; there were no plows, no horses, no food, no money, no credit—and no man outside the Territory cared whether the Indians lived or died. The thriving civilization that the Territory Indians had built up in the thirty-year period following the relocation of the tribes was gone forever.

Fortunately there was still game in the Territory. It had reappeared in unremembered abundance. Most of the Indians reverted, threw away their civilization, and became hunting Indians again in order to live.

. . .

Though his crops had been burned for four straight years, Hannali Innominee had planted more corn than ever in the spring of 1865. He was one man who still had seed corn; the raiders had never been able to find all his caches. He had plows and mules—wherever he had kept them hidden. He and a few others led the comeback in the Choctaw North.

Hannali, Natchez, Hazel, Famous-George, Peter-Barua, Charles-Chitoh, Martha-Child, Thomas-Academy, Helena, Anna-Hata—ten of them (and seven of them were children of ten years old and under) were left to reconstitute a clan. But would not the great sons be coming home?

Travis Innominee came home first, but he did not remain. He said that he did not wish to see his brother Alinton—not till several years had passed and they might be easy with each other again. Travis went across the river to North Fork Town in the Creek Nation to live. He built a house on a town lot that had been willed to him by his uncle Pass Christian Innominee—for Pass Christian had bought property here and there on that long ago visit up the river. Travis had some money that he had picked up as a card shark during his Union service. He opened a store, and for a long time he did business on promise of future payment.

Alinton Innominee came home, a crippled man who walked with a cane but who still rode horse easily. Alinton said, as had Famous-George and others, that his brother Famous Innominee would not be coming home. Famous had visited Alinton just after he had died, and they had a long talk into the night. Famous was in contingent form and could not take either coffee, tobacco, or whiskey, although he said he still enjoyed the smell of all three.

"How is it with my great son where he is now?" Hannali asked.

"Oh, he says purgatory is not the best land beyond the world, a little better than Texas, not at all up to the Moshulatubbee." They grinned, but Alinton had told his father, even in a riddle, that he knew his brother Famous was dead.

"So now I have but one brother," Alinton said, "I'll go over and see him and won't put up with this reluctant business of his what are we white men that we should be enemies and we brothers?"

Alinton stayed with Travis a week, stayed at the Big House a further week, then rode off to Texas to buy cattle with gold that Hannali dug up from one of his hordes. Man, you can't stand around and let the world do nothing. When the bottom is out of everything is the time to go back in business.

"We are a twice-crucified people," said Hannali, "but this second time they have nailed us up on the cross grotesquely by one hand and one foot and flopping like a caught turkey let us not be impatient I am feel that very soon they be along to drive the nails they have forgotten."

Yes. They came. They drove the nails they had forgotten. It had been an oversight. A full crucifixion had been intended.

The two nails now driven by the federal hammer were these: First, all Indian treaties and all Indian rights to Territory land were voided because of the adherence of the Indians to the Confederacy (though only half of them had adhered to her). Second: The Five Tribes Indians must forfeit *one half of their land for punishment.*

The white men of the southern states did not have to forfeit one half of their land. It was different with Indians. Well, what would they do with the one half of all the land then? Bring in other Indians on it.

Indian tribes were uprooted in every portion of the United States and piled in on top of the Territory Indians. Mostly they were looted of their old land without payment. Most of these new Indians were civilized and settled, had forgotten that they were Indians, in many cases were prosperous farmers of three-quarters white blood who fell victim to the new rampant racism.

The new transported Indians began to arrive before word of the declarations came to the Territory. Most, it is true, were from the immediately surrounding territories and states—Texas, Arkansas, Kansas, Missouri, Colorado, and were of tribes which already had clans living in the Territory. But others came from both the Atlantic and Pacific coast and from the Canadian border.

Skip the following if you want. It is but a partial listing of the tribes uprooted again and loaded in on newly stolen land, the names of nations going to their extinction and absorption.

Chiricahua Apaches, southern Arapahos, Cahokias, Cayugas, southern Cheyennes (from Colorado and elsewhere), Chippewas (from Kansas), Conchos, Quadhadi Comanches, Delawares (from Kansas, from Missouri, from Illinois, from everywhere), Illinois (from Kansas, Missouri, and Illinois), Nemaha Iowas (from Nebraska, Missouri, and Kansas), Kansas, Wildcat Kickapoos (most of them from Texas, but also from New Mexico, all these Indians had to come from somewhere else), Kiowas, Lipans, Miamis, Michigameas, Modocs, Nez Perces (from Oregon and Idaho), Osages, Otos, Ottawas, Pawnees, Peorias, Poncas, Prairie Band Potawatomis (from Iowa), Woods Band Potawatomis (from Kansas), Quapaws, Sac and Fox Indians, Senecas of Sandusky, Mixed Band Senecas (this was now made into an omnibus tribe for government convenience, to include remnants of Wyandots, Ottawas, Peorias, Kaskaskias, Weas, Piankashaws, Eries, Conestogas, Cayugas, Oneidas, Mohawks, Onedagas, Tuscaroras, and smaller groups from twelve states), Shawnees, Stockbridge Indians, Tamoroas, Tawakonis, such Tonkawas as had not already fled from Texas into the Territory, Wacos.

That's the most of them. There are others, but they are cousins of those listed here. Many of the new Indians had no idea to what tribe they had belonged when they were really Indians, and they would be added to whatever group of Indians was then being transported and told that they were that sort of Indian.

It couldn't have happened at any other time, but there was a hatred in the United States at the close of the war and it took the form of rampant racism against the Indians. It was the modern doctrine then that the Indians were the unfit who must be extinguished to make room for the manifest destiny race.

But in the robbery of the lands of the Five Tribes Indians to make room for the new arrivals, there was one most peculiar thing. The Chickasaws and Choctaws had been officially for the Confederacy; they did not lose one acre of their land. All that was taken from them was the western region, called the Leased District, which had been vaguely reserved for their future use, but upon which they had never built expectations.

But it was the Seminoles, Creeks, and Cherokees, of whom either a huge minority or a majority had been loyal to the Union, who were robbed of much more than half of their land. The Cherokees had 2220 men in the Union forces, and about 1400 in the Confederate. The Creeks had 1675 men in the Union Forces, and 1575 in the Confederate.

But the Seminoles were robbed of 80 per cent of their land. *All the land* of the followers of the Alligator and Bolek and Tustennuggee—those who had thrown in with Opothleyahola's Creeks and whose remnant had later fought for the Union—all their land was taken. Only the solidly Confederate Seminoles were permitted to retain their land.

The Cherokees lost two thirds of their land. It was the land of the full-blood Pin faction, either neutralist or Unionist, that was taken. The Confederate Cherokees did not lose any land at all.

All the land of the Upper Snake Creeks was taken. None of the land of the Lower Confederate Creeks was taken.

Who won the war anyhow? It was to punish friends and award enemies that the land was divided.

There had to be an explanation to this selectivity of the robberies. There is one. It almost seems a just one, if the robberies had to be carried out, and if no protests were to be heard or modifications permitted after it was drawn up on paper.

The eastern, mixed-blood, slave-holding, Confederate-adhering Indians held their land in severality—they held individual titles to their individual acres.

But the western, full-blood, freeholding, neutral or Union-allied Indians held their lands in common as belonging to the tribe. A man would have life tenure to as much land as he needed, occupied, and used; his heirs could have the same land, or more if needed. But these western Indians did not hold individual title to land, no written title at all.

The land administrators could say truthfully or half-truthfully that only the land owned by nobody was assigned away, and that every Indian title to specific land was respected.

3.

Whatever happened to all those Ottawa Indians?
When saw you last a Fort-Snelling Sioux?

But would there not now be intolerable crowding in the Territory, with more than fifty other Indian tribes and remnants brought in? As a matter of fact, there would not be, even though there would be deaths by starvation for a full decade while the Indians tried to get things going with no help at all from outside.

But compassion finds its own tools, and the Territory Indians— now completely destitute themselves—adopted and somehow provided for the new Indians. Besides, there weren't so many of them.

The estimate has been given that more Indians died on these removals after the Civil War than had died on that earlier removal from the old South. If so, then more than half of them died on the removal, for there were only about twenty thousand new Indians who came into the Territory after the Civil War. But, somehow, the states had gotten rid of three or four times this many Indians. Many of them, of course, hid in the white communities and ceased to be Indians.

The Ottawa Indians were given twenty-three sections of land in a region southeast of present Miami, Oklahoma. Twenty-three sections of land for a tribe which not too long before had numbered seventeen thousand persons? What will you do with them? Stack them on top of each other? No. That would not be necessary. There were not now seventeen thousand of them; there were not seventeen hundred; there were not even one hundred and seventy. There were one hundred and forty-nine of them, and no more of them left in the world; twenty-three sections of land were plenty for such a small group. Sometimes we wonder whatever happened to all those Ottawa Indians.

And what happened to all the Minnesota Indians, for Cyrus Aldrich of Minnesota was the most avid of all U.S. congressmen for removing and extinguishing the Indians. Most of those Indians were surely swept out of Minnesota, and just as surely most of them did not arrive in the Indian Territory. Some Ojibways (Chippewas) came into the Territory, but most of them came from Kansas—having arrived there from Minnesota fifteen years before. Where are the and the Fort-Snelling Sioux? Where are the Ouiskonche, Songes-kiton, Manchokatonx, Mantantan, Assiniboin, Menominee? Along the way, they lost their names or they lost their lives.

The Territory Indians had built up a thriving civilization between the years 1828 and the time of the Civil War. This Indian civilization Teton, Yankton, and Santee Dakotas? Where are the Nadoues-Sioux —parallel to and friendly to the white culture—was yet a thing utterly Indian. It was a solid civilization that had been built up in about thirty-five years.

It had been built up and destroyed. Could it be built again?

CHAPTER EIGHTEEN

1.

The Children's Decades. Underground thunder in Congressional Cemetery. Poor Peter Pitchlynn!

It had come an Indian summer to the Territory—that frostbit second spring that is the end of things and not the beginning. But the community of that period was a youthful one rather than aged.

The Indian summer was the Children's Decades. A people faced with extinction will either die, or they will reproduce lavishly. More than one third of the Territory Indians were killed in the war years. More than one half of the men of the prime years were dead. But in anticipation of this disaster—for both nature and human nature are prescient in these things—there had been a great number of children born just before and during the wars; it was like a wave. And the children lived through all the hardships; the Territory orphans were cared for. Families took strange children whose language they could not understand, and raised them up. And the new Indians coming into the Territory seemed to be made up entirely of children and old people. The old people were passing over the hill, but never had there been such a children's world.

Let us put it into context. This was the *beginning* of the Old Wild West Days. In most ways it was a retrogression. The lawlessness of the Old Wild West Days was a new lawlessness following on the extinction of old civilizations. Many of these civilizations appear small from our own eminence, but they were real things. The Indian Territory civilization of the Five Tribes had been the genuine article. The thin-spread civilizations of New Mexico and California had been real. The prairie peace of the Plains Indians had actually obtained. They became warlike now—as a new thing—only when threatened with final extinction. The old French and Spanish veneers had represented real civilizations. The great trading empires—the Bent St. Vrain and others—had stood for something. The Old Wild West Days came in an interlude following civilizations, not leading them.

Abilene and Dodge City and Wichita had not yet become the raucous towns of the trail ends. Texas longhorns had not yet been driven north in their millions nor had they been introduced onto the Montana and Utah ranges. The great spreads had not been developed, the Montana column had not marched, Custer had not pursued the Sioux, the banditti of the Plains had not gathered, nor the vigilantes. The great wave of homesteaders had not begun. But the Territory civilization had already built itself, lived its short life, and been murdered.

That old civilization was gone, and another would attempt to push up through the ashes. Let us veer off a little into the then future and bury the man who—more than any other—had been the symbol of that Five Tribes civilization of the Territory.

After the Civil War and his term as chief of the Choctaws, Peter Pitchlynn lived out the remainder of his life in Washington, D.C. He lived quietly, though he had many friends. He sometimes served as an expert to Congress on Indian affairs. He was a tireless—though some said tiresome—advocate of justice for the Indians. But he had become a white man.

There is an interesting question in the *Summa* of St. Thomas Aquinas and also in an old science fiction story, the name of which I forget, concerning the paradox of free will and predestined fate. It asks whether a man in making a great decision that will forever set the seal on his future does not also set the seal on his past. A man alters his future, and does he not also alter his past in conformity with it? Does he not settle not only what manner of man he will be, but also what manner of man he has been?

Peter Pitchlynn died in Washington, D.C., January 17, 1881, a white man, the son of white man John Pitchlynn. But—by an alternate recension—he had been born a full-blood Indian named Ha-Tchoo-Tuck-Nee.

There was another aging man in Washington in those days. He was the Moses emeritus who still wore monstrous Indian trappings. Men had either forgotten or never known what had happened earlier.

The old man asked for it, and none of the friends of Peter Pitchlynn understood who that man really was or what he had stood for. The man had some old Indian connection, and he was said to be a great orator.

Albert Pike preached the funeral eulogy over the grave of Peter Pitchlynn. Peter was buried in Congressional Cemetery, and the second Devil of the Indians boomed sonorously over his clay. There was an angry rumble from under the ground and nobody understood what it was. They had forgotten that old Pushmataha was also buried in Congressional Cemetery.

Peter Pitchlynn had been the Choctaw star all of whose rays had pointed upward. And Albert Pike had been what he had been.

Poor Peter Pitchlynn!

2.

In the old Indian manner on the second syllable.
The White Eyes use words curiously. A sharp
thing with galena and niter mixed in.

The Innominee clan thrived once more. It would always do that. Hannali had money, not only in New Orleans of the bankrupt South, but also in St. Louis. He also had gold coin at home; he had but to dig up his caches. He had always known how to grow money as well as corn and cattle.

There were a lot of the Innominees left, and after an interval there would be still more. They grew and prospered, and perhaps the Territory trick could be done again. If the Innominees could pull it off, why could not others?

But there was one thing wrong, and for a long time Hannali could not put his mind or finger on it. Things were not as they had been; that could not be expected. But the new thing was stubbornly of a different nature from the old thing.

"They are not Indian any more," Hannali said one day as the realization came over him.

"No, they are not Indian people," said Natchez, "they are now come to be white-people people even the darkest of them. Maybeso we are the last of the Indians, Papa Hannali."

And there Natchez herself let it slip that she was no longer completely Indian. When she said "Papa Hannali" she intoned Hannali on the first syllable—as the white people and the new Indians and the children pronounced it. She had been the last one who accented the name in the old Indian manner on the second syllable, and now she had slipped.

Should anyone ever wonder how the "Hannali" in the title of this study is pronounced, it is this: If you read it before the end of the Civil War (some hundred years before it is written) you accent it on the second syllable. If you read it at a later date, you accent on the first.

Never mind, they were all splendid children—for all that they had become white-people children under their ruddy brown skins. There is no thing wrong with white people other than that they are not Indians, but how had it come about?

It had come about by smashing the old civilization and by the accretion of new Indians of fifty tribes and remnants. But do you get white people if you mix enough Indians together? In this case, yes.

There were new Indians from New York State, from Ohio, from Pennsylvania, from Indiana, from Michigan, from everywhere. Most of these had never heard a word of any Indian language spoken in their lives. They were white people except in their forgotten ancestry, and they had never thought of themselves as Indians until their land was stolen and they were removed to a strange country. The intent had been to settle the new Indians in groups, but the practice was different. There was no town or clan or neighborhood in the Territory that did not receive families of the new Indians.

Few of the new Indians spoke anything but English. Almost all of the Territory Indians could get along in English as their second language. Now, from the necessity of communication, English became the tongue of all, and the old Indian languages were set aside. It was in the 1870s that the old tongues of the Five Tribes went out of common usage. There would always be old people who could speak them, there are old people who can speak them even today, but they were gone as common things. And with the English language supreme, there came English-language thought patterns.

It was so with clothing, tools, housebuilding, even plowing the land. The old Territory Indians had built very good timber and stone buildings, and every one of them looks Indian in every line. The new houses looked just like those in Illinois and Missouri and Kentucky. Compare sets of Territory photographs taken ten years apart and you will see it.

Even shirts. The old Choctaw calico shirts had been completely Indian. Never mind the material, they had had the shapes and lines of fitted deerskin. But now the Choctaw looms turned out white-man shaped shirts.

The new schools were white-people schools in their instances and examples. The children learned the bits of history of the colonies and of New England, but no longer anything of their own past. What would the Choctaw or Creek past mean to Iroquois or Chippewa children or to children who had no idea from what tribe they derived?

"What is Pale Face? What is Red Man?" grandson Thomas-Academy asked one day when he rode home from school. "History book has them. Why am I ignorant? Why have I never heard of them before?"

Hannali tried to explain.

"The White Eyes have the belief that sometime somewhere some Indian called them pale face which I disbelieve," he said. "They also believe that sometime somewhere someone called the Indians Red Men which is likewise questionable."

"But why?" asked Thomas-Academy. "It is they who are ruddy red rosy people and not we. We are bark-brown people."

"The White Eyes use words curiously," said Hannali.

The mind itself changed—the way that ideas are put into words. The constitution and laws of the Choctaw Nation printed at

Doaksville in 1852 was completely Indian. But the Permit Law of 1867, the Timber Law of 1871, the Coal Law of 1873 are white-man things in their thinking and wording.

Indian art ceased for two decades. When it resumed it did have a remarkably vivid Indian strength to it again, but now it was nostalgic and reminiscent. It was no longer contemporary in feeling.

It wasn't the little things; it was the whole world that had changed. The Territory Indians woke one afternoon and found that they had been turned into white men. The Indian thing was gone and nobody could find it again.

. . .

Along about 1870, Hannali loaded the four smallest children into a spring wagon and took them up to the Osage country to be baptized. There had used to be a priest come through the Choctaw North every five years or so, but there had been none during the war years or for some time after. But sometimes one came to the Osage country, and then Indians of the various tribes journeyed there.

It is not the same raising grandchildren as children. The grandchildren were better and prettier than the children had been. There had been too much of Hannali himself in the three great sons to allow them to be really handsome. Man, but those tall men had beaks on them! In their own way they were handsome, perhaps, but they were so sudden and strong as to overshadow it.

Now there was also real strength and character in Famous-George and Charles-Chitoh and Peter-Barua, and it was beginning to appear in Thomas-Academy. But there was also a new gentleness, a readier wit, an adaptability, a softhearted foolishness that their fathers had lacked.

And the granddaughters, though less beautiful, were much prettier than their mothers. Luvinia had been a beauty. Sally had been until she became somewhat empty-faced from her troubles. Nobody would deny that Hazel was still a great beauty. But there was something rather stark and sheer about their beauty and their talents. It was as though they had accomplished it all by a great surge of effort.

The granddaughters carried their beauty more easily, and really (except for Anna-Hata) they had less of it. Martha-Child was droll and pleasant. She had a bubbling humor and plenty of salt in her, but it was refined store salt. The salt in her mother Luvinia had been compounded at the Territory salt seeps—a sharp thing with galena and niter mixed in.

The children had been, in their abrupt moments, savage creatures. The grandchildren were not. It was with pride that Hannali said that these grandchildren hardly did a bad thing in their lives, but he did wonder sometimes how they had come from his nest—smooth-skin creatures with hardly any bark growing on them.

"The world is getting worse but the people in it are getting better," he said, "how do you figure that one out how can it be like that."

3.

Powerful stuff up out of the cellar. When the towns moved to the railroads. A house at the top of the hard hill.

One night long ago Hannali had played the fiddle for the pleasure of himself and his guests. Then Peter Pitchlynn who was staying at the house that week took the instrument up. And in his hands it became a violin, and no longer a fiddle.

Now in his latter days when Hannali played in the evenings it was a violin he played. He didn't fiddle jump tunes—except sometimes at dances. He bowed old powerful stuff up out of the cellar. There was great depth and richness in his playing.

Hannali had about given up reading. The Territory newspapers were now printed in English, and Hannali knew all the news before it came to them. He finished out a few corners of Plutarch and Leviticus that he had not read before; then he had it all in him. Whatever he had read carefully he had by heart for life.

He went over very old French letters. He smiled when he found that his father-in-law had been named Alinton Duchesne, and not DuShane. Hannali had once had a wonderful wife who intrepidly taught them all to read and write when she could not even spell her own name. Hannali, as a matter of fact, had had a handful of wonderful wives.

Say, but that country had changed! The new railroads did not go where the old towns had been. *Every* town in the Territory had been destroyed in the war years. They had hardly started building again when the railroads came down into the country and ignored those trivial old town sites. There was only one thing to do. The towns up and moved to the railroads, and forgot their names when they moved. Doaksville moved to Fort Towson, North Fork Town moved to Eufaula, Skullyville moved to Spiro, Boggy Depot moved to Atoka, Perryville moved to McAlester. The old continuity was broken, the old towns were buried in buffalo grass.

Time moved more rapidly. Hannali said that he went out to shoot a turkey once, and five years slipped away from him like minutes. It wasn't that he was getting old. He was only sixty-three at the end of the Civil War, and the following decades did him no harm. He still had plenty of green branches growing out of him, he was made out of primordial stuff that was not subject to aging. Sometimes Hannali, trying to touch old things again, went out and lived for a few weeks with the blacks and mixed blacks. There was a twenty-year-time lag during which the Choctaw Indians spoke English, and the Negroes still spoke Choctaw.

Anna-Hata had married. How could a little blue-eyed Indian-white girl be married almost the day after she was born? She had grown up in a moment when Hannali wasn't looking. She was the least Indian-appearing of the grandchildren and the closest to Hannali.

What had that old bear Hannali come to look like in his afterlife? He was still of the *pansfalaya*, the long-haired people, though many of the Chocs had cropped their hair. Often he wore his hair loose and nearly waist length, and he was in all ways informal in his appearance.

So then he was an old character when he went to town like that: flowing haired and shirtless, sometimes barefoot, rosary around his neck, and him nine colors of brown and a little dirty by white man's standards? He was not! Hannali had too much character ever to become an Old Character. Long hair and deerskin pants and all, he was *Senator* Innominee when he went to town anywhere in the Choctaw, Creek, or Cherokee nations. White men who laughed at young pushing Indians did not laugh at Hannali. He was Senator Innominee when he went down and talked in the new brick Tuskahoma Council House in the shadow of Nanih Waiya, and he was also Senator Innominee when he shot pool in Eufaula. You did not know that he was a pool shark? He could clear a hundred dollars a week, now that monied white men had begun to come in who would bet against a sure thing.

. . .

In 1874, Father Isidore Robot came to Atoka and built St. Patrick's Church. This was in the Choctaw South, but the families who had not seen a priest for more than a hundred years came in— knowing intuitively that this Bohemian Benedictine was of the same species as the French Jesuits known to their great-great-great-grand-fathers. There had been a sustaining influence in the Choctaw North—French blood, some green-Irish blood, the Rileys and a few others, and priestly visitations once or twice a decade; but there had been no contact at all with the Choctaw South. But the people recognized and remembered.

After this time Hannali used to ride down to old St. Patrick's several times a year. It was seventy-two miles at the beginning, and he was seventy-two years old. Thereafter the distance seemed to increase about a mile a year—keeping pace with his age—till finally it was rather a hard ride for him.

At least once a year he led the whole caravan of Innominees down there, on horseback and in buggies and wagons. He never gave up the journeys. He made the last one in the year of his death.

But it was a long time coming back to the Choctaws.

It was all right after that. There would be a house at the top of the hard hill.

CHAPTER NINETEEN

1.

The garish old light. The cloud of dust that lasted twenty years. Green Interlude. The sign in the sky it say one hundred and sixty acres no more and no less.

Boomer! Boomer! Who remembers the Boomers? David L. Payne was king of the Boomers. And were not the Boomers those who sought to steal the Indians' land?

But the funny part of it is that the Indians always liked Payne and his poor-man following, and hated the men who killed him.

The Boomer movement was part of the farmer-fencer settling that ended the Old Wild West Days—the part peculiar to the Territory—and the men of that movement were hatched out of the Wild West background. And just what were the *Old Wild West Days*—(the lettering should be burned in billboard letters on shingle-wood with a branding iron)—that stand pre-eminent in song and story and melodrama?

The Old Wild West Days were only twenty years long (from about 1867 to 1887) and not of really wide extent. The heart of the complex was the cattle drives from Texas up through the

Territory to the Kansas railheads; and the cattle drives to stock the ranges being opened up in Montana, Idaho, Wyoming, Utah, Nebraska, and Colorado with the same Texas longhorn or mixed cattle; and western mining and prospecting added their condiment to the Old Wild West Days stew. The costuming of the thing was Spanish-Mexican, and it was already three hundred years established when it moved up into the states.

There are two dates to be noted. The Homestead Act was passed in 1862. This sentenced the period to death five years before it was born, but there is a time lag in these things. And barbed wire, invented by J. F. Glidden of DeKalb, Illinois, was first marketed in 1874. It was barbed wire that killed the Old Wild West, and it took only thirteen years to do it.

In coming to the episode of the Boomers and to the end of our account, we pass lightly over the Old Wild West Days. This period still catches the garish old light, but the thing was not really important in the Territory. It was only a cloud of dust that lasted twenty years. Nevertheless, the heart of the Wild West saga was the Texas trail drives up through the nations, the B.I.T., and we must list at least some of the dusty names that echo out of that cloud.

The trail drivers usually referred to the Territory as the nations—it was driving up through the nations. But in their private slang it was "Up through the B.I.T." The abbreviation of the Beautiful Indian Territory was used sometimes in derision, but often seriously. It was the beautiful country—the Green Interlude—between the raucousness of assembling the herds in Texas, and the pop-skull nightmares and viciousness of the Kansas railhead towns.

The trails of the Old Wild West Days drives were the Great Western Trail, the New Western Trail, the Jones and Plummer Trail, the Dodge Trail, the West Shawnee Trail, the East Shawnee Trail (mostly identical with the Texas Road that went through by Hannali's Landing), the Cox Trail, the Chisholm Trail.

The great river crossings were at Spanish Fort, Doan's Store, Red River Station, Colbert's Ferry. The main Texas towns of the herd stagings were Preston, Denison, and Fort Worth, though many of the herds originated below San Antonio. The Kansas railhead towns were Abilene, Wichita, Dodge City, Caldwell, Baxter Springs, Ellsworth, Hays City, Newton.

The railroads of the thing were the Hannibal and St. Joe; the Leavenworth, Pawnee & Western; the Kansas Pacific; the Missouri Pacific; the Santa Fe. The stage lines of the area and period were the Sawyer and Ficklin, and the Butterfield Overland Dispatch. Well-known promoters were Joseph McCoy, T. C. Henry, Charles Goodnight, Shanghai Pierce. The name hotels were Drovers' Cottage, Abilene House, Grand Central Hotel, the Occidental, the Texas House, the Douglas Avenue Hotel, the Southwestern Hotel.

The raiding Indians of the period were the Apaches, Quahada Comanches, Cheyennes, Kiowas, and Arapahos. The battles and ambushes were at Adobe Walls, Pawnee Fork, Cimarron Crossing. The Army forts were Lyon, Dodge, Harker, Hays, Wallace, Sill, Reno. The Indian leaders of the Plains tribes were Dull Knife, Little Wolf, Quannah Parker.

The vice areas were McCoy's Addition, Nauchville, Hide Park, Delano, and several Hells' Half Acres in different towns. The saloons ran from the Alamo and Joe Brennan's to the Keno House and Red Beard's Dance Hall, with a hundred of them to be found in the chronicles of Drago. Whether or not they were all alike, they have become identical in popular imagination; one stylized set serves for them all in dramatic representation.

The name sheriffs and marshals were Pat Sughrue, Mysterious Dave Mather, Bill Tilghman (the best of them), Bat Masterson, Wyatt Earp (whose deeds are more fiction than fact), Tom Smith, Wild Bill Hickok, Brooky Jack Norton, Billy Brooks, Mike Meagher, Charlie Brown.

These are the dusty names that echo out of that cloud of dust that lasted for twenty years and is called the Old Wild West Days; and out of these names has been built an authentic American folklore.

But the Innominee family, more than most Indian families in the Territory, had strong connections with the Wild West trail driver affair. It was a connection that began with Jemmy Buster and Famous Innominee when trail driving was only a shadow of what it later became, and which now continued in Alinton Innominee. The Indian Territory was becoming more than the Green Interlude in the drives north; many of the herds now originated in the Territory. In the spring of 1870, Alinton Innominee drove one thousand of his own cattle north to Baxter Springs, Kansas. On this drive Alinton was accompanied by his father Hannali; it was one of the pleasant and expansive events of Hannali's life. The following year Alinton made a second trail drive north to Kansas.

Then he began to act as factor for other Indians—taking their cattle on commission or outright purchase and trailing them north. And in the spring of 1884, his father Hannali was in Dodge City, Kansas. He had ridden west to meet a trail drive conducted by certain friends of his, and he had gone on up to Dodge with them.

Do we not skip too many years here, going suddenly from 1870 to 1884 with no explanation? No. It will be all right. We will perhaps come back to some of those years several times, and to some not at all. The fact is that years do not follow a consecutive order after a certain number of them have been piled up. It was not that Hannali was confused in his thoughts and no longer mindful of the years, but when a man has finally become full and mature, then he is lord of the years and can move through them as he wishes. And he was in Dodge in the spring of 1884.

The twenty-year dust cloud was nearly over with. A slim white man, a fat white man, and fat Indian man sat and talked together, for they found each other interesting. The slim white man was David L. Payne, the king of the Boomers. The fat white man was the foremost immortalizer of the Old Wild West Days on canvas, in bronze, and on paper. The fat Indian man was Hannali Innominee.

"A man without land is not truly a man," said David Payne. "He is only an unbodied abstraction of a man. A man does not properly have either a body or a soul until he is set down on his own plot of land."

"Land is the people," said Hannali.

"No. Land is a person," insisted Payne, "the person who is the other half of man. If they are not one, then neither half can have a meaning. God created man to stand six feet tall and to own one hundred and sixty acres of land."

"You fall quarter inch short," said Hannali.

"You have a fine eye; so I do. And you stand six inches over. Do not blunt my point. Man is of a certain general measure, and so must his land be. Wherever there is one hundred and sixty acres of land that is not occupied by one man in his full rights, there is laid up one hundred and sixty acres of injustice."

"The land you talk of is Indian tribe people land," said Hannali with good humor, "Go file on your own tribe people land."

"God did not make any land to be forever Indian land or white-man land," said Payne. "He made land so that every man might own one hundred and sixty acres of it. That the Indians have suffered injustices I know, but that has no point of contact with the present subject. There are three million acres of unassigned land in the Territory; there would be thirty million acres unassigned if every Indian were compelled to accept one hundred and sixty acres, no more and no less, in severalty. Two hundred thousand men might file on that land and so be complete men."

"Where have God say this to mete and measure all the land," asked Hannali.

"It's shot all through the unwritten testament in golden colors," flamed Payne. "It's proclaimed by the sign in the sky."

"The sign in the sky it say one hundred and sixty acres no more and no less," Hannali chuckled.

"Yes. The sign in the sky, the sign on the earth says that man does not properly have either a body or soul till he is set down on his own plot, and the one quarter section, the one hundred and sixty acres, becomes that natural plot. But I am mocked when I try to convey God's truth, and my enemies surround me."

"You do not know your enemies," said Hannali. "They are not the Indian men name me one Indian man who oppose you strongly or unfairly name me the name of one."

And David Payne could not name one, for oddly Hannali was right in this. The opening of the Territory to white homesteaders—sometimes given as the culmination of all the wrongs to the Territory Indians—was opposed by those Indians hardly at all. Some of the Indians believed that they should receive fifty cents an acre for their land, and some of them would receive half that. But the Indians did not oppose white settlement.

Then what men did oppose the settlement—even to the point of murder? There is no doubt that Payne was murdered. We come to that.

This man Payne, who had the mystique of the land, was born in Indiana in 1836. He came to Kansas early. He believed so strongly in the Homestead Law—that a man could file on one hundred and sixty acres of land—that he availed himself of it twice, once in Doniphan County, Kansas, and once in Sedwick County. He saw service in the Union Army during the Civil War, and later service in the disputes with the Plains Indians—as captain in the 18th Kansas Cavalry, and with Custer as captain in the 7th U. S. Cavalry. During this cavalry service he became obsessed with the shoulder-high grass in the B.I.T. and believed it should all be broke to the plow. He went with the opinion that the unassigned lands in the Indian Territory, those taken from the Territory Indians for penalty after the war and never assigned to other Indians, were public lands subject to the Homestead Law.

Five times David Payne organized parties of homesteaders in Kansas, took them down into the Indian Territory, filed claims on the land, settled them and broke land, and announced that they were there by law and right. And five times Payne and his followers were arrested by U.S. troops out of Fort Reno and thrown out of the Territory.

Who were the men who opposed David Payne's Boomer movement? Who came to the defense of Indian rights so vehemently and so late and under such peculiar conditions? They were the cattlemen of the Cherokee Strip Livestock Association, cattlemen of other associations, and of no associations at all.

The point is this: Those white men were already in illegal possession of all the unassigned lands in Indian Territory. They had come into possession and use of the lands by fictitious leasing arrangements with paper Indians (names put down on leases to which there were no corresponding live Indians), and by connivance with the commanders of the U. S. Army posts. The Indians had already been excluded completely from these unassigned lands. The cattlemen would fight to the death for the exclusion of the white homesteaders also.

On the evening of November 27, 1884, Payne addressed a rally of his adherents in Wellington, Kansas. He would be able to mount one more Boomer homesteader invasion of the Territory, and likely it would be successful. National opinion was behind him now. The law had been on his side through all his five arrests and deportations. The unassigned lands *were* U.S. public lands by every legal definition, and they *were* subject to the Homestead Law.

After the rally, Payne went to bed in the Barnard Hotel in Wellington. In the morning he arose, ate breakfast, and then died in excruciating agony. He was an active man forty-eight years old. His enemies boasted openly that they had poisoned him, and this is likely the case.

But in dying he won his battle. Not only were the unassigned lands in the Indian Territory thrown open to homesteaders, but lands in a dozen states that had been held out of it by cattle interests were now thrown into the homestead stream. The trim man with the trim moustache and the mystique of one hundred and sixty acres of land had finished off the Old Wild West Days.

It didn't matter much to the Territory Indians. Their peculiar civilization had ended twenty years before, and they had never taken the Wild West Days seriously. They would as soon be farmer fencers as ranchers.

2.

Is it the Kiowas or is it far thunder? The last night but one of his life. "Hell, let's swim it," said the horse. The old Adam voice.

In those latter days, Hannali usually lived in the Big House alone, or with only the ghost of Robert Pike for company.

"It is good to have someone to talk to in the evening Robert Pike," Hannali said, "there were the years when I could not see you now there have come the years when I cannot hear you well unless I force my voice on you why are you so unclear Robert and we friends."

"It is that I am not here save in your mind," said Robert. "The stories are that I haunt your old house, that I am a ghost. Everybody fears the ghost of Robert Pike except yourself and Anna-Hata, but nobody feared Robert Pike very much while he was alive. What you see of Robert you see in your mind."

"Was it only in my mind that two white men came last Friday

sundown and they were scared silly they had seen that crazy coot of a Unionist ghost others have seen you also ye be a haunt Robert but a friendly one I knew you had died when you did not come back to visit us after the years."

"You should go and stay with some of your people, Papa Hannali, or have some of them stay here with you," said the ghost of Robert Pike. "It is dangerous for you to be alone at your age."

"I be not alone spook Robert think ye that ye are the only familiar ghost that I own Robert do you know that I thought to see the new century just for the hell of it three weeks ago then Anna-Hata says no you have not done it Papa Hannali the first day of 1901 is the beginning of the century not the first day of 1900 damme but she is right now I have to stretch myself to make it."

"When you are dead there will be no more Indians," said the ghost of Robert.

"It is true they are almost all gone," said Hannali, "Quannah Parker is now a tame Indian at Anadarko Agency why do I laugh Hannali Innominee is now a tame Indian in his own house where are they all who have seen Buffalo Hump or Dull Knife or Gray Ghost who have seen Pock Mark or Roman Nose Thunder or Powder Face or Black Kettle where are my friends Opothle and Bolek and Alligator where is strong Nitakechi and good Pitchlynn where is my own father Barua and my good brothers where are the Tribes Indians where are the Plains Indians is it all a good thing that even the terror have gone out of the Indian name was one time when even Indians were in terror of Indians when they would listen at night and say is it the far thunder or is it the Kiowas is not the world weaker when we lose the terror where is the fun to be always tame people on tether."

It had been those terrifying Kiowas sixty years before who had named Hannali "The Man with the Talking Horses." This was because of a device that Hannali had created for the amusement of his own children, and because the Kiowas (those terror raiders) were a very childlike and credulous people. Hannali, a consummate horseman, was able to flick any of his animals on the side of the throat and the beast would always give out with a good-natured nickering or neighing. Hannali's trick was to ventriloquize words to go with this carrying neigh so that it would seem that the horse spoke.

Of course Hannali's young sons understood the trick for what

212

it was, but visiting Plains Indians were sometimes fooled. One day one of the Kiowas watched and listened fascinated.

"If that horse is so all red smart let him talk Kiowa," the Kiowas finally said. "Then we will know whether there is a Choctaw throat in the middle of this."

"My horse has never been in the Kiowa country," said Hannali. "Let us see how well your own horses talk Kiowa."

"Our horses do not talk at all," said the Kiowa. "Never in our country have we had a talking horse."

The Kiowa language is like no other Indian tongue. Hannali could speak it, but not like a Kiowa would. But he had more devices than one.

"Kiowa horse let me hear you talk Kiowa," he said as he went up to one of the animals and flicked it on the throat, "your masters say that you do not talk at all surely your masters have something the matter with their ears how would a fine horse like you not talk."

"I am no Kiowa horse at all," said the Kiowa horse in imperfect Kiowa, "I am a Creek horse and I was stolen two years ago by this Kiowa man down below Tukabatchee Town it is a devil hard language the Kiowas have I wonder that they can talk it themselves."

"Oh, that horse lie!" howled the Kiowa. "He is no stolen horse, he is born a Kiowa horse and no part Creek horse. The Creek horse stolen was twin brother of this horse and have same markings. Oh how I beat this horse when we are alone! Horse must learn not to blurt out damaging things like this."

But Hannali had recognized the peculiarly marked horse and remembered where and when it was stolen.

Now it was sixty-four years after that, and Hannali sat in the back room of a drugstore in Eufaula and talked and drank with friends. He had ridden into town and had supper with his daughter-in-law (daughter), the second wife and now widow of his son Travis—with her and with her small daughter Catherine. And later he had sat in the back room of the drugstore—which room also served as saloon, for the blight of prohibition was early on the Territory—and played cards and drank with several men.

Hannali sat late that night—the last night but one of his life—and enjoyed the pleasant company. There were eight of them. All were of some Indian blood—Hannali found it out of the eighth that night—but only Hannali and one other would have been taken for Indian.

It was after they were far along and had become somewhat slushy with the drink that Hannali learned that the eighth man of them (a tow-headed heavy man with a German name) was a Kiowa Indian in his one-quarter ancestry. On learning this Hannali laughed and told the old story of the talking horses that he had not thought of for more than half a century.

And later as Hannali rode his big horse home he chuckled over the thing and flicked the horse.

"Horse my horse," he said, "talk to me see if I can still make horses talk."

"Man my man," said the horse, "maybe I flick you with a foot some day then I make you talk horse and not talk man."

"Horse my horse," said Hannali, "do you know that there is a wonderful tonic to be had for two bits a bottle it is print on the bottle 'Is not alcoholic' and under is Choctaw words that look like a motto 'Oh the hell it is not' they say I tell you horse that this stuff put you clear over the edge I tell you with pride it is made and bottled by one of my own grandsons Hey that boy mint money out of it even the bottle will test one hundred proof when it is empty."

Hannali was as ripe as a fall pumpkin and as round. He was tall as a tupelo tree and wide as a False Washita swamp. He had a bucket of the old juice in him, and he was one hundred years old by the count of his grandchildren. More likely he was only ninety-six, but he had lived more than four years while others slept. He was Senator Innominee on a big plow horse, for a riding pony could no longer carry him. He was clay-footed Hannali, the Choctaw fiddler. He was the son of Barua who had told Pushmataha that he sucked white men's eggs, he was the father of Famous Innominee who had been afraid of nobody. And the old Hannali vine itself had enjoyed a third and fourth growth. He now had more than fifty great-grandchildren they told him. He was a full man in every way possible.

They came to the river. The ferry did not run at night; in any case it was an inferior ferry, not like the one Hannali used to have there. There was a raft that Hannali could have used to drift himself and horse across, but he did not.

"Hell let's swim it," said Hannali.

"Hell let's swim it," said the horse, for horses still talked to Hannali when he wished them to. Hannali dismounted, and man and horse swam separately. It was easy ice on the river, hardly more than paper thin, and it broke and tinkled for them as they swam into it. People, that was a pleasant night!

But as Hannali—dripping and crusted lightly with ice and all aglow—bulked through the great door of his own Big House, the old Adam voice told him that this was the last time he would ever walk through that door.

CHAPTER TWENTY

1.

It bedevils me if I can even think of a witty way to die. What are we, white people that we kid each other? He was a Mingo.

Hannali was taken by sickness in the night and he knew that it was all over with him.

"It bedevils me if I can even think of a witty way to die," he told himself, "shall I die like everybody else it is that most people die with no imagination at all it comes to me that I cannot joke about it how big is a man all his life how he blow and carry on but how does he go through that last door how does he die."

He chuckled, and it choked him up.

"I die all right," he said, "not a big show just do it neat and proper."

He sent out a call that one of his people must come to be with him. He sat up in his big bed—the buffalo bed—and worried that he was not heard. Then he lay back with his mind eased of that care. Twenty miles away, a forever-young matron lady of the Territory—a blue-eyed girl, by some not known to be an Indian—slipped out of bed.

"I start now, Papa Hannali," she said, "I be there in the pretty early morning."

"Is no big hurry, Anna-Hata," said Hannali, "only that you be here by noon I cannot guarantee to wait longer."

In this extremity, Hannali and his granddaughter Anna-Hata were old Choctaw Aliki people who could talk at a distance without apparatus. So Anna-Hata went out to hitch up horse and buggy and drive down to the Big House. It was still several hours before dawn.

Had they not a telephone? No. Hannali had talked on a telephone only once in his life—in the previous year—and had not been impressed by the instrument. "It is not a man talking on that thing," he said, "it is a bunch of birds talking whoever will pay out money for an instrument that carries only the voices of birds who needs telephone."

Hannali and his granddaughter did not need one. Sure she heard him; sure she was coming; sure she understood what was wrong. "All right old grandpapa bear I come I come be you behave till I get there."

Anna-Hata told her husband—a white man (did you know that there were now more white men in the Territory than Indians?)—to get a priest in Muskogee and bring him down to the Big House. There was then no priest resident in Eufaula. The husband did not grumble, nor did he wonder any longer how Anna-Hata communicated with her grandfather.

She was down at the Big House well before the middle of the morning, coming up with a music of harness and buggy bells and a clear voice that she had from her grandmother Marie DuShane:

"I come I come, old bear grandpapa, we fix everything right will be left nothing undone," she burst into the room.

"This we cannot fix," said Hannali. "I die Anna-Hata."

"Oh, I know that. What are we, white people, that we kid each other?"

White people! Anna-Hata was white people from her mother Hazel and her grandmother Marie DuShane—white people French. She was white people from her father Jemmy Buster—white people Texas. She had eyes like blue cornflowers and hair like corn. But Hannali, looking at her there, knew that the world had not run out of Indians yet.

"I turn white people myself," said Hannali, "I die of white people pneumonia that is better than the new Choctaw fashion to sicken and linger with white people tuberculosis to what lengths do the people not go to prove that we are now white."

Hannali was born when Napoleon was still on his surge upward. As a boy and young man he had heard all three of the Medal Mingos speak: Pushmataha, Apukshunubbee, Moshulatubbee. Who else still living had heard all three of them? He had been in every nation of the Plains during his long life; he had been in Florida of Spain and in Louisiana of France; he had been in old Mexico and in Texas of Mexico. He knew the nations of the Creeks and Seminoles and Osages and Cherokees, of the Quapaws and Absentee Shawnees, of the Wichitas and the Quahada Comanches and the southern Cheyennes, of the Kiowas and the Arapahos, of the Caddoes and Tonkawas. He had known nations of Indians that have since disappeared in every man of them.

He had learned every common trade that a man may carry on with his hands. Never in his life had he availed himself of the services of a doctor, lawyer, or sheriff. He had not backed down from any man in his life, and he came fearless to the hour of his death.

He was a Mingo.

2.

Why we gathered here then, to play pinochle?
Hell is full of men who die with dignity. The
smoke has gone up.

The husband of Anna-Hata, along with the priest, arrived late in the afternoon.

"Hasn't the doctor been here?" the husband asked. "I thought you would long since have the doctor out from Eufaula."

"Why no," said Anna-Hata, "they're not particular friends; I saw no reason to have the doctor out. About a dozen people have come— those who knew to come without being sent for, little Catherine and her mother, most of the good friends. None other of the kindred lives close enough or would know to come without being contacted."

"I do not mean the doctor for friendship, Anna-Hata," said the husband. "I mean to have the doctor out professionally. Papa Hannali seems very low to me."

"Low as a snake's liver, good husband. Doctor is in the way with sick people."

"The doctor is *not* in the way with sick people, Anna-Hata. I'll ride to get him now. Papa Hannali might die."

"But of course he will die! We agreed on that much. The priest is here and ourselves. What shall we do, make a show of it?"

"She is right," the priest told the husband. "Hannali will die, and there is no use bothering his dying with a doctor. Get out of here, Anna-Hata, and take your husband. I have my own business to transact with Hannali."

So Hannali was confessed, counseled, and composed, and made ready for the journey about which he showed great curiosity.

"I'll know in a little while," Hannali said, "I'll know it all there's a dozen things I've argued about and I bet I'm right about every one of them that all knowledge is given to us immediately after the particular judgment is one of the things I've argued why have a man to wait so long to know everything."

Anna-Hata and her husband came back in, and the priest gave Communion and Extreme Unction to Hannali. Thereupon Hannali went to sleep till midnight, and Anna-Hata sat with him. Into his breast pocket she slipped a corn cake that he could eat on the journey. Hannali wakened at deep night and talked to Anna-Hata:

"I tell you little straw-colored bird I have just arrived at the solution of it all call the two men in and we finish with it."

"Come you in the men," called Anna-Hata going to the door, "we have decided to make the finish to it."

"It is like this," said Hannali, "the priest will have to get back to Muskogee the grave still has to be dug I had put off doing it as I hadn't intended to die till later in the year other things must be taken care of if the key act waits till morning then we will all lose valuable time O.K. then I die now we fix it all."

"No, no, do not talk of dying," gasped the husband of Anna-Hata.

"Why we gathered here then to play pinochle," asked Hannali, "I do it now it take me about five minutes when I make up my mind then husband get busy dig the grave coffin is already made in the big room behind also rollers to get me out the door in it I am very heavy these I make myself others will do other things and all can start home by sunup."

"Only God can say when you will die, Hannali," chided the priest.

"So then He say it to not keep these good people waiting Hannali He say how do you know which ear He talk to me in He tell me to get with it now I die in five minutes watch and you learn how to do it."

"Death is not a joke, Papa Hannali," said the husband of Anna-Hata.

"What then should I die with dignity," asked Hannali, "Hell is full of men who die with dignity sure it is a joke the last one of all to get out of every life trap get away clear watch this old operator operate I bet I can do it in five minutes and me not even very sick right now."

"Sure you can, Papa Hannali," said Anna-Hata, "go get that old thing. Don't wait him come get you, old buffalo bull grandpapa. I bet you can cut a minute off it."

"Anna-Hata, this is ghastly!" protested the husband.

"What? To laugh and smile at the old thing when it comes along to one of us? What are we, white people, that we use such words as ghastly? Look! The old bear will do it with plenty of time left over."

Hannali did it in good time. He died in about three minutes after he really put his mind to it. It would have taken most strong men twice that long.

He was clear in his mind to the end. He had never been anything else. He remembered every name or word he had ever heard—every scent he had ever smelled—every object to which he had put his hand—every notion he had ever entertained in the dark of night. He remembered every blade of grass he had ever seen.

His memory was unimpaired. Nor did his eyes really grow dim till he shut them by his own effort.

He was really the last of them.

. . .

The smoke has gone up. The talk is over with.

. . .

In the beginning was first the Okla—the people.
This is the story of what happened to the people.